July, 2015

It's time to break my oath of silence. The death threat kept me quiet for twenty-three years, but the keepers of the yellow metal are probably too old to care by now. Besides, I'm not telling the location. But live or die, the story of the biggest treasure deposit on the planet has to be told.

Matt Howard

TWENTY DAYS TO TREASURE

Phyllis Gunderson

Onesimus Publishing 2015
Copyright © 2015 Phyllis Gunderson
All rights reserved.

ISBN: 1511831804
ISBN 13: 9781511831802
Library of Congress Control Number: 2015906418
CreateSpace Independent Publishing Platform
North Charleston, South Carolina

CHAPTER ONE

While dinosaurs contentedly chewed on each other, sudden violence spewed across their world. Earth vomited itself from its own bowels, bursting through the crust into sulphuric air. When the carnage settled, dinosaurs were extinct and the Uinta Mountains had trembled into existence.

Heat from volcanic fury had liquefied a yellow metal which spilled into lava tubes, filling huge caverns with soft, purified gold…worthless until Homo sapiens discovered the pretty stuff and learned to dig it, mold it, cast it…and kill for it.

Shortly thereafter, counting in geologic time, my mother's cousin once-removed left me her house. Thus began my twenty days to treasure.

July 1992. Scottsdale, Arizona

It died an agonizing death, groaning and rattling into oblivion. The air conditioner had served the house for twenty years under my parent's constant care. They'd been gone for ten years and the machine had earned the right to join them. The timing of its demise couldn't have been worse. I planned to spend the summer writing a textbook on prehistoric pottery dating, but cockroaches are the only life form that can survive the heat of an Arizona desert.

The repairman shook his head and muttered the obscene number of dollars it would take to resurrect the cooling system. Even *he* choked on the amount. "It'll be cheaper to replace it," he suggested.

"I don't have the money and it's July," I reminded him. "Nobody can live in Arizona without a cooling system."

He shifted his feet. "Go north," he advised.

I thanked him anyway and he left, discounting his usual service fee by ten percent. It was the decent thing to do.

I sat in my little Scottsdale house, the sun pounding on the roof to get in, and tried to write another page of textbook on my old electric typewriter. My colleagues raved about computers but I considered it a passing fad, an example of technology looking for an excuse to exist. I expected to laugh when everybody wanted their small, inexpensive typewriters back.

Zeus positioned his large body directly in front of the fan, panting mouth open, tongue lolling, drool flipping against my arm from the force of the wind. I had to choose between circulation and saliva. The dog would have to go.

I rose to get the mail outside, ordering Zeus to come. The giant animal, part Boxer, part Great Dane, pretended he hadn't heard and hunched in the stream of air.

"Come on, Zeus." I switched the fan off. "If I have to go outside, so do you. I'm not leaving you here to drench my work."

Zeus heaved himself up and wobbled to my side. The Great Dane portion reached my hip. The Boxer part stared up with dark, soulful eyes, anticipating banishment.

"Stupid dog," I muttered. The creature wasn't even a thoroughbred and still cost four hundred dollars. I bought him after a divorce when I needed something big and dumb to replace a husband. I had defied the rules of ownership: first you get a fish; if that goes well, you add a bird; if the two survive, you pick up a cat. When you successfully acquire a dog, you're ready for a husband. Unfortunately, I did it backwards. Zeus was my rebound.

In spite of the fact I'm female, my name is Matt Howard. Thirty-five years ago, which is also my age, my parents burdened me with the name Mathilda, which I shed like the skin of a snake as soon as I could legally wiggle out of it. A framed piece of paper on my wall proves I have a doctorate in Archaeology. I'm an adjunct professor at my university when I'm not in the field getting bit, stung, scorched, fried and frozen in dirt holes around the world: Lamanai in Belize, Angkor Wat of Cambodia, Egypt's Nag Hammadi site at Seila, Turkey's underground city of Derinkuyu, to name a few.

Along the way I have discovered that I prefer dead people. They're nicer than fresh ones. My favorite folks are mostly deceased, like Hammurabi, first ruler of Babylon, and Ankhesenamun, King Tut's wife. An Assyrian sage named Ahiqar left his good sense on papyrus sheets in 500 B.C. *"I have lifted sand and carried salt,"* he said, *"but there is nothing heavier than rage."* None of my living friends say profound things like that.

The instructions of an ordinary Egyptian father to his son are carved in a wood plaque on my desk: *"Do not talk a lot. Be silent and you will be happy. A man may fall to ruin because of his tongue."* I should tattoo that advice on the back of my hand where I can't lose it. My tongue and I often run on separate tracks, to my detriment.

After meeting these long-gone people, I became an Ethnoarchaeologist. My official title is Dr. Matt Howard. Since I need to move up the hierarchy ladder to earn more money, I'm writing a pottery textbook to fulfill the demand of publish-or-perish.

Zeus followed me obediently to the front door where I slid into rubber-soled sandals to prevent fried feet and we entered the Arizona oven for ninety seconds, roasting until well done. I grabbed a handful of mail as the dog hopped around me in a hot potato dance, without so much as a blade of grass to rest his paws on. My house, part of the family for three generations, is landscaped with cactus, mesquite bushes, and a phony river of rocks. It looks drab against the lush green lawns of my neighbors, but they're hostages to watering and mowing. I, on the other hand, am free of such foolishness.

The dog and I tore back to the medium high heat of the house. At my office I closed the door on him. The great lump of animal spread himself on the floor outside the portal, nose stuffed into the crack. The sound of my whirring fan covered his whimpering.

The mail is usually bills and advertisements. If an envelope looks official but is addressed to "Mr. Matt Howard," I know the sender has copied my name from a marketing list and thinks I'm a man. It gets an instant pitch to the garbage. On this day, one legal-sized packet said, "Dr. Matt Howard." I glanced at the upper left corner, printed with *"Law Offices of Hutchins, Eyring, and Lowe"* from Detroit. Warily, I opened the envelope and skimmed the first page, something about me being the closest living relative of someone who had died a month ago, leaving property that was legally mine if I wanted it.

On page two I saw a description of the property written in lawyer-speak. As close as I could figure, a woman named Hilda had owned a house and five acres in the Uinta Mountains bordering the Uinta-Wasatch-Cache National Forest. Page three caught my interest.

Renunciation of Inheritance

The undersigned renounces any and all right, title or interest in and to any gift, inheritance, bequest or other property or assets of the Estate of Hilda Hathenbruck…

These guys wanted me to refuse my inheritance from dearly departed Hilda, whoever she used to be. I consulted the family tree my mother had embroidered to see if Hilda was there. The large framed picture leaned in the back of the office closet. I smeared dust off with my hand to find the elusive Hilda, only child of my mother's cousin Alice, which would make Hilda my mother's cousin once removed and maybe my cousin twice removed. I could look it up later, but knew I never would.

The chart showed Hilda had married a man named Theodore Hathenbruck and that's where their family ended. No children. My name beneath my parents was also the termination of the tree. The fact that Hilda's house in the mountains had no one to fight over it was a sad commentary on our family's lack of procreation.

I called the phone number of Hutchins, Eyring, and Lowe. A young girl's high-pitched tone assaulted me. You'd think a group of professional men would hire a mature voice to answer their phone, but men are visual. The teenager connected me.

"Lowe here," he spoke nasally.

"I'm Dr. Matt Howard and I've inherited property from Hilda Hathenbruck bordering the…" I read from the document, "…Uinta-Wasatch-Cache National Forest. Where is that?"

He rustled papers. "Are you calling on behalf of Dr. Howard?"

"I'm Dr. Howard." There was a short silence. I filled it with unnecessary facts.

"I'm not male. Matt is my legal name. I'd like to see the property. Where is it?"

More rustling. "It's in the mountains between southern Wyoming and northern Utah. Be advised there's a time limitation to renounce the inheritance."

"I think I'll look at it before I give it away. Is there a town I can fly into?"

The man exploded a short laugh, as if he'd heard a dirty joke. "It's a wilderness area," he said. "I have a phone number for the real estate agent who's had the property listed for the last five years."

"It's been for sale that long? What's wrong with it?"

The lawyer turned verbose. "Our dealing with Mrs. Hathenbruck's estate doesn't include personal knowledge of this particular asset. It was among her husband's possessions when he died. He hadn't mentioned it to her. She inspected the property and decided to sell. That's all we know." He detoured back to the renunciation. "You have thirty days to decide whether or not to accept the inheritance."

I brusquely thanked Mr. Lowe, dialed the real estate number he offered, and got a machine.

"Hi. This is Jack Jamison. It's a great day here because I've got what you need *and* what you want. Leave your name and number."

Zeus howled under the door. I left a quick message for Jack to return my call, took pity on the dog, and let him in. He rushed to sit on his haunches in front of the fan, spewing dog spit and smell into the air. I got out of the house. Ancient pottery couldn't compete with an air-conditioned movie theater, where I took a nap. On the way home, I purchased a private fan for Zeus.

Next day I was cooling my head in the refrigerator when the friendly real estate agent called. "Got a message you're interested in a piece of property." The man's voice smiled through the wire. "I see your number is in Arizona."

"I've inherited a house and five acres," I said. "Your name was provided by Hutchins, Eyring, and Lowe."

"Inherited?" His voice dropped a disappointed decibel. Maybe he wouldn't get as much money off an inheritance. "It wouldn't be the old Hathenbruck place, would it?"

"That's the one."

"So poor old Hilda died." I could imagine his head shaking. "You might want to sign a renunciation."

My back hackled as I wondered why everybody conspired to cheat me out of my inheritance. "Even if the house is a run-down shack," I reasoned with the man, "five acres bordering a national forest should be worth something. What's the going price?"

"Well, all things considered," he said, "and being as the house is more than a hundred years old, and the place is totally isolated...." I waited patiently for the bottom line, which he finally supplied. "It should sell for $500,000."

I felt my jaw hinges loosen. For the last few years I'd been having an out-of-money experience and the sudden prospect of half a million dollars left me dizzy. But something about the man's tone yanked me back to reality and I asked the obvious question, "What do you have it listed for?"

He hedged and procrastinated. "You know, it's been on the market for five years. Housing is down. Mrs. Hathenbruck and I conferred several times and agreed that—"

I cut him off. "How much?"

He sighed. "I have it listed for $200,000."

I nearly swallowed my tongue before I could get it in place to say, "And nobody's buying?"

"I get a lot of bites."

"No buyer in five years?" I sent a command sizzling between phones. "Tell me what's wrong with the house."

"It's a nice house," he answered too quickly. "Mrs. Hathenbruck invested quite a bit to restore it, added a generator for electricity, a pump to bring water from the well, propane---"

"Outhouse?"

"Indoor toilet."

"Mr. Jamison," I announced. "I'll be there day after tomorrow."

He gave directions to his office in a little town called Kamas and we said goodbye. The words of the repairman flickered into life. "Go north." A month in the cool Uinta Mountains would give me time to decide about the property while I worked on my book. No heat. No stress. No....

Zeus.

The dog couldn't be left alone. I once tried a kennel while I was gone on a dig in Iraq, but Zeus chewed at the bars until his mouth bled. I had to pay extra for the stitches. Neighbors had also proved dismal. People on my street could barely be persuaded to throw food and water at the beast for a few days, much less a month. Nevertheless, I approached four of them and got a variety of lies:

"We're not sure what our plans are for July."

"We'll be gone." Nervous laughter. "Getting out of the heat."

"My husband's uncle's second wife is very ill. We expect to be flying out for a funeral any minute."

"Look Matt," the man next door said. "We can't take care of your dog for a month. You shouldn't have an animal. You're gone too much."

"I appreciate your honesty," I replied. "But I sort of like him."

"He's not a child," my neighbor said kindly. "He's just a dog. You should get rid of him."

I called two airlines to see if they could transport Zeus in their baggage hold. The woman at one company said she was sorry, but they didn't take animals over a hundred pounds. Another air carrier explained they only allow animals small enough to fit in a cage under the passenger seat. I responded that a dog that size was only a cat in disguise. She laughed before she hung up. Freight haulers told me they're limited to inert objects on flatbeds. I had to face the likelihood that my journey north had turned into a road trip with a large dog.

I should have kept the husband. At least he could stay home by himself.

CHAPTER TWO

The deafening fan pushed hot air at me, rattling the map while I figured out the shortest route to the Uinta Mountains. Twelve hours through the least populated area of the Arizona/Utah desert would take me to the rural community of Kamas. The end of my poverty was only half a day away.

I crammed my old Chevy station wagon, nicknamed the Shove-it, with snacks, water, dog food, dog, and cash emptied from my meager bank account. The credit card, which was entirely responsible for my money mess, deserved to be left behind. Not having access to plastic money would force frugality on me. It sounded virtuous at the time. Hindsight is ugly.

The car resembled something out of *The Grapes of Wrath*, piled with everything that could be tied on. I expected the best, planned for the worst, and prepared to be surprised. We departed at 1:00 a.m., hoping to reach the Kamas real estate office in the late afternoon. The Shove-it coughed itself to life and rolled from the driveway. In the ten years I'd been its master, it never failed to start…which is better than a lot of people.

It was dark on Interstate I-17. The heat still attacked, but its effort was halfhearted. Zeus flopped across the middle seats and snored for a hundred and fifty miles until we reached Flagstaff. The map demanded I find highway 89 and stay with it. Two hours later we reached Page, Arizona where I filled the car, allowed the dog to empty, and returned to 89 going west. The desert had morphed from Arizona's friendly man-sized cactus with arms raised in the air, to a flat, colorless plate of gray dirt, with patches of weeds desperately clinging to life.

Suddenly, the sun rose behind us, slapping the landscape into life. All glory broke loose. Radiance spread across the desert in a fan sparkled with rainbow colors of light. I drove with a grin on my face until the angle of rays shifted into normal and the desert changed from a butterfly back to a dreary, sluggish caterpillar. Seventy-three miles later, the landscape formed hills, then mountains, and we slowed to enter a small township named Kanab where the road nosed north.

Outside of town I stopped for a meal, something that didn't crunch like Fritos when I chewed it. Zeus settled under sparse shade with dry dog food and water. "We're halfway there, boy," I told him. "Only six more hours." I didn't have the heart to tie him up. Feeling guilty, I scratched the dog's pointed ears before entering the small cafe. Twenty minutes later I'd downed a hefty breakfast and waited for the bill. Stretching and yawning, I wandered outside to check Zeus.

Two empty dog bowls stared at me, minus the dog. Calling his name and jogging around the cafe didn't produce the animal. Back at the front entrance, my worried gaze searched the horizon. A man sat at a small, round wire table with coffee and a newspaper.

"Lose yer dog?"

I nodded. "He doesn't usually wander off."

The man stared up the road. "Big feller? Short hair?"

Relief washed over me. "Did you see him?"

"He might be headin' east in the back of a truck bed."

Alarms clanged behind my forehead. "Did someone force him in?" Zeus was too big to force.

The man put down his newspaper to explain. "The skinniest kid I ever saw patted a big dog's head, then got in the cab of an old truck. There wasn't a tail gate and the dog jumped in back while the boy cranked the truck over and left."

"How long ago?"

"Maybe five minutes."

Mumbling thanks, I dashed to the Shove-it, ground it into gear, and left permanent tire marks on highway 89 going east.

Stupid dog. I could save everybody trouble if I let the boy keep him...serve them both right. I roared along, eyes riveted on the road ahead, searching for signs of a truck with a Great Dane/Boxer vacantly staring backwards at the scenery. Henceforth, that dog would spend the rest of his life on a tight leash, maybe hog-tied from neck to tail, fastened to a post or tree.

In the distance a swirling dust devil moved north toward the base of the mountains, a signal that something, maybe a truck with a dog in back, had taken a dirt road off the main highway. I turned in hopeful pursuit, catching sight of a truck camouflaged by dust. Leaning on the horn to get attention, I waved my arm out the window and honked SOS in Morse code. The driver, his head covered in a baseball cap, looked behind at my car closing in on him and accelerated. Rotten kid. My loaded Shove-it fell behind as I struggled through sand and ruts. Somewhere on the wretched road, I remembered that I hadn't paid for breakfast. In a little town like Kanab, the police could already be after me.

A few miles later I heard wheels around a corner churning in something loose. The beat-up truck came into view, throwing sand from the left back wheel like a badger tossing dirt from his burrow. I parked far enough away to avoid the soil storm and exited my car. Zeus had stretched out on a couple of old tires in the truck bed, surrounded by assorted buckets, rags, bumpy black trash bags, and enough rope to climb Mt. Everest. He lazily wagged his tail stub at me. "Thanks for nothing, Zeus," I growled as I walked to the driver's side window, nervous over confrontation with a teenage boy.

"I think you need to let up on the gas and stop digging in deeper," I advised. It seemed like a friendly introductory statement.

The kid stopped gassing it, turned on me and snarled in a high-pitched voice, "Mind your own business."

It was a girl. Great drops of sticky sweat rolled from under the baseball cap into her eyes. She removed the salty substance with the back of her hand, wiping the wetness on her worn-out Levis.

I stopped being friendly. The girl was not a threat unless she had a gun. "You *are* my business," I replied. "You took my dog."

"He's *your* dog?" Surprise tinged her voice. "I thought he was a stray."

I pointed out the obvious. "He's got tags around his neck held in place by a chain that could hoist a motorcycle."

She rested her forehead against the wheel and mumbled, "I thought he was a lucky sign." Raising her face to look at me with resentment, she opened the door and jumped out. "I shoulda' known it wasn't good luck. So take your dog and go."

Marching to the back she hurled another statement behind her. "And tell them I'm not giving up." I followed and watched her kneel in the dirt to examine the left wheel, half submerged in sand. A little mew escaped her throat.

I took pity on the young woman. She was in a mess and even my underdeveloped conscience couldn't leave her there. "Maybe," I offered, "I can help you get out."

She stood, slightly shorter than me, skinniest girl I'd seen since elementary school, dressed in a long sleeve cotton plaid shirt over a pair of jeans that didn't fit, baggy in the bottom, legs lengthy enough to leave a snakelike trail in the sand. She seemed too covered up for the heat of the desert.

Her anger seeped through her words. "Who sent you?"

"Nobody," I answered. "I followed my dog. His name is Zeus, mine is Matt." I bent for a closer look at the pit the girl had dug for herself. "Do you have any water? Let's try that first."

Her mouth pursed itself and moved sideways in a sign of doubt. "What do you need water for?"

"To pour on the sand."

She put her hands on her nonexistent hips. "The last thing I need is mud."

"Sand," I said with authority, "doesn't turn to mud."

She studied me a few seconds. "How do you know?"

"I'm smart."

Still deciding how much of me she could trust, she wearily climbed into the truck bed to push forward two five-gallon containers. "Is this enough?"

"We'll find out."

We took everything out of the truck to lighten the load. Zeus refused to leave his tire throne and it required both the girl and me to physically force him off. He took it personally and sulked under a gray bush. The skinny teenager got in the cab and geared low to avoid spinning while I sprinkled water on the sand, creating a firmer base to crawl on. It was too little too late. She rejoined me, closing her eyes in disgust. "Well, there goes most of my water."

"Don't give up yet," I encouraged. "Let's take some air out of the tires."

She mocked the idea with a loud laugh. "You've done enough, lady. Thanks anyway."

Sarcasm is my weapon of choice. Sometimes I can draw blood. "You wanna know who I am?" I stood and folded my arms, ten o'clock sweat dripping down my neck. "I'm your only chance out of here. But I'm close to taking my car, and my little dog, too, and you can bake in the oven." She probably didn't catch the wicked witch irony, but she saw the reality.

Her voice rose in a slight panic. "Fine. I'll let out some air."

With an empty truck and the tires half size, I sat in the cab to drive while she lifted and pushed…her idea, since she figured I knew what I was doing. Fact is, I once saw a TV comedy where a couple were stuck in a sand pit and they tried a bunch of silly things until the water and tire deflation got them out. For all I knew, the whole thing was a farce, and we should have kept the truck heavy for traction. But I figured if the truck didn't move, I'd take the girl home and my conscience and I could continue our journey north.

We escaped the sand pit in thirty seconds, another endorsement for what can be learned from mindless television. The girl jogged to catch up and stood at my driver's window, beaming with excitement.

"Thanks," she said. "I can take it from here."

I let the truck idle as I calmly spoke. "In some cultures, if you save a person's life you're responsible for them. I can't leave you here until I know you'll be safe. What's your name and where are you going?"

Her smile disappeared. She wiped liquid from her brow, this time with the edge of the plaid shirt, and said, "I have to get moving."

I swept my short, soggy hair off my forehead and attacked through the window in a mini-tirade. "Hold it, missy. I'll need a chiropractor from lifting and pouring heavy water. My Gucchi shoes are covered with wet sand. I've ruined my manicured nails removing everything from your truck, I didn't pay for my breakfast and I'm considering pressing charges against you for stealing my dog. What's your name and where are you going?""

17

She noticed my ragged fingernails and Wal-Mart tennis shoes, then turned away to begin replacing the truck's belongings. "My name's Candy," she said, stooping for a tire, groaning to lift it. I dragged my weary, hot self out of the cab to give her a hand.

The girl softened at my willingness to help. "The whole name is Candy Robison. My great-grandfather was the only man in town who believed Freddy Crystal's story and invited him to live at the ranch so Freddy could prospect." She paused, expecting a response from me, but didn't get one. "Don't you recognize the name?"

We loaded a second tire next to the first as I grunted, "Should I know Freddy Crystal?"

Candy retrieved a large backpack from under a bush. "In 1914, Freddy rode into Kanab on a bicycle, with a newspaper article about Indian picture writing."

"Petroglyphs?"

"Yeah, that's the word. So he convinced great-grandpa Robison there was gold in the Kanab hills. Great-Grandpa grubstaked the search and, after several months, Freddy found the carved pictures in Johnson Canyon, but no gold." She looked at me in triumph, as if everything must be clear. It wasn't.

She sounded disappointed. "I guess you're not from Kanab."

"Not in this life," I stated, folding two rat-eaten blankets to throw over the tires. Zeus settled on top like King of the Mountain.

Candy breathed a weary sigh, knowing she'd have to tell a long story. "Freddy searched the canyon for two years and came up with nothing. The whole town made fun of him and he left." We hefted a jack onto the truck. "He came back in 1921 with an old map drawn on cactus fiber…said he'd found it in a monastery in Mexico City. The map was four hundred years old, drawn by one of those priests who wears a black dress and lived during the time of the Spanish explorer guys, Pizza or Cortez, I don't remember who."

"If Freddy's map came from Mexico City, Cortez was the conqueror."

She considered the information while we shared the weight of a tool box. "Cortez sounds right. Anyway, he tortured lots of the Inca guys---"

"Cortez defeated Aztecs," I cut in. "Don't confuse South American Incas with Mexican Aztecs."

She shrugged the detail off and positioned the toolbox toward the back. "The priest---"

"Friar," I corrected.

"Friar," she gave in. "The Friar drew a map from what one of the…uh…Aztecs," she looked at me for approval and I nodded agreement. "…what the Aztec guy said while he was being tortured. The map ended up between the pages of a big book in a Mexican monastery. Freddy recognized some of the marks on the map as the same from carvings in Johnson Canyon."

"So you're going to Johnson Canyon."

She ignored me. "It took a few years, but Freddy followed the map to a canyon with seven mountains. He found steps, like the map showed, going up one of the mountains to a cave plugged with blocks and some kind of cement. When he broke through, there was a tunnel that ended in another cemented wall, then more tunnels. It was too big to work alone. He got people from town to help him dig out the mountain in exchange for a share of whatever they discovered."

I placed a couple of shovels and some rope next to the tires. "What did they expect to find?" Zeus yawned noisily during Candy's explanation.

"They weren't sure, but figured somebody went to a lot of trouble to build those tunnels. Booby traps were everywhere, big boulders set to fall on people, pits to drop into. Folks figured something valuable must be in there. Seventy-five percent of the town got involved, even built a tent city close to the mountain so they could search the caves every day."

"How many caves?"

She tossed a rusted hammer into a truck corner. "Who knows? The mountain is still full of tunnels, like mazes leading to mostly empty rooms."

"Mostly?"

"They found some statues like guards at one of the entrances, and a pair of rotting leather sandals. Somebody picked up rusty trinkets. One room had a big skeleton sitting in it. They named him Smiley. But after three years of digging, there wasn't any gold. Everybody got discouraged and went home to farm potatoes. Freddie stayed for awhile, but one day he disappeared. People thought he might have found something and sneaked away so he wouldn't have to share it. They never saw him again, but didn't forget him, either. My family spent the next eighty years living down the fact that they fell for his story. We don't talk about it, but I'm not giving up."

I loaded Candy's two water containers onto the truck bed, refilled from my Shove-it supplies, while she threw the last item into the truck, a crowbar that clattered against the side. "That's it," she said. "Thanks for the help." She walked toward the cab.

I followed her, crammed with questions. "Do you know where the steps are?"

"Sure. Everybody in town knows. The Boy Scouts camp out there and practice making fires where they can't burn anything down." She entered the cab and slammed the dented door behind her.

I draped my elbows over her open window. "How old are you, Candy?"

"Fifteen."

I smiled. "You're driving illegally."

She exhibited the gleeful expression teenagers get when they defy rules. "Not only that, I took the truck without permission and I'll be grounded for the rest of my life un-less…" She stopped abruptly.

"Unless?" I encouraged her to finish.

She thought before completing the sentence. "Unless I go back home with the gold."

I leaned my back against the grimy truck, adding its dirt to the collection that already covered me. "So you're going by yourself to explore an old, booby-trapped gold mine?"

"Nope." She took a swig of bottled water, certainly hot by now, then added the punchline. "Freddy studied the map again before he left and figured the upper tunnels were a decoy to throw people off the real entrance. I found the new directions he wrote."

I stifled a yawn. The story was older than the hot dust I was standing in. Every failed gold mine pointed to a real one just around the corner. "Candy," I said, leaning against her window frame, "Freddy didn't find anything after years of searching, even with the whole town helping. There's no chance you'll discover a new tunnel of gold. Go home, be a cheerleader, enjoy the Junior Prom. There's no gold mine out here."

Her head leaned slightly toward me. "Did I say it was a gold mine?"

"You said you'd go home with gold."

Candy's dour little mouth spread itself into a sneer. "But I won't dig for it. All I have to do is find it and pick it up."

I waited blankly for more information. She looked straight into my eyes, her face the picture of sincerity and truth. "It's the Lost Treasure of Montezuma."

CHAPTER THREE

Montezuma! Candy couldn't possibly know all the nuances that came with that name. *Montezuma's revenge* for one, or the Marine song that begins with *From the Halls of Montezuma*. There's Montezuma's castle, his well, and two or three mountain peaks resembling his head. Lakes and streams bubble with his name, while the Treasure of Montezuma is hidden in every nook, cranny, and cave from Mexico City to the Grand Canyon. Arizona's Lost Dutchman Mine is my personal favorite. Kanab can't compete.

I lowered my head to hide a smirk before asking, "What do you know about Montezuma's treasure?"

"I know it's out here and this is my day to find it." Candy turned the key in the ignition, giving the truck life. "So either come or leave, because I have to get going." With her right hand on the wheel and her left elbow out the window, she addressed me. "What's it gonna be?"

I feigned surprise. "Do you want me to go with you?" The girl nodded. Something in the air puffed at the edges of my imagination. Maybe Candy knew nothing, but I would always regret driving away without knowing. "I'm in," I announced.

The frail-looking teen hit the side of the truck with enthusiasm. "Great! Maybe this really is my lucky day."

I returned to the Shove-it for my "plan-for-the-worst-in-the-desert" kit: a fanny pack for me with two bottles of water and assorted snack items; a second doggy pack for Zeus to carry, with a tin water bowl, the word "doggy" stamped into the side. I threw on a lightweight, long-sleeved cotton shirt with thick purple stripes, originally purchased to make me look skinny. It failed and deserved to fade in the sun. There were two red, round scarves filled with a gel that expanded in water. When wet, they kept both human and dog necks cool. Zeus wore his pack behind his shoulders, the tin bowl hooked to his neck chain. My outlandish outfit was topped by a large red and yellow umbrella hat, designed to fit on the head with straps. When I entered the truck's passenger side, Candy grinned and quipped, "We usually wait until October to celebrate Halloween."

I removed my hat. "Show some respect. I'm your lucky day."

Candy pushed in the clutch and ground the gears into first. "Look," she said, "maybe the dog really was good luck. I feel like I can trust you." She lurched forward.

"Ah, but Sweetheart," the words bounced from my mouth as we struggled through a rut, "can I trust you? Gold brings madness, and your story is already insane. I should take you back to town."

"Please," her voice cracked with desperation. "I know exactly where I'm going this time." *This time?* I stayed silent and she continued. "If you promise not to get greedy, I'll cut you in." She gave a weak smile. "Besides, I need you to be my adult supervisor so I can legally drive."

"Agreed." I laughed.

The truck thrashed through sand on its half-flat tires. "So," Candy down-shifted into low for a hill, "Tell me about Pizza and Cortez."

I uttered a sigh. "Pizzaro had nothing to do with Montezuma's gold." I happily launched into a history lesson for my captive audience. "Cortez is the Spanish explorer who defeated fifteen million Aztecs with six hundred Spanish soldiers. The Emperor Montezuma ruled from his very wealthy city of Tenochtitlan, which," I added wistfully, "is buried beneath Mexico City and can't be excavated."

I silently lamented the inaccessibility of Tenochtitlan until Candy brought me back with a question. "When did Cortez take over?"

"In 1519 he invaded eastern Mexico and made his way to the capital. Montezuma met him outside the city, offered lavish gifts of gold, and politely asked him to go away. But when the Spanish saw the treasures of the Empire, they wanted it all and easily took Tenochtitlan. Cortez had to leave town to fight a small army from Spain, sent to arrest him for disobeying orders."

Candy spit out the open window before commenting, "He fought his own countrymen?"

"And made them his prisoners. But they slowed him down on the march back to Tenochtitlan, so he left them behind. They were captured by the natives and eaten." Candy's eyes grew bigger. I laughed and continued. "Meanwhile, back in Tenochtitlan, two thousand Aztecs and a host of pack animals carried away the national treasure. By the time Cortez returned, Montezuma had been murdered by his own angry people and the rooms once full of gold were empty."

"Why didn't Cortez follow their trail? It must have been big enough with all those people and heavy gold."

"He and his men had to battle their way out of Tenochtitlan, with dead bodies from both sides filling the moats and bridges. Cortez barely made it out alive. It took two years for him to build a new army and defeat the Aztec Empire again."

"I'll bet it was harder the second time," Candy said.

"Harder and longer," I agreed. "By the time he succeeded, clues to the treasure trail were cold. He used extreme torture to discover where the riches had been taken. But all Cortez could get before death took his victims was an agonized *north* or *seven cities*."

Candy gave me a quick sideways look. "What was *that* supposed to mean?"

I shrugged. "Nobody knew. For four hundred years the Spanish and later Mexicans built trails north trying to follow Montezuma's treasure. Eventually, the search narrowed down to what was called The Seven Cities of Cibola."

"What did *Cibola* mean?"

For a teenager, the kid asked good questions. Fortunately, I knew the answer. "It might have been a Spanish corruption of the Zuni word for "Bison."

Candy scrunched her little face into wrinkles. "Isn't a bison just a buffalo?"

"Right. The maps and legends pointed straight to the American southwest. Archaeologists have found parts of the Old Spanish Trail in Arizona, Colorado, Southern Utah, and California, but not a shred of treasure."

"How come you know so much?"

"Like I said, I'm smart. How come you don't know so much?"

"I'm just a kid," the girl quipped. "I'm not old enough to know everything…like you."

We both shut up, bouncing through the desert dirt. Rattles from Candy's decrepit truck filled the silence. The thought that Montzuma's riches could be hidden in the hills of Kanab tickled the back of my neck, but I didn't laugh. Stranger things have happened, like the discovery of Troy by a German businessman who believed Homer was telling the truth; or the emergence of Sumeria at the feet of a bored French government worker idly kicking at dirt. A British housewife on a leisurely stroll stumbled across the first dinosaur fossils, and Egyptian hieroglyphics were finally cracked by a French teenager. Anything is possible. Kanab could be the hiding place of one of the greatest treasures of the world.

Yeah, right.

Candy suddenly swerved off the road and parked on top of dry weeds poking from a patch of hard dirt. "This is it," she announced, jumping to the ground. "We walk from here." She slipped into her pack, adjusted the straps, and headed for a canyon entrance. I grabbed my gear, plopped the umbrella hat over my head, and followed her through knee high desert scrub. Zeus peered over the top of the cab, his big, dark eyes analyzing whether to stay or follow, but he knew he needed me to give him water in the bowl chained under his neck and the lunch strapped to his back. He bounded out to join us and we trekked away from the truck, the hot noon sun agitating air into waves of motion.

Twenty minutes later I dragged into a canyon, eyes glued to Candy's slithering pants trail in the dust. Drops of sweat dried up almost immediately, depositing salt on my skin. Zeus pushed against me trying to get shade from my hat brim, his dog bowl banging against my knees.

"Time out," I begged, settling on a small ledge big enough for one, shaded by the cliff.

Candy spoke casually. "You should always look for rattle-snakes before you sit." I leaped away from the seat and she laughed, dropping into my place. "I've already checked," she smiled wickedly. She drank deeply from her canteen, wiping her shirt sleeve across her mouth like a man. Candy probably wouldn't be nominated for Prom Queen.

I leaned against the cliff, conscious of red sandstone lifting itself into the sky. Inert air settled around us, small creatures scurried under the changing shadows of rocks. I unhooked Zeus' bowl and filled it with water. He noisily lapped at it, then placed his giant head against my thigh, dribbling slobber on my pants. I was grateful for the cool wetness and rubbed behind his expensive ears, specially cut to stand straight up. After the surgery, he wore a clown-like collar to prevent him from scratching his ears and ruining the effect. The whole image…

"Whoa," I exclaimed, startling Zeus by stepping forward. "What's that?" A panel of petroglyphs unexpectedly came into focus above the canyon floor, its large size a perfect camouflage. The wall must have been eight feet high, maybe ten feet long.

I turned to Candy. "This is something I should examine."

"We don't have time to climb up there," she answered.

"I'll make time."

Candy stood to leave. "It's just a bunch of chicken scratches. Freddy used his Spanish map to figure out what the scratches say. The treasure is in a canyon with four forks, surrounded by four peaks. In the center is one mountain where the treasure is hidden in a cave. It matches Johnson Canyon and the White Mountain. That's where we're going." Buckling her pack, her skinny legs strode away. What could I do? I shrugged and plodded after her. Zeus lagged behind, sniffing at crawling things under rocks and ledges.

We trudged toward a mountain colored in shades of light gray. When we reached it, Candy retrieved a paper from her pack and compared it to the landscape during our hike. We passed a mound of rubble piled high against the slope, as if a giant animal had made its den in the rock above and shoved the leftovers out. I craned my neck to find the source.

Candy noticed my pause in our journey. "It's from the Kanab people eighty years ago," she explained, "cleaning out all those tunnels. Freddie wondered if they covered up the real entrance, but ---"

"The tunnels are up there?" My mind danced at the thought. "Where are the steps carved into the mountain?"

She waved her hand behind us, bending her head to examine the paper left by Freddy.

I followed her direction, scanning the sandstone cliff, irritated that Candy, after all I'd done for her, didn't guide me. Zeus ran past, scrambling after a thick-tailed lizard about the size of a rat. As my attention turned from the dog, I noticed Candy observing me, a mean smile playing at the edges of her thin little mouth. "The steps are really hard to find," she said unnecessarily. "It took Freddy two years."

My patience stretched to a thread as I snarled, "I don't have two years."

She relented under my anger. "Oh, alright, I'll show you."

Candy strutted past me several yards, stopped and turned like a Hollywood star, gesturing with both arms to a wide crag in the mountain. "Freddy had to climb another mountain around here before he could see the steps."

My eyes searched the area she indicated, but all I detected were a few foot-size holes dimpling the sandstone. Suddenly, the image came clear, like looking at one of those pictures that turn three dimensional if you stare long enough. "Amazing!" I cried, and climbed up the hollowed depressions before Candy could protest. I had ascended several steps when she found her voice.

"Come back down," she ordered. "We have more important things to do."

"I'm going to the cave," I announced, scaling the steps carved obliquely across the mountain. Glancing over my shoulder, I could see the desert floor below but realized no one at the bottom would be able to spot the holes. Candy's voice pleaded at me. "There's nothing there anymore. The tunnels are filled with sand again."

I fitted a foot and hand into place and pulled forward. "What about the statues that guarded the tunnels?"

"They're probably under the big mound of dirt and rocks on the canyon floor."

I froze. "Are you telling me," I shouted down, "that the most valuable things at the site were thrown over the cliff?"

"The most important thing to them," Candy yelled back, "was the gold. Come down."

I moved to the next handhold. "Where's Smiley?" I hoped the skeleton was still covered with shreds of clothing to identify his origin.

"He's sitting in a shed somewhere. Or maybe they buried him. Nobody knows. You're killing my time. It's five hundred feet up to the cave."

The vision of scrambling over one and a half football fields stopped me. "You win," I called to the girl below. Rummaging for a foothold down, I realized it would take a long time to descend.

A shriek rumbled through the canyon, like a piercing train whistle or a dog in pain.

"Zeus?" I bellowed the dog's name. "Candy! Is my dog in trouble?" The yelping, howling wails filled the air, bouncing between rocks to double the fearsome effect. I heard Candy's answer in spurts, as if she was chasing something. "He's running...all over the place. Something's...hanging from his lip." *A Gila Monster's got him. Zeus will die of poison before we can get out of here.* I increased my efforts to move backward, suddenly aware of the danger in our isolation. The sound of bedlam continued, interspersed with calm words from Candy and echoes of Zeus's attached bowl banging against rocks. By the time I reached bottom, Candy had disconnected the source of my dog's pain and it had scurried away.

I comforted Zeus, questioning Candy. "Was it a Gila Monster?"

"No," she said. "Just a big lizard that got tired of being chased. I lit a match under its tail and it let go."

I smiled at her creativity. "Let me take care of my dog before we move on with our..." *use nice words, Matt. Wild goose chase? Scavenger hunt? Snipe search?* I allowed the sentence to trail off and checked Zeus' jowl for broken lizard teeth. Candy walked along the cliff floor, still hoping to find a door with the word "treasure" carved on the lintel. Zeus whimpered while I cleaned the bite.

"Ms...uh...Lady?" Candy sounded unsure. She knew my name but never spoke it. I ignored her.

"Lady!" Candy spoke forcefully. I pretended not to hear and bent to the task of repairing my dog's mouth.

"Hey, Matt!" I raised my head, acting surprised to hear my name, and saw her squatting on the ground inspecting something in her hand. She stood and walked to me. "These are funny little pebbles."

She transferred five items to my hand and I rolled them with my fingers. "They aren't pebbles," I told her, "They're made of metal. Where did you find them?"

Candy pointed to the base of the cliff. "Over there. What are they?"

I enlightened her as we walked. "These, my dear, are bells worn by Spanish horses." We stopped at a four-foot pile of dirt against the mountain, widening at the base. Candy crouched to collect more bells scattered across the mound. I followed the trail of bells until my focal point riveted to the black slit of an arch peeking over the rubble. It was too symmetrical for a natural crevice.

"Candy," I announced, "the bells may have come from this opening."

She joined me, briefly inspected the void, then pulled a folding shovel from her pack and began digging while I cleared debris. When we'd finished working, a decent-sized black hole sat ominously before us, big enough for a hands and knees crawl.

"Something pushed the bells out," I warned, "and might still be living in there."

"I know," Candy replied. "That's why I'm glad the dog volunteered. Plan B is to send him in to sniff things out." She picked up a short stick and threw it into the cave. Turning to Zeus, she said, "Fetch, Boy."

Zeus looked up at her, stubby tail beating at the heat, missing the command entirely.

I laughed. "Allow me to introduce you." I scratched behind the dog's ear. "This is Zeus the Cowardly."

The girl physically forced the dog's nose into the hole and pushed on his tail. Zeus bent his big body away from the cave and circled back to her. Candy stood. "I guess Plan A will have to work." She put her baseball cap in her pack.

I spoke with concern. "Did you bring a light?" I, of course, hadn't.

She fitted a small headlamp over her dung-colored hair. "Duh," was her response as she positioned herself on hands and knees, slowly disappearing into the void.

When the soles of her shoes were in shadow, her voice drifted out. "Matt? You're gonna wanna see this."

"What's in there?"

"A whole bunch of rusty stuff."

"What kind of 'stuff'?"

A scuffling sound was followed by a long blade emerging at my feet. It was peppered in black, the cup-hilt shaped to fit a hand...a Spanish sword, typical of the 1600s.

I dropped to the dirt. "Put it back exactly where you found it," I ordered. "Move over, I'm coming in. Don't touch anything."

Once inside, there was space to kneel upright. Candy's headlamp swept over items that didn't belong in a desert den: a rusted helmet; a long chainmail gauntlet with two fingers still attached; myriads of tiny bells scattered across a dissolving leather horse harness. The size of the room vanished behind the dark periphery, light unable to penetrate, and Candy scooted farther inside. I stayed close behind her right elbow. We had inched a few feet into the cave when the girl gave a quick intake of breath and switched off her light. We entered the blackness of the blind.

"Don't move," her voice rasped out a whisper. "Don't breathe."

The sound of soft movement scraped against the dirt floor. I closed my eyes tightly against the dark, hoping to block out the stirring. Candy's arm shuddered, the involuntary movement of terror which transferred to me when I felt an undulating slither across my outstretched ankle. My natural reaction was to jerk away, but horror paralyzed me. The thing caressed my skin in a cool, oily motion, gradually getting smaller, the end finally dropping to the dust.

We remained motionless for an interminable time until we heard Zeus barking beyond our abyss. Candy finally whispered, "Back up...slow. Where there's one, there's a bunch." My movements were so sluggish not even the pebbles beneath me scraped a sound. During the exit my hand hit something rectangular and heavy. I gripped it instinctively for protection, realizing how useless it would be against the bite of a snake, but I pulled it with me as I backed from the cave. Zeus, the stupid, cowardly dog, greeted me with his wet nose against my neck and I stayed on all fours to collect strength, leaving the strange rock on the ground. I figured the snake had moved on after meeting Zeus and it was safe to remain in the dirt until Candy made it out. When the shock wore off, we stumbled to our feet and stared at each other. My thoughts were how lucky we were to be alive, but she opened the conversation with, "What's the black thing on the ground?"

I looked down, too drained to analyze it. "If you have the energy to pick it up," I offered, "you can have it."

To my surprise, she did. Agile teenagers don't appreciate what they're capable of. "It's really ugly," she commented, studying it in her hands. "Why is it so heavy?"

My stupor dissolved and I straightened to examine it. "I think it's a silver bar."

"No it isn't," she said. "Silver is…silver. How come it's so black?"

"It's old and tarnished. The Spanish must have smelted silver into a bar and cached it here."

"Cashed? Like at a bank?"

"They hid it here, expecting to come back later. Obviously, they didn't." I smiled broadly. "Young lady, I don't think you'll be grounded when you put this on the table. Spanish silver isn't Aztec gold, but it's still an impressive find. I'll bet there's more in there."

Candy cheered and jumped in a circle, holding the black rectangle with two hands above her head. "I'm rich," she crowed.

I popped her balloon of innocence. "You know, of course, about the Antiquities Act. The cache is on public property and you'll have to report your discovery. An archaeologist will come and assess the place and you might get a small finder's fee in time to help pay your college tuition."

The girl's eyes darkened. "It's mine," she said flatly, turning and striding back through the canyon. "I'm spending it all."

I caught up with her. "When you try to sell it, the dealer will have to call the authorities and you'll be considered a thief. You might even go to jail. It's better to inform the state and be grateful for what they give you."

"The state doesn't need it," she protested, venom in her voice. "It isn't fair."

"Life isn't fair," I said bluntly. "Get over it."

Candy looked at me with squinted eyes of distrust. "How come you know all this stuff?"

"Because," I said indifferently, "I'm an archaeologist."

She stopped walking, alarm clouding her face. "Would you rat on me?"

"Yes." I continued to saunter forward.

She brutally kicked a rock. It skipped down the canyon like a flat pebble across a stream. "I knew it," she grumbled. "You and your dog were not good luck."

"Don't forget," I goaded her over my shoulder, "you promised me a cut."

She wasn't amused and hurried ahead, leaving a chill in the heated air between us.

CHAPTER FOUR

Fortunately, Candy waited for us at her truck, but deliberately ran over every bump and hollow in the road, barely slowing down to let us out at the Shove-it. By the time we settled into our car, dust hung in the air from Candy's hasty exit. Maybe I shouldn't have mentioned the Antiquities Act, the small finder's fee, or that she promised me a cut. The lure of gold had struck again, capable of destroying the best of friends and partners, which didn't describe my relationship with Candy. The girl was devious, disobedient, churlish, rude, and obnoxious. I liked her. I hoped she would remember to fill her tires with air, knowing she wouldn't. Oh, well.

After the dust settled, Zeus and I returned to the little restaurant where the day's adventure had started. I paid for breakfast and ordered dinner while Zeus stayed on a short leash under a tree. It was six p.m. when we rolled north again on highway 89.

"We've wasted the day, Zeus," I told the animal, "and our budget doesn't include a motel. We have to keep driving." The dog cheerfully thumped the remnant of his tail against the middle seat, which I took as a sign of agreement. Thus encouraged, I continued on the two-lane narrow road that the map optimistically called a highway. We wove through mountain canyons and high deserts, with tiny hamlets sprinkling themselves like measles on the face of the landscape.

Two hours later, highway 89 ran through a real town with multiple gas stations and fast foods. I gratefully utilized everything gas stations offer, stopped for milkshakes and French fries, and checked Jack-the-Real-Estate agent's directions. In thirty miles I needed to connect with Interstate I-15. We returned to the road as the sun glided behind the horizon, coloring the sky in pinks and yellows until black erased everything. The dark desert swallowed my headlights and I lost a sense of movement. A dashboard clock ticked away time.

One drop of water splattered like a bug against the windshield, followed by its playmates, turning the shower into an attack. The car wipers couldn't keep up with sheets of water rolling off the windshield and I slowed to a crawl, rummaging for sunglasses. I'd read somewhere that dark lenses could improve vision in the rain, but this time the trick did as much good as a sieve in a tsunami. Five minutes later I became vaguely aware of buildings on both sides of the road. A red light, distorted by rain, stopped me at an intersection. I edged onto a side road that turned up a hill to a parking lot where I waited for a pause in the weather. And then the Shove-it did what it had never done before.

It died.

I twisted the key in the ignition. It ground out a rattle, running itself to a final silence. The howl of pounding rain filled the car. I stared morosely out the window into the maelstrom.

"Well, Zeus," I spoke to the creature inhabiting the middle seat, "we're stuck here." The dog was already comatose, his large head resting on my only pillow, drool spreading below his tongue. Reaching for a blanket, I pounded it viciously into a ball, stuffed it under my neck, and squirmed the night away.

Dawn pierced the clean-washed air and Zeus whined his need to visit the great outdoors. A crick in my neck competed with leg cramps as I hobbled to clip a leash on the dog's collar. The parking lot was halfway up a hill with manicured grass under tall pines, white spires of a church peeking through tree branches to our right. After Zeus contaminated a bush, we climbed toward the top of the hill to check out the view. To the west, houses and farms were snuggled into a valley stopped by foothills. At my left, on the crest of the rise, I was startled to see a bent figure sitting on a large boulder, staring east toward the massive Rocky Mountain range.

"Hello," I greeted his back. "Can you tell me where I am?"

He pivoted slowly on the rock to meet us. Gray hair and a short, grizzled beard framed light green eyes under bushy eyebrows. His tanned leather face was pale at the forehead where a hat usually sat. I'd seen better skin on Egyptian mummies.

"I don't git too many guests at my sunrise," his voice rasped. "Sit yerself down 'til the show's over." *My sunrise?*

It was a quaint way to describe the daily event. His speech had an uneducated background, matching his dirt-farmer appearance, with overalls so ancient the original color could only be surmised.

"I need to find I-15 going---"

"Shhh." The man touched the rock in a silent order for me to take a seat next to him and shut up. I obeyed, hoping to question him when "his" sunrise ended. He gazed at the diffused light dripping like paint down the east mountains, and his hands began waving in front of him as if conducting a symphony. With each upbeat, the faded overalls produced a soft rustle. Illumination from the sun moved over scrub oak, grass, and the ever-present sagebrush, while the man's arms increased their tempo, his body rocking to fit the gestures. As the radiance rolled up our hill, the old guy pushed himself to a standing position, wobbling slightly at the effort, and performed a flourishing finale. When the full force of sun hit him, he stood with arms raised to the sky in a victorious end.

He relaxed and turned to me. "It's not safe ta' look enymore," he warned. "A sneak peek is all we git. He doesn't like ta' be watched." My face couldn't conceal the astonishment I felt at his bizarre performance. He paused before asking, "Da' ya' think I'm crazy?"

Absolutely yes, I thought. *You just conducted the sunrise.* "Absolutely not," I humored him. "My name's Matt Howard. This is my dog, Zeus. We got stopped by rain last night and my car died. I need to get it fixed and find I-15 going north."

"I'm Ezra Snow." He rested his hands in the bib of his overalls. "Folks around here say I'm a little crazy. If they saw me greet th' sun, they'd say I wuz a *lot* crazy. Ya' passed th' I-15 turn-off thirty miles back. Right now, yur standin' on Manti Hill." Ezra's stream of consciousness meandered beyond its banks. His tone lifted higher. "Would ya' like ta' hear about th' hill? T'won't take long."

I'd seen other wrinkled faces in my life, begging to be heard, gray little people in nursing homes, full of memories destined to die with them. I made a quick study of the elderly man. If he turned out to be dangerous, he was too skinny to win a battle against me. "I'd like to hear about your hill," I said.

His clear green eyes sparkled under their folds of skin and he positioned himself on the rock again, this time his back to the sun. "My gran'pa wuz only nine years old when he come ta' this valley with th' first settlers in 1849. He told me th' secrets a' th' hill."

I joined him on his rock. "I like secrets, Mr. Snow."

He rested his arms on his legs. "Two hunderd twenty-four people stopped here. Th' snows begun that night. Next day th' men and boys started diggin' caves in th' hill fer shelters. Injuns warned 'em th' hill wuz sacred. If they lived there, they'd die in th' Spring. But it wuz too late ta' build cabins, so th' families set up housekeepin' in twenty-seven caves an' stayed all winter. My gran'pa worked with th' men in three feet a' snow ta' find grass fer their cattle, but most a' th' livestock starved. Those folks thought it couldn't git worse..." Ezra grinned his uneven brown teeth at me, "...but it did."

Zeus folded himself on the grass next to me and I rested my hand on his warm neck, nodding for Ezra to proceed. "Spring finally come," he said, "an' one day, jest after sunset, a rattlin', hissin' sound come frum ever'where at once, an' spotted rattlesnakes dropped ta' th' ground. Th' men grabbed torches and killed three hunderd of 'em th' first night. Next day, th' wimmen found snakes curled in cupboards, restin' on beds, coiled under tables, an' th' battle kep' up ever day 'til th' snakes wuz mostly gone."

"That's a fascinating story, Mr. Snow." I stood to leave. "I'm glad I got to hear it."

Ezra reached out to stop me. "That's jest th' beginnin'."

"I don't have much time," I apologized.

The man whined his response. "But th' best part is comin'." His eyes had the same hungry look Zeus gets when I put a piece of meat on the grill. My next decision proved I wasn't totally devoid of human kindness. "I'm glad there's more," I lied, and returned to the rock. "Tell me the rest of the story." I figured I could use extra credit when I died and went to wherever I went.

The old guy hurried to finish his story before I could change my mind. "My gran'pa said there wuz sumpin' mighty strange 'bout those snakes. Some fell frum rocks and ledges higher on the hill, but lots of 'em came frum th' back walls an' ceilings a' th' caves. Th' dirt wud move like it wuz alive, an' out wiggled a black spotted snake."

I tried not to be intrigued, but it was too late. "Where were they coming from?"

Ezra sat straighter and folded his arms, speaking in triumph, "Frum inside. Them snakes hibernated in manmade tunnels leadin' ta' th' center a' this hill."

"Slow down, old timer," I raised my hands to ward off his lunacy. "How do you know the tunnels were manmade?"

"My gran'pa got th' story frum Injuns that lived around here. They said a big bunch a' people come through a long time ago, too many years ta' count, an' they dug tunnels like a maze ta' hide sumpin' inside this here hill." He turned his head toward me. "They put the snakes in ta' protect a treasure. But th' settlers killed th' snakes an' filled in the tunnels without explorin' first. Everthing's blocked off now." The man waxed angry eloquence. "I keep tellin' these people ta' tear down th' hill an' git rich. No more dry farmin', or milkin' cows or savin' chickens frum skunks. We all got televisions an' we kin see how th' other half lives. Those rich folks could be us."

"Doesn't anybody listen to you?"

"Durn fools, that's whut they are. When I'm gone, th' truth'll die with me."

"Did your grandfather tell you what kind of treasure is in this hill?"

Ezra Snow raised his eyes to the branches of a tall pine next to us. "Stuff made 'a gold," he said to the tree. Lowering his head he faced me. "Lots a' gold."

My words held a touch of derision. "Maybe Montezuma's treasure is buried under our feet."

Ezra's eyes clouded in confusion. "Who?" He had never heard of Montezuma.

I stood, thanked him for his story, and Zeus and I escaped to my car. The Shove-it, having had time to repent, coughed to life in its usual cheerful manner.

We found I-15, grateful to enter the real world. I briefly considered the possibility that Montezuma's servant with all those slaves hid their Aztec treasure under Manti Hill.

Nah.

Over the next three hours, Jack Jamison's directions took us past modern cities and through mountain gorges cradling reservoirs and ski resorts. Eventually, road signs for Kamas pointed to a steep route going east into the mysterious Uinta Mountains, the only major range on the continent running east and west. Someday I'd ask a geologist to explain how that happened.

My introduction to Kamas began with a trailer park on the left. I drove past two forty-ish women sitting at three card tables by the side of the road, a large "SELL" sign which should have been spelled "SALE" propped against a table leg. High cheek bones and round faces identified them as Indian, probably Ute. They were dressed in long full skirts topped by billowing blouses, their thick ebony hair pulled into single braids down their backs. I figured they must live in the trailer park. Three chubby toddlers sat in the dirt by the tables, playing with rocks.

On a whim I stopped, left Zeus in the car, and strolled over to see what I could buy. I smiled warmly at the two ladies and our eyes locked. I halted in my tracks as if I'd been hit. They had constructed a barricade of loathing and I crashed into it, like the proverbial brick wall. The hate was so strong and viable it became a living thing with power, something wild and dangerous. I backed up, still clinging to an artificial smile, then turned and hastened to my safe little Shove-it and my friendly dog. I locked the doors and drove into town.

Mr. Jamison's real estate office was in a strip mall, sandwiched between a Day-old Wonder Bread store and a video rental place. Zeus stayed in the car while I opened the single glass door with *Jamison Real Estate* painted on it. The one-room office had mismatched K-Mart files against the walls and a metal desk piled high with papers.

I called out a timid "Hello?" Curly brown hair popped up behind the desk, followed rapidly by a head, shoulders, arms, and a T-shirt that said, *Eat well. Stay Fit. Die anyway.*

"Hi," the man said. "I'm Jack Jamison. I've been under my desk getting grape jelly off the carpet. What can I do for you?"

In my book, a man who eats grape jelly and cleans up his own mess is a good guy. I smiled broadly. "My name's Matt Howard. I've inherited a house in the Uinta Mountains."

The man was in his late thirties, possessing a face smooth enough to exude the confidence of youth, but included enough wrinkles to suggest experience. "I expected you yesterday," he said with a touch of resentment.

"We were delayed by a storm."

"We?"

"I had to bring my dog."

He pursed his lips. "That'll make it hard when you try to find a place to stay. There's a Motel Six down the road that might let you keep the dog with you. The price is right, but it should be called Motel Three-and-a-Half."

"I plan to stay in my potential house." *Given the fact that my cash is low.*

"Not a good idea." Concern edged his voice.

I ignored his tone. "You said it had electricity, running water, and an indoor toilet. Have bears moved in?"

"Well, it's...um..." *Um? He's looking for excuses.* "It hasn't been cleaned in awhile."

"I've got a mean hand with a broom," I lied. "Dust is my specialty." The truth is, my mother was addicted to housecleaning, but I never picked up the nasty habit. "Besides," I added, "I don't have the money to stay in town."

He thought for a second. "Is your dog big?"

"A Great Dane-Boxer mix."

Mr. Jamison spoke under his breath, more to himself. "Then you should be okay."

"Terrific," I said with pretended enthusiasm, nervous about why I might *not* be okay. "I'll pick up supplies, meet you back here, and follow you in my car." I showed my I.D., signed temporary occupation papers, shook Jack's hand and drove a few blocks to a modern grocery store.

By noon we were behind Jack's car on a road that scraped against cliffs on our left and plunged on the right into a valley of scattered homes. In twenty minutes, even isolated cabins vanished, yet we drove higher. Jack's sudden left turn onto a dirt side road made me wonder how often he visited the place. Cousin Hilda Hathenbruck must have had confidence in the guy, but I doubted she made many trips on this winding trail. If we came face to face with a bicycle, one of us would have to swerve into the trees. Zeus' head jerked with the twists and turns of the car until we drove over a slight hill and stopped in front of a grass-covered clearing, wildflowers adding tiny bits of color.

Backed against a cliff stood a two-story yellow brick house with a wrap-around porch, its gingerbread trim dripped like cake icing around the eaves. We exited the car and Zeus bounded off into his private puppy nirvana. I leaned against the Shove-its hood for support and stared at the exquisite house...my house. Primeval forest grew beyond the meadow, but a peculiar half circle of bare dirt sat directly in front of the house, a few patches of straggly, straw-colored weeds stabbing through the ground.

Mr. Jamison was halfway to the porch when he turned. "Are you coming?"

I put my feet in low gear and walked dreamily through the green field before crossing the ragged barrier of vegetation-free clearing. It reminded me of an unfinished fairy ring without the mushrooms. "Who keeps the growth down in the front yard?"

"Nobody." Jack walked across a single small step to the porch and front door. I noticed the house had been built directly on the ground, an unusual design. Even cabins were normally raised a few feet from the land.

My interest turned back to the yard. "Somebody has to kill weeds and keep trees out."

"Nobody comes up here." He wiggled a key in the lock of the front door, which boasted the original stained glass flower design framing both sides.

I surveyed the irregular ten-foot half circle of dead dirt, then followed Jack Jamison into the house. The door fronted a steep, straight staircase leading to a landing on the second floor. On the main floor to the right of the stairs, a long hallway was lit by a single bare bulb in the high ceiling. The house had a typical turn-of-the-century floor plan, starting at the left with a dining room. The original chandelier, designed for candles, had countless glass prisms to reflect light. It hung over an oak table with six chairs upholstered in needlepoint. An aged, ornate mirror topped a sideboard.

Jack led the way to the kitchen, jabbering something about an electric pump bringing water from a well. He twisted the flower-shaped ceramic faucets that coughed up spurts of water, and grinned broadly when a decent stream emerged. The kitchen had a small wringer washing machine connected to an old-fashioned electric socket protruding from the wall. I followed the wire's course, which disappeared through the ceiling. A small bathroom jutted into the room with a tiny toilet as alternative to an outhouse. The added luxury of a mini shower stall made me grateful to Cousin Hilda, who had thought of everything.

A pantry brought us full circle to the hall, which we followed toward the front door. A touch of cold hit my right side.

"Why is it chilly in the hall?" I asked Jack, touching the wall.

He had already reached the end of the corridor and turned left into the parlor. "It's warm in here," he called back.

I let his evasive statement pass and joined him in the final downstairs room, the parlor. It contained ornate Victorian furniture with red velvet cushions. Above the fireplace hung a huge 3 x 5 foot oil painting of a man dressed in fringed buckskin. He sat on a tree stump with blue sky and white clouds as backdrop. A double-barreled rifle rested against his left leg to point to the heavens, held in place by his left hand. The right arm hung limply at his side, the fabric clinging to itself as if no arm were there. The guy, maybe in his early forties, had a handlebar mustache, a short goatee, and a high balding forehead with thick wavy hair past his ears.

I stood in front of the picture. "Who's this?"

Jack spoke from the door, ready to move on. "That's F.W.C Hathenbruck, the man who built the house."

"Was something wrong with his right arm?"

"He lost it in a mining accident."

I examined a thick gold chain leading inside Hathenbruck's shirt. "Whatever is on the end of the chain," I commented, "leaves a big bump. It's strange the artist didn't smooth it out."

"Hathenbruck," Jack answered, "had a watch set into a large gold nugget that he was very proud of. He wore it everywhere." Jack showed no interest in the painting, finishing with, "You know, there aren't any phone lines to this house. Are you sure you want to stay up here?"

"Kamas is thirty minutes away," I reassured him as he led me from the parlor. "My car is reliable, I have a ferocious dog, and I'm ready to see the rest of the house."

We turned up the stairs. "In a few years," Jack said, maneuvering the narrow steps, "everybody will have phones without wires that they can carry with them, like *Star Trek*."

Yeah, right. "I see you like science fiction," I countered behind him.

The landing served three rooms, one on the left, two at the right. Jack opened the first door and I stepped inside a space filled with dark wood furniture, broken beds, tables, a wardrobe, and rolled rugs leaning against the wall. Several items had been covered with gray, tattered sheets. Jack stayed at the door while I maneuvered around obstacles, dust rising to fill my nose.

"This is the only room," I said to Jack, "that hasn't been cleaned in decades. Who takes care of the rest of the house?"

"Nobody," he insisted. "Storage rooms always seem dirtier than empty ones."

I decided not to push the obvious and allowed Jack to guide me across the landing, where a framed black and white photograph of an Indian stopped me. The man had heavy wrinkles in a round face, even though his hair was still black. Two white mustaches accented each end of a solemn mouth. It looked like the man had eaten a couple of small animals whose furry little tails drooped from the corners of his lips. A cowboy bandana wrapped his neck.

"Who's this?"

Jack opened the second bedroom door. "I think that's Chief Tabby."

"Why is his picture in the house?"

"He and Hathenbruck were friends. Tabby traveled through a winter storm to help Hathenbruck get a lease for a gold mine on the Indian reservation." *So,* I thought, *the guy who built this house was into gold mining. He must have found something to have a watch set into a gold nugget.*

Jack ushered me into the second, smaller bedroom, which held a crib with two slats missing. It had been placed against the wall next to the door. Above the baby bed someone had painted an angel with crooked wings, one eye larger than the other, a billowing pale blue robe spreading to match the size of the crib. It was a sweet effort at amateur art.

We moved to the larger third bedroom where a double bed with sheets and a quilt had been pushed into a corner. A dresser minus the usual mirror supported a collection of old-fashioned sepia photographs in antique frames. A Mason jar full of brass buttons seemed out of place among the ornate pictures. The buttons appeared to be from soldiers' uniforms. I picked up one to check the design, a raisèd X bordered with a scroll. I returned the button to its plebian container and focused on the only other item in the room, a trunk in the exact center of the floor, its rounded top covered with embossed silver.

I ran my fingers over the lid. "This has value," I said to Jack. "It's barely tarnished. Cousin Hilda must have polished it. I'm surprised it hasn't been hauled off."

He laughed. "Go ahead and move it."

I kicked at it with my foot, producing not a smidgeon of change. Leaning into it with all my weight didn't budge it. "What's in this thing?"

Jack shrugged. "Nobody knows. It's been locked for eighty years."

Suddenly, I became Nancy Drew, girl detective in a house with not just one, but three mysteries. "Does the trunk go with the home?"

"If it doesn't, the owner will have to remove the roof and winch it out with a crane. I think the trunk is permanent."

A grin wrapped around my face. I liked the house settled at the edge of a bare, half fairy ring, with a cold spot in the hallway and an ominous, heavy trunk in the middle of the bedroom floor. When Jack left, I parked the Shove-it next to the back porch and hauled my possessions through the kitchen door. The house had been built so close to the cliff that there was no space between the railing and the rock. It was a strange setting and I wondered what Hathenbruck had been thinking.

I claimed the third bedroom for myself, then settled Zeus downstairs in his oversize foam bed facing the hall.

He raised his expressive dog mug up at me, thick eyebrows lifted in an accent of worry. My finger massaged the indentation between his eyes.

"You know the rules, Zeus," I told him. "You can't be in my room. Stay here."

That night I slept like the dead.

Fortunately, so did they.

CHAPTER FIVE

Zeus was gone.

With doors locked and windows shut, he had to be in the house. Apparently, he didn't like the location of his bed and now, guilty with disobedience, he ignored my insistent calls. I shook a box of doggy snacks in each downstairs room, switching to an unwrapped slice of ham that could entice even a human nose. In the pantry I spoke his name and caught a plaintive, mumbled moan that seemed to come from inside the wall. I put my mouth against yellowing wallpaper printed with pots and pans and shouted, "Zeus?"

A whine above my head led to the second floor. I found him cowering under the crib in the middle bedroom, body fused against the baseboard, jowls drooped over his paws. Something had frightened him. I slid my back down the wall to sit closer, like a parent confronting a naughty child. The dog slinked to my side, laid his head on my thigh, and

I, like all good mothers, dissolved into forgiveness and gave him the ham. "We'll try again tonight," I told him.

My house inspection/cleaning was done wearing the dog like a growth on my leg. If I looked under a table, he fell to his stomach to be near me. I found a ladder on the back porch and used it to explore the top cupboards while Zeus stood under the frame. As I sanitized the tiny bathroom, the odor of dog filled the space. At the top stair landing, the first room on the left seemed too gloomy to tackle. I decided to let sleeping grime lie and moved on to the remaining bedrooms, Zeus tripping me at every step. But when I scrubbed spots off the worn hall carpet, Zeus backed against the front door, watching intently.

I sprayed and brushed my way down the hall, aware of an increasing chill. At the halfway point, the wall released a frigid aura. Searching for a hole or opening, I ran my hand over the busy pattern of faded blue wallpaper. A slight depression met my fingers and I traced it from the floor to above my head. It was a door, boarded up and disguised, but no breeze could account for the cold.

As an intelligent, educated adult, I knew a logical explanation would surface, but an eerie discomfort persuaded me to scrub faster away from the area. At the end of the hall I raised my eyes to see Zeus the Cowardly sitting against the front door.

"Come, Zeus," I ordered. "Here, boy." His front paws trembled. I rose to my knees and commanded in a fearsome dog-owner voice, "Come." The animal reluctantly began to submit, then turned to avoid the hall, detoured through the dining room and kitchen, and joined me by the pantry door. The decisive move required more intelligence than

I thought he possessed. I couldn't get angry. He had, after all, complied. But his behavior went beyond my experience with him. I finally decided to reward his indirect obedience by patting him on the head. "I don't like the hall, either," I confided. His tail stump moved like a metronome on steroids, pumping its beat into the air.

That night I dragged the oversized dog bed into the kitchen away from the pantry, beyond sight of the hallway, and ordered Zeus to stay. Then I avoided the hall myself by circling through the dining room to reach the staircase. Laughing at my childish fear, I hurried up the stairs before the hall could grab my ankle.

Sometime during the night a great, heavy body heaved itself up the steps, toenails clicking on the wood floor leading into the second bedroom. I resigned myself to reality. "My dog gets a room of his own," I thought, rolling over to face the wall.

On the third day at Hathenbruck House I hauled the dog's foam bed up to the second bedroom. Then I set up my electric typewriter in the parlor to work on my pottery textbook. There was only one power outlet in each room, easily located by the round cord that snaked up the wall. My forced location was at a window. Squinting at white paper inside the roller, I typed the title "Pottery Paleography: Shards of Ostraca," and made my first mistake of the day: I looked through the window.

Tall Quaking Aspen waved at me with twisting leaves, undersides winking lime green. Ripping my eyes away from the scene, I resolutely placed my fingers back on the typewriter keys... and wondered about the sanity of staying indoors when I had five acres to explore.

"Get up, Zeus." The dog had settled on my toes and scrambled to get out from under the table. "We're going on an adventure."

$$\Longleftarrow\!+\!+\!\Longrightarrow$$

The forest looked as if someone had stripped the trees of their lower branches, resulting in a top canopy of forest without a lot of ground vegetation, creating a civilized, friendly jungle. The trees reminded me of Roman soldiers in a siege, bare legs planted firmly on the ground, green plumes on their helmets swaying in an attack by the wind.

My five acres, according to the plat Jack Jamison had given me, butted against the boundary of the national forest on the east. North showed a large flat area with a gully and stream running northwest to southeast. West revealed cliffs backed by layers of hills introducing tall mountains. The road returning to Kamas lay south. I cradled a cheap round compass in my hands and twisted my body until the needle pointed north and we headed through Lodgepole pine, Spruce, and Douglas fir to look for open ground.

Twenty minutes later a meadow emerged from the forest like a city park, except willows in scattered patches replaced swings and teeter-totters. Snow-covered peaks extended themselves above the opposite tree line and I stood in awe until a warning at the center of my head murmured that something must be wrong. Nobody wanted to buy the place. I chased the voice away with the thought that the universe had saved this spot for me. It was my reward because... I had to think a minute. I don't go out of my way to do good deeds or be friendly, and I tend to tell lies if the situation needs a touch of perjury. I'm not malicious but, all things considered, I'm not a totally nice person and don't deserve special favors from the universe. On the other hand, the universe isn't nice, either. It's a dangerous place, perpetually threatening mankind with extinction. I concluded that the universe and I had a few things in common, and it had given me the Hathenbruck Estate.

Meanwhile, my compass and I did not respond to each other. Its needle struggled to obey the laws of magnetism, while I turned too fast to let it settle. I kept Zeus on a long leash, one of those internal winding jobs that allowed him to wander when I needed to consult the map. It was on one of those occasions that he stretched the wire to its maximum. When I pulled to let him know I was ready to walk again, the leash might as well have been tied to a tree. Zeus stood like one of those pointer dogs, nose even with a straight spine. If he'd had a tail, it would have been horizontal. I walked back slowly, letting the wire on the leash rewind into its compartment until I saw what had captured the dog's attention.

Forty feet away stood a man knee deep in a stream, struggling to submerge what might have been a dirty sheep. It looked like he was determined to drown the animal. Whatever it was, it didn't put up an active fight so it must have already been dead. Zeus and I moved closer to get a better view. The guy wore a turquoise, billowing shirt that ended below his hips, topped with a short black vest. From a navy blue knit cap, his auburn hair fell in a long ponytail across his shoulder and halfway down his chest. Obviously, Samson-like, he never cut his hair. A bright yellow scarf was wrapped around his neck, peeking from under a brown beard dusted in gray, clashing against the reddish ponytail. He made a garishly colorful picture. Zeus rustled in the grass and the man glanced up.

"But soft," he said, stretching his hands in greeting, "What light through yonder window breaks? It is the east, and Juliet is the sun." He quoted Shakespeare with the stream lazily lapping past his knees.

"Are you talking to me?" I asked.

He lowered his hands to remove the stage presence. "Yes, I'm addressing you. You're the only one here."

"You could have been talking to the dog," I reasoned, "but neither of us is named Juliet."

"Just follow my lead," he said, slightly annoyed at the interruption. He raised his hands again and proceeded with *Romeo and Juliet*. "Arise, fair sun, and kill the envious moon, who is already sick and pale with grief, that thou her maid art more fair than she."

During my high school years I'd had the audacity to try out for Kate in *Taming of the Shrew*. I was smart enough to memorize the lines, but not pretty enough for the part. They let me be the understudy. Now this strange Romeo spoke of the sun and the only lines I could remember belonged to the masculine Petruchio in *Shrew*, insisting the sun was the moon.

"Good Lord," I said in a deep masculine voice, "How bright and goodly shines the *moon!*"

He looked blank before catching my switch in Shakespeare's plays, then sparkled in his new role as Kate, putting his hands on his hips, one leg cocked to emphasize a feminine stance. "The moon?" His falsetto tone enunciated the words. "The *sun*: it is not moonlight now."

I folded my arms across my chest in Superman style. "I say it is the *moon* that shines so bright."

He waded out of the stream, leaving his fluffy dead thing in the water. "*I know* it is the sun that shines so bright." His levis, heavy with water, dripped rivulets onto his boots, but he stood there in the role of a prideful woman who knows she's right.

I strode toward him, stressing the words in low tones. "Now, by my mother's son, and that's myself, it shall be moon, or star, or what I list..." The rest of Petruchio's speech wandered off while my mouth uttered a series of "um's."

The wet man rescued the scene by moving to the end of the dialogue, his high voice pleading. "Forward, I pray, since we have come so far, and be it moon, or sun, or what you please. And if you please to call it a rush-candle, henceforth I vow it shall be so for me."

I recalled Petruchio's challenge to Kate. "I say it is the moon."

He spread his turquoise shirttail like a skirt and curtsied in agreement. "I *know* it is the moon."

Laughing aloud, I applauded his performance and shook his wet hand. "My name's Matt Howard. What's a Shakespeare buff doing in this wilderness?"

He smiled through his hedge of beard. "The name's George Murdock. I'm working this area to earn a scant living." He nodded at the stream where parts of the white object showed under the water's surface. "Excuse me." He splashed back into the water, explaining, "I need to save my income and anchor the sheepskin."

"Sheepskin?"

George plunged his arms to their pits, spreading the submerged item on the stream bed. "Though this be madness," George took another stab at Shakespeare, "yet there is method in it." He rolled a heavy rock under the water. "It's an ancient mining technique," he huffed. "According to both Strabo and Plinius, sheep skins were used to gather gold in the Caucasus." He saw skepticism in one upturned corner of my mouth and added more evidence. "Appian, in Volume Twelve of his *Roman History*, also described using sheepskins." Sloshing downstream, he continued to secure the skin. "I like the method. It doesn't require mercury or cyanide." He caught his breath, doubled over with hands on knees. "No chance of burning out my brain cells."

I figured Mr. Murdock had already scorched a few cells. "Experts agree," I said kindly but firmly, "that the Uinta Mountains don't show typical geological signs of gold deposits. What makes you think there's gold in this particular stream?"

"Not only this stream." He worked in the water, his arms soaked to the shoulders. "I've got half a dozen skins gathering gold from these mountains. As for experts," George stood upright, "they need to take lessons from ancient civilizations who knew about the gold of the gods." He spit in the stream, the phlegm floating away with the current. "This," he said, spreading his arms to the landscape, "is the source of the greatest gold deposit in the world. This is the land of Colchis, where Jason and the Greek Argonauts stole the Golden Fleece." He gestured to the sheepskin anchored in the stream. "I'll have a golden fleece in a few days."

"The Golden Fleece," I insisted, "is a myth. You're implying Homer wrote history and Colchis was in the western part of North America."

"The Land of Colchis," he spoke slowly to make sure I understood his words, "was in the valley below these mountains, around a lake that was four times its current size."

My eyebrows lifted. "Are you saying Jason and his Greeks sailed around the world?"

"Are you saying they didn't?" He sloshed to shore.

I spoke with the authority of a scholar who had earned a doctorate degree. "They didn't."

George stood taller to emphasize his surety, reaching a full five feet eight inches. "The earliest civilized world," he announced, "knew about the gold in these mountains. King Solomon called it the Land of Ophir and sent his ships on a three-year journey to get gold. This is the fabled land of El Dorado and the Seven Cities of Cibola." He stared into my eyes to find incredulity and said. "Have you heard of the treasure ship, Atocha?"

"Not lately."

"It was part of a Spanish fleet that carried gold from Mexico to Spain. The ships were hit by a storm in 1622 and sank off the coast of Florida. In 1985 the Atocha was discovered. It carried a treasure worth $400 million. The guy who made the find had the gold analyzed. Guess where it came from."

"Is this a trick question? The ships were Spanish, the cargo came from Mexico, the gold had to come from---"

George interrupted me. "The Uinta Mountains!" His eyes sparkled with excitement.

"I'm not sure what that means," I said dully.

The sparkle vanished. "It means," he said impatiently, "that the Spanish melted Mexican gold into Spanish coins, but the raw gold came from," he lifted his arms into the air, "right here!"

My eyes narrowed. "You're kidding." I presented my best deadpan expression and he understood I wanted solid facts

"Listen," he began. "Both the Aztecs and their gold originally came from here. They migrated south and built an empire in Mexico. When Cortez conquered them, Tlahuicle brought the gold back."

"Who?"

George slowed the story so I could catch up. "Montezuma's servant, Tlahuicle, brought their treasure back to these mountains."

Montezuma, again. I couldn't escape the old emperor. "Scholars don't believe the Spanish came this far north," I told George. "They agree that Montezuma's treasure, if it even existed, might be scattered across Arizona and the southern part of Utah."

"Some of it was left behind in various places," he agreed, "but the bulk is in the Temple of Towats." George tended to toss strange names out like corn to chickens.

"Towats?'

"The name of the Ute Indian god."

"So Towats is an Indian god who has what?...a cave, or a temple?"

"Yes." George Murdock grinned at my confusion. "Let's sit so I can dry off."

I followed him to settle on a hillock of grass where he stretched his legs out for maximum sun exposure, balancing his upper body on his elbows, chin bowed to his chest. I sat, resting my arms on bent knees, knowing it would take two days to dry his Levi's.

The man's beard flapped against his chest in rhythm with his words. "Gold is strange, inconvenient stuff found in dust, flakes, nuggets, or deep in the earth embedded in rocks. Some theorists believe meteors deposited gold on this planet when it was forming."

I let go of the leash in my hand and Zeus, the traitor, extended himself next to the bearded man. Mr. Murdock scratched my dog's ears and kept talking. "The Uinta range is full of gold deposits in lava-tubes, but the Towats cavern is in a class by itself. It filled up with gold that melted over the heat of ancient volcanoes. The filtered gold was about as pure as natural gold can be and offered easy digging for ancient people. All they had to do was shovel it out and haul it home. Artisans pounded the soft metal into jewelry, masks, whatever. Over decades of digging, workers left pillars of gold in the main room and carved pictures on the gold walls. The place became a temple."

"How big is this cavern supposed to be?"

George thought for a second. "The main room is as big as a three-story house, with nine corridors leading to other rooms."

He's making it up. "Have you seen it?"

The man shook his head. "No, but eight other men claim that distinction. Their stories float around and hang in the air like smoke from a campfire. If you're here long enough, you breathe it in."

"Eight? Name a few."

George sat up, clinging to his bent legs. "You haven't heard of them. Names like Isaac Morley, Thomas Rhoades, Caleb Rhoades---"

"I've heard of the Lost Rhoades Mine. It's a companion story to the Superstition Mine in Arizona."

"The Rhoades family had their own hidden mine, but they were also shown the Towats temple." He turned his head to look at me. "Maybe you've heard of Butch Cassidy."

"The outlaw? I saw the movie twenty-three years ago."

"He was a friend to the Indians. They allowed him to see the temple."

We stayed silent, studying the flow of the river in front of us. Zeus put his head on the man's knee and I picked up the leash to reel the dog in. George ignored the struggle and offered a random comment. "One of the Aztec kings used to put gold dust on his body to make his skin glitter."

I remembered a Shakespeare poem and thought this was a good place to recite it.

"All that glitters is not gold.
Often you have heard that told.
Many a man his life hath sold,
but my outside to behold.
Gilded tombs do worms enfold."

"Merchant of Venice," George said in a low voice. "A lot of men have died in the tombs of these mountains." He sat straight, intermission over, and addressed me again, teacher to student. "The whole Uinta range, from Kamas to Flaming Gorge, is about a hundred miles, with at least seventy-nine recorded mining claims. Some of the digging goes deep into the earth. But the Towats temple has two entrances, one at almost ground level and another high on the cliffs." He glanced over at me and abruptly changed direction. "Where are you staying?"

I avoided his question. "Where do *you* stay?"

He pretended not to catch my avoidance of his question. "There are hundreds of decaying cabins left by old prospectors. I've remodeled a few in the areas I work. I used a tent when I first started this summer job ten years ago, but didn't feel safe from bears. In the cabins, my sheepskins dry out on plank floors and it's easy to shake out the gold."

"What kind of park permit lets you fix up old cabins and pan for…" I changed terminology "…skin for gold?"

"I don't know," George laughed. "I don't include the Park Service in my little hobby and I move around enough not to get caught. This particular place is private land and nobody bothers me."

I felt my spine straighten. *This is MY private land. The guy's stealing my gold.* Then I remembered the Hathenbruck land wasn't mine yet. Carefully, casually, I asked, "So, how much gold do you get from this stream?"

His beard scratched along his chest from side to side as he shook his head. "Not enough to make it worth my time. That's why I have six sheepskins going all summer."

"Mr. Murdock---"

"Call me George."

"George." I took a deep breath. "If there's plenty of gold in the mountains, why are you gathering grains in streams instead of finding the real treasure?"

He shrugged. "Life is too good to take a chance on losing it. If you get close to the Towats Temple, you could get killed."

I hesitated to ask the next question, afraid I'd be pulled deeper into his dark bog of a brain. "Why would you get killed?"

He spoke as if the answer was obvious. "The Ute Indians still guard the sacred places."

"If they know where the gold is," I asked, "why don't they use it to improve their lives?"

George rolled onto his stomach and scooted to a drier section of grass. "It isn't theirs to use. Only a few chosen priests protect the treasure for Towats."

"What does Towats want it for?"

"The legends say Towats has plans for the gold in the future. Until then, the Utes have orders to keep it safe. They take the job seriously."

"So, let me get this straight: there are hundreds of gold mines around here but only one cavern full of pure gold and Aztec treasure." He nodded, the ponytail undulating like a red snake down his back. I continued. "So let's say I find the entrance to a mine. How will I know if it leads to the Towats cavern?"

"If you're still alive, it's just a leftover Spanish mine, or it could be one of their hiding places full of gold bars. As for the Temple of Towats, you'll be shot if you get near it."

"Even today?"

"Especially today."

We stared at each other for a brief moment before George Murdock abruptly stood and said, "Well...duty calls. Come back in three days and I'll show you my personal Golden Fleece." The guy unwound his yellow scarf to its thirty-inch length and struck a dramatic pose, one hand on his heart, the other with the scarf held high. "Bell, book and candle shall not drive me back, when gold and silver becks me to come on! I leave your highness." He bowed low, his arm in the air resembling a weathervane with a yellow flag. He straightened again, presented the scarf to me, then turned and walked east. I examined the flimsy material and wondered what use George had for such delicate fabric. It wasn't thick enough for an ordinary nose wipe, much less a hearty blow.

"Thanks," I called after him. "Where did you get the 'bell, book, and candle' quote?"

He yelled the answer behind his back. "King John, Act three, Scene three."

I stood and brushed my pants, watching him disappear into a stand of Aspens. Stuffing the swath of yellow silk in my pocket, I recited a line from Twelfth Night.

"If this were played upon a stage now, I could condemn it as an improbable fiction."

CHAPTER SIX

The compass needle jerked itself to point north and I walked south, but the yellow brick house did not appear within a reasonable thirty minutes. My childhood *Girl Guide* training had taught me to make necklaces of pine needles, weave dandelions into crowns, and how to sell cookies…but not to use a compass. I adjusted my position to a southwest reading and walked another ten minutes. "We should have brought bread crumbs," I told Zeus, "to mark our way back home." The dog wrapped his leash around a tree and we circled a few times to untangle him. Orienting south again, the compass pulled me deeper into the forest, hiking on flat ground.

An area at my left whispered an out-of-place item. The old Sesame Street song rolled into my head. *"One of these things is not like the other…"* I gazed through the scene of tall trees, low bushes, knee-high weeds, and short growth. *"One of these things just doesn't belong."*

At the center was a poisoned fairy circle, a three-foot round version of my front yard. Slowly, I walked past living green things to step inside the ring. A single large stone jutted four inches from the dead dirt and I squatted for a better look. My fingers followed its straight shape to the top, which curved to create a hole, half filled with solid soil. I quickly removed my hand, thinking of small snakes and spiders, but put my head close to the ground to see inside the clay-packed cavity. If it were cleaned out, it would be a perfectly round hollow. Mother Nature had not been involved in its construction.

The ground was too hard to clear with bare fingers, so I searched surrounding trees for a stick. Returning to the strange stone, I jabbed at the earth inside the hole, finally clearing away enough to stand in shocked comprehension. Whatever was buried in this defunct circle had a three-inch bore. I kneeled to scrape dirt layers off the top, eventually scratching into metal. Encouraged, I rubbed harder at the spot, finally dropping the stick to use my hands. Crusted grime fell in clumps to reveal the rich hue of bronze. Only one thing could be made of bronze that ended in the lip of a three-inch aperture. I yearned for a shovel. All I had was a dog.

"Here, Zeus," I reeled in the animal and pointed to the dirt. "Dig!"

The dog stared up with liquid brown eyes and, thinking I wanted him to sit, obediently perched his slender behind on the muzzle of a buried bronze cannon. I lowered my head in frustration. "Stupid dog," I mumbled. "I'll have to go into town for a shovel." Scanning the area, I looked for a memorable sign, an irregular tree, a glitch in the land-scape to help me locate the spot again. I thought of the yellow scarf in my pocket. Tying it to a tree branch, I hoped it would make the spot visible when I returned. The long fabric lifted and danced on a tiny breeze, waving cheerfully.

With dusty clothes and sore fingers, I pulled Zeus into the west woods, reviewing what little I knew about bronze cannons. *Bronze was preferred over cast iron because...* I searched for the cliff my house settled against...*because cast iron heats too quickly and explodes the powder, killing the men who fire it.* An outcropping of small boulders made the area unique, a beacon to aid my return to the yellow scarf later. *Who would bury bronze cannons?* The story of Coronado, a Spanish explorer, leaped from a subconscious memory. During a campaign, he and a thousand men buried bronze cannons on the southern border of Arizona. Since bronze isn't magnetic, the buried artifacts were never found with metal detectors. A monument now points to the approximate spot of burial. *Why would those men bury heavy weapons?*

Zeus and I moved west through the xerox forest, an exact copy of itself in all directions. My compass and map had stopped speaking to each other, but I trusted if I found the cliff and followed it south, it would lead to my back porch. *1540! That's the date on the Coronado National Monument. So the Spanish used bronze at that time. Is it possible the buried cannon on my property is Spanish?* I shook my head. The Spanish were never this far north. I was left with no answer for how or why a bronze cannon got buried in the Uinta Mountains.

The terrain tilted up, pebbles and rocks replaced soft undergrowth and we stumbled into a cliff. Rising hope took precedence over Coronado and his Spanish cannons. Zeus pulled the leash to return to flat ground, but I jerked at him mercilessly to stay on course, both of us slipping on loose rock, climbing over boulders. I studied a large crack in the cliff, widening into a fissure, hoping to use it as a guide through the forest when I hiked back to my yellow marker. As we moved south, I noticed gaps large enough to explore. Zeus took it as a personal invitation, fighting against his restraint.

"Later, boy," I yanked him into submission. "We'll come back another day." The sun no longer breathed its light through the branches, but hid behind the cliff we were hugging. "When we get home," I encouraged Zeus, "I'll give you a whopping bowl of dog food, you lucky bounder."

I yearned for Zeus to reply. I wanted to hear him say, *"Oh, thank you, gentle mistress, I adore my dog food."* Or even, *"Think again, lady. It's steak or you're losin' a dog."* At that moment I craved another human voice. It could offer insults, taunts, even criticism about my lack of compass skill. *"You fool,"* would have satisfied my need.

"You fool," it could say, *"why didn't you learn how to use a compass?"*

"Because in my day," I would answer, *"girls didn't. They didn't do sports, either, and they could only be elected class secretary."*

"You're not a girl anymore. How did you get a doctorate in anything and not understand compasses?"

"Even in my undergrad fieldwork," I sniveled to my imaginary nemesis, *"somebody else found the site and did readings. I hated it and managed to avoid it, since it wasn't on the test. It's not my fault."*

"Well, now you're lost and it IS your fault."

The need for a human voice vanished. I pulled Zeus against my hip. "Good dog," I said, rubbing the pointy ears at their base, the way he liked. His cut-off tail moved fast enough to create a breeze. Suddenly he barked, heaved forward, and pulled me into view of a yellow brick house with white trim and a wraparound porch. Even though it didn't really belong to me, the tiny glow of a place to call home warmed my central core. I liked the gingerbread trim, the isolation, the forest, and the mystery that surrounded it. We slid off the mountain to the south side of the deck and ran across the porch to the kitchen door. It was locked, the keys hanging inside on a nail. We maneuvered the porch corners on a sprint to the front door. I fumbled for the key in my pocket and opened the lock in great gratitude.

The long hallway assaulted me with its peculiar dark boding. Zeus and I automatically nosed into the dining room and entered the kitchen where I emptied the last bag of Kibbles into Zeus' bowl, realizing a trip to town would have to be made immediately, for both dog food and a shovel. I left Zeus in the house with the downstairs lights on, figuring it would be dark when I got home, and crawled into the car for the journey.

The thirty-minute drive took me into town and I passed Jack Jamison's Real Estate Office. On impulse I swerved into the strip mall, slammed into park, and exited the car. Jack stood by one of his filing cabinets, transferring manila envelopes from one drawer to another. It looked like a wretched way to make a living. This time his T-shirt said, *"I plan on living forever. So far, so good."* He turned when I entered.

"Hello, Ms. Howard."

I'm at the awkward age when 'Miss' or 'Mrs.' could be insulting. Covering all options, Jack slurred both names and continued. "How's it going up in the mountains?"

"Great," I said. "I'm in town for supplies and a shovel."

Jack halted his filing for a microsecond, barely enough to show his unease at the word 'shovel' but I caught it. He recovered quickly. "What do you plan to dig?"

"I'm curious about the dead yard around the house and I'd like to see if there's anything under the dirt that could solve the mystery."

Jack straightened papers and stapled them together. "The Law Firm will collect heavy fines if you damage their property before you accept the inheritance." He glanced at me with a smile. "So don't dig any holes in the yard."

"Can I uncover the hall door?"

Jamison's eyebrows slanted in confusion. "There isn't a door in the hall."

"It's been covered up," I said evenly, as if hidden doors were common. "Does the house have a root cellar under it?"

"Let's find out." Jack walked to a cabinet behind his desk, rifled through the third drawer, and held up a rolled parchment. "These are copies of the original drawings," he explained, pushing aside papers on a small table to spread the yellowed plans. I held one end, he anchored the other, and we peered at the old paper looking for clues.

Jack spoke first. "I don't see anything indicating a basement or root cellar."

"I don't either," I said, then pointed to the hall on the plans. "Doesn't that line indicate a door?"

Jack placed his finger on the spot. "It shows a small closet."

"Somebody boarded it up." I cocked my head in a question.

He moved around the table to read numbers. "Judging from these dimensions, there wasn't enough head room in this closet for people to stand upright. And they were short in those days."

"Why," I asked, "would somebody board it up, wallpaper over it, and camouflage it?"

Jack rolled the plans and tied it with the original thick twine. "I wouldn't say camouflage; they just didn't need a small closet."

The answer didn't satisfy me. "So the house is just an ordinary two-story brick house built directly on the ground." I leaned against the table for emphasis. "Didn't they usually have the house off the ground, for flooding or snows or something?" Surely Jack could see the place was not a normal house.

He shrugged. "They didn't have planning commissions in those days. Maybe Hathenbruck figured a brick house didn't need air space."

"The same Hathenbruck in the parlor picture?"

"The very same, famous in his day."

I spoke in my usual brusque manner. "I never heard of him until two days ago."

Jack sat at his desk, arms crossed on top. "He showed up around these parts in the 1850s. He was educated, a doctor, knew music, married a local girl, eventually made claims to several gold mines, and was a true friend to the Indians."

I grinned. "That's a good thumbnail summary of a man's life."

"That's all I know," he shrugged. "Hathenbruck had the house built but didn't live in it. His mines petered out. At the end of his life he sold sewing machines door to door and died a pauper in the late 1920s. But he never sold his house. It stayed in the family and remained empty."

I was incredulous. "You're telling me nobody has lived in the house, yet it's still in good condition after all that time." I cut to the bottom line. "Somebody takes care of it."

Jack ignored my challenge. "Your cousin Hilda fixed the place up a few years ago. I expect it will deteriorate, like all of us." He glanced briefly down at his wristwatch, a motion that told me it was closing time. For Jack's benefit, I looked at my watch in surprise. "It's five o'clock," I exclaimed. "I have to hurry. Thanks for staying to answer questions."

He opened the door for me. "Drop in anytime. You have a few more weeks to make a decision."

The Shove-it and I drove to a small strip mall with a decent-sized grocery and hardware store. I began to fill a grocery cart that refused to move unless I applied force. I jerked the thing back and forth and kicked at the offending wheel. I was in the middle of bending over to straighten the wheel with my hands when I had the distinct impression someone was watching me. The feeling created an electric buzz down my back. Slowly I stood, still staring at the rubber circle that was giving me so much trouble. *"Don't look,"* I commanded myself. *"Keep your head down, eyes to the floor. Don't…"*

I looked.

The dark eyes that pierced mine belonged to a middle-aged woman standing at the end of the aisle, her round face characteristic of the Ute Indians. She was dressed in a colorful patchwork skirt topped by an untucked white blouse, her thick black hair fell over her shoulders. In a measured motion of disgust, she held her eyes on me while her body turned to saunter away.

"Wait a minute," I called to her, forcing my cart into a noisy, uncontrolled chase. She, of course, did not wait, and I pursued the hateful woman around the corner, determined to ask why she detested me so thoroughly. The wheel suddenly righted itself and I catapulted toward her. At the last second I swung the cart against some shelves before it hit her heel. She languidly turned to face me.

I heard myself pleading, something I rarely do. "Look, lady, I've never met you and I'm sure you don't know me, so---"

"We know you," she said, her tone toxic in the clipped words. "You drove into town three days ago with your Arizona license plates." Her eyes narrowed. "You will break the promise."

"What promise?" I spoke in frustration. "I haven't made any promise to you."

She turned away to disappear down the next aisle, leaving me grateful she hadn't pulled a knife. I pride myself on creating enemies during a battle of wits, but out-of-State license plates didn't give the same satisfaction. She had used the word "we," meaning, I assumed, the other Indians in town. Why would they dislike Arizona? Maybe there was some cultural rift between Utes and Navajos. I moved to the opposite side of the warehouse hoping to avoid the woman, almost wishing my cart had hit her Achilles tendon.

With shovel and supplies in the back of the car, I drove into the dusk, noticing houses in the gully just turning on their lights. My mind bounced between the stranger who hated me and the bronze cannon in the middle of my five acres. If I actually owned a sixteenth century cannon, every museum in the country would be offering delicious deals. That yellow scarf marking the small, lifeless circle in the forest would lead me to wealth.

The Shove-it cleared the ridge to my flat little meadow, where the house illuminated its porch from the front windows. I intended to drive to the south side of the house to park and unload groceries, but abruptly froze. Words from my subconscious replayed themselves: *"One of these things is not like the other. One of these things just doesn't belong."*

Tied to a post of the front porch, highlighted by a soft glow from the windows, hung a yellow scarf. The long fabric lifted and danced on a tiny breeze, waving cheerfully.

CHAPTER SEVEN

I unloaded groceries through the back door into the kitchen, intense irritation growing in my gut. George Murdock had shadowed me, removed his scarf from the tree, and tied it to my porch. I got violent, slamming cupboards, pummeling counters. The refrigerator received especially harsh treatment as carrots and potatoes hit against its sides. I kicked chairs out of the way, tipped over the garbage can, and threw a package of paper towels against the wall, the way a man throws a baseball, foot forward, full-armed, back muscles adding force. If the item had been a can of soup, the law offices of Hutchins, Eyring, and Lowe would have billed me to replace the wall.

"That red-headed weasel," I muttered. "That aging Shakespearean hippie." Did he think I'd be intimidated? Should I be frightened that the man had stalked me to my home? I called for my trusty dog. "Zeus!" I waited and called again, a queen commanding her army. "Zeus!" I was so angry I went through the cold spot in the hall to reach the stairs, climbing and protesting. "One shrimpy man can't begin to terrorize a heavy-set woman backed by a brute of a dog with teeth."

I found Zeus in the second bedroom under the baby crib, the amateur painting of an angel above it, her wings crooked on her back, one eye larger than the other. The sight of Zeus cowering defused a portion of my anger. The poor animal must have heard my lunatic ravings and had enough sense to hide. "C'mon, Zeus," I said in a soft, loving tone, which the dog didn't respond to. "C'mon, you useless dog," I amended, "I'm going out to the porch to get the scarf and I need back-up." Zeus crawled from his shelter, stretched, and followed me downstairs through the front door. I tore the scarf from the post, lifting it into the air, feeling dramatic as the wind whipped it into a flag of defiance.

"If you're out there, George Murdock," I yelled to the shadows of the forest, "it didn't work and I'm not scared. So crawl back to your cockatrice den." The yellow fabric fluttered out of my fingers into the night as I quoted Shakespeare. "Rich gifts wax poor when givers prove unkind! Hamlet, Act Three, Scene One." I did a regal turn into the house, Zeus padding behind me, and I bolted the door. Moving through the downstairs, I checked every possible entry to make sure George couldn't sneak into the house. In the parlor, I discovered the window open above my desk. I shut it viciously, locking it with the old-fashioned twist closure. "Let's see you get through there," I challenged under my breath. I had taken three steps up the staircase when I happened to glance above at the left bedroom door and froze mid-step as a chilling thought formed: George was already in the house.

Every Grade B horror film I'd ever seen got caught in my throat. The first bedroom at the top of the stairs would be perfect for him to hide in, skulking among the large pieces of furniture shrouded with sheets. A scene from the movie "Psycho" flashed before me: A man climbs the stairs to the landing, music ascending the scale with each step. Suddenly, violins emit a screeching, staccato noise as a figure throws itself from the left bedroom door and forces a knife into the man's chest. The victim turns, falling, while the knife again flashes and sinks again, this time into his back. He drops to the floor, his blood spreading across the carpet as the murderer backs into the bedroom and quietly shuts the door.

Paralysis fell like a net. I had passed that door a few minutes earlier, searching for Zeus. George could have jumped out and...what would he do? Probably use the leather thong tied around his ponytail to strangle me. Or he could just use the ponytail. Gathering courage and a plan, I retreated backwards down the steps, prattling to the dog as if everything were normal. "Hey, Zeus, are you hungry?" *Too loud, can't talk too loud.* "I've got a new brand for you to try." *Too fast. Take it easy. Don't give George a clue that I know he's here.* I entered the kitchen, rattled some dishes and poured dog food, making noise to cover opening a drawer and fumbling for a large, serrated knife. I turned the faucet on. "Here's water, boy. Good dog." Zeus heard my words but didn't see the expected food or water on the floor. His animated eyebrows twisted in confusion while I clipped a leash on his collar, grabbed my pack, and quietly opened the back door, shutting and locking it from the outside.

As I pulled Zeus to the car, the thought slinked into my brain that George could be crouched, waiting, in the back cargo. When Zeus bounded onto the middle seat, I hoped he would act like a real dog and bark or growl or, preferably, bite. A large slurp of saliva escaped from his hanging jowl. If George was hiding back there, he'd be drowned in drool.

We drove without incident. Gruesome George must still be in the house.

The Kamas police station had shut down for the night, with a single sergeant manning the desk. I kept my voice low and calm, so he wouldn't discount me as a frightened female. "I think there's a crazy criminal hiding in my house and I don't dare go back until an officer checks it out."

He studied me as if he should know me, then brightened. "You're Ms. Howard in the old Hathenbruck place."

"How did you know?"

"News travels fast, ya'know, in a little town." His right eye winked, too fast to be interpreted as a joke. "You've given people something more to talk about than the weather, although that's always a good subject because, ya'know, in the mountains the weather changes every hour." His right eye quickly shut and opened again. Maybe he had a tic. "The weather in these mountains can be sunny one minute and pouring rain the next. There's been hail in July, ya'know." He winked, definitely a tic. "Is your dog outside?"

"He's in the…" I stopped and stiffened, resenting my status as a topic of gossip, which even included my dog. "Can I get an officer to follow me home and check the place out?"

His sociable side retreated so the professional policeman could surface. "It's getting late and I don't like to get one of our guys out when there's no emergency. You look like you're safe enough. Why don't you come back in the morning and somebody will go up there with you."

"I can't go home tonight," I objected. "What do you suggest I do?"

The night officer screwed his mouth to one side in thought. "There's a Motel Six off the highway. It's cheap."

At the north end of town I found the Motel that Jack-the-real-estate-agent had called "Motel Three-and-a-Half." I was so shocked at its run-down condition that I neglected to tell the desk clerk about Zeus. By the time I remembered, the dog and I were already settled on the bed watching an old game show featuring a skinny lady in clingy clothes turning large letters to make words. I couldn't concentrate. There was an enemy hiding in my house. When I had met George that afternoon, he seemed nutty but harmless, even amusing. At the time, I questioned whether I needed a camera or a gun. Obviously, a gun was the better choice. Curling under worn covers, I left the flickering TV on to calm Zeus and hypnotize my frazzled nerves.

Hunger woke us better than an alarm clock. I foraged Motel Three-and-a-Half for a free breakfast roll, but the service wasn't offered. Zeus and I were forced to use our dwindling cash reserves at a gas station snack shop while filling the Shove-it. We returned to our room armed with enough sugar to guarantee a two-pound weight gain, and waited for 10:00 when the rest of the town would be awake. First stop: the police station.

"Hello Ms. Hathenbruck," the new cop at the desk eyed me with interest. "Shorty said you'd be comin' in."

"I'm not Ms. Hathenbruck," I told him. "My name is Dr. Howard." I loved using the "Dr." moniker. It was worth all those years of tests and thesis hassles just to be able to say, "Dr. Howard."

The officer at the desk changed his attitude to respectful. "Sorry, ma'am," he apologized. "I just assumed…you're stayin' in the Hathenbruck place, right?" I nodded and he stumbled on. "I figured you were a Hathenbruck, seein' as how you might inherit the place."

"Does the whole town know about me?"

He ducked his head. "Yes, ma'am."

"I suppose 'Shorty' told you there was a man hiding in my house. I need an officer to go back up with me and make sure the place is safe."

"It'll be about an hour before somebody's free."

I couldn't suppress a groan. "Is there anything to see around here?"

"The town has some great 18th century architecture. The Assay Office down the block is native sandstone, two feet thick, a hundred and fifty years old."

A modicum of interest surfaced. "Does the place still analyze gold and silver?"

"Nah. It's a landmark now. Belongs to the State Historical Society, but old Ben's there to take school kids through and you can get pamphlets and such."

I drove two blocks south and one block north to a gray stone structure styled like a box, tall trees providing shade. Iron bars on the windows protected long-gone gold that once collected inside. A large sign above the right window announced in fading letters, "Assay Office, Test and Hallmark Precious Metals." A short, crumbling stone fence surrounded the property and I followed a cement path to a portico sheltering an old wooden door. It opened noisily, its hinges squealing for oil. 'Old Ben' would have to be deaf not to hear it.

The interior had a museum ambiance, dark and cool, two windows framing the entry providing the only light. I leaned against a long saloon-type counter holding tourist maps, tracts, and brochures about the historic building. Stairs curved to a second floor where I imagined men once worked with nitric acid to reveal the worth of samples brought in by hopeful prospectors.

The building, designed to keep gold in and thieves out, was now filled with colorful grade school displays and dioramas. A sign titled "Teacher's Corner" publicized the spot where children could pin their crayon masterpieces about what they'd learned in the museum. The mock-up of a dredge, created with sticks and egg cartons, led to a diorama showing a mining camp. The scene looked like a meteor had hit the spot, leaving a lifeless depression with tiny toy miners in various stages of gold recovery. The scene of man-made destruction produced sadness. I turned to the next exhibit where a gold-painted bar was stamped with its purity content. It sat on a pedestal, ready for small hands to examine.

A male voice startled me. "I wasn't expecting a class until this afternoon. But you're not a class, are you." I turned toward the voice that came from the stairway. It belonged to an older man topped by gray hair, his loose trousers held up by green suspenders. Square glasses fell halfway down his nose.

"No," I replied. "I'm a tourist with an hour to spare." Impulsively I added, "You wouldn't happen to have an antique Spanish cannon around, would you?"

"Actually, we do," he said. "It's outside." I swallowed a surprised reaction and he led me through a back room full of assaying equipment that resembled instruments of torture. He opened the back door, allowing me to step outside. A brass cannon hung upside down by chains under a tin roof. I walked reverently to it, my fingers tracking the swell of the muzzle, moving up to the trunnions protruding from the sides. I wasn't tall enough to touch the cannon's breech at the top of a sturdy crossbeam. Returning to the muzzle, I explored the three-inch bore. It was about the same size as my buried cannon in the forest, now lost to me thanks to George Murdock.

I faced the museum curator. "Where was this found?"

He shrugged. "Gold hunters found it somewhere in the high Uintas. It was still on its carriage and they muscled it down...ruined the carriage, of course."

"Did scientists examine it? Is it Spanish? What did archaeologists say?"

"Said it was an elaborate hoax. The Spanish didn't come this far north."

"Can I talk to the finders?"

"Nope. It's been eighty years and they're all dead. "

"Is this the only cannon found in the mountains?"

"Folks say they've seen others real high, up on the ridges, but this is the only one that's been brought down. There's lead cannon balls up there, too. One was found inside a dead tree." The museum man shook his head. "It's a mystery, all right."

I ran my hand down the gun barrel. "Is there something about brass that would kill grass and weeds?"

The old guy grinned. "Living things don't like tin, copper, and arsenic, which is the recipe for brass. Lead cannon balls wouldn't help, either."

"So," I reasoned, "if a brass cannon got buried, it could poison the ground."

The old man's eyes squinted at me behind his glasses. "What sane person would bury a brass cannon?"

I studied the five-foot long Spanish barrel, its eight hundred pounds hanging from the crossbeam like a hog curing for winter. My reply was terse. "Somebody who was desperate to get rid of it."

About noon the Shove-it and I rounded the curve onto my meadow. The cop car that followed was driven by a young man in his twenties who didn't want the assignment. I'd heard the one-way phone conversation behind the door. "She says there's a man in her house." Pause. " Just go on up there, Dave, and check it out...Sanders is on that today...Because I said so."

The house seemed normal, its lights still on from the night before. "You scoundrel, George Murdock," I thought. "At least you could have turned off the lights." We parked on the south side and I let Zeus out to run. Dave and I entered through the back door, stepping around overturned chairs, avoiding spilled garbage. A few potatoes and carrots were scattered around the roll of paper towels I'd used to attack the wall.

His clean-shaven face turned to survey the damage. "Is this the way you left it?" I nodded, slightly embarrassed. "So," the cop proceeded, "the guy attacked and you protected yourself by throwing vegetables?" He moved toward the pantry door.

"No," I admitted. "I never actually saw him. I just… knew he was here." If I said George had tied a scarf on the porch to frighten me, I'd have to explain the meeting at the stream, pilfered gold in a sheepskin, and a buried cannon that was none of the cop's business. Rather than sound like a silly girl, I spoke harshly. "Please just do your job and check my house."

The young man, annoyed at my rudeness, inspected the pantry, circled through the dining room and entered the parlor. I tried to be helpful. "This window was open," I pointed out. "He probably got in through here before I closed it."

Dave studied my desk under the window, papers neatly stacked in piles. "Nothing's messed up," he observed. "A man entering here woulda' had to jump over the typewriter and the papers would be on the floor." The cop was right and I felt dim-witted for not noticing. We left the parlor and my polite policeman tested the front door. "Are you the one who bolted this?" I nodded and he continued. "Then he didn't leave this way. The kitchen door was also locked, so he didn't use it, either." He paused, then added with a sideways glance at me, "unless the guy had a key."

"He did not have a key," I bristled at the suggestion. "He's probably still holed up in the first bedroom at the top of the stairs. It's an old storage room with lots of places to hide."

The man's brows lifted in doubt. "You think he spent the night in your storage room?"

Yes, you dense moron, that's why I went into town to get help. I bit back the words that formed, the ones that would antagonize and inflame, a speech that started with insults and ended with wounds. Instead, I chose better sounds to send into the air. "I don't know where the man is now, but I appreciate you coming all the way up here to make sure my house is safe."

Dave nodded in a glad-to-be-of-service-ma'am way, squared his shoulders, and headed up the staircase, un-clipping the holster of his pistol. At the top he faced the door on the left. "Police!" he called. "Come out with your hands up." No response. He opened the door and stepped back, then moved inside. I heard the sound of shoes on the floor, wardrobe doors opening and closing, soft thuds of fabric falling to the floor. He emerged again with the words, "The room's clear." He crossed the landing and dis-appeared from my view, but I heard him rustling in the sec-ond bedroom. Soon, his heavy boots tromped across the hallway ceiling and the door to the third bedroom creaked open. There were muffled noises and a kick at something before the man returned to the landing. "What have you got in the trunk?" He descended the stairs. "It's so heavy I couldn't kick it out of the way."

"I don't know what's in it." I shrugged. "It's been locked for eighty years."

He reached the bottom and faced me. "Well, Ma'am, whoever was here is gone now. I suggest you keep everything locked up tight. Do you have any idea who it might have been?"

I decided to reveal the essence. "I know exactly who it was. A crazy old hippie named George Murdock. He was using a sheepskin to gather gold in a stream. I met him yesterday and knew he wasn't normal, but didn't think he was dangerous."

The cop's mouth contorted into a partial grin, topped by raised eyebrows of recognition. "Ms. Hathenb…Dr. Howard… I know Mr. Murdock. He was my high school drama coach… took us to State competition my senior year. He spends summers up here, winters in town, and still directs productions that are better than movies." The cop studied me. "What makes you think Mr. Murdock was in your house?"

The stupid scarf couldn't be avoided anymore. "He gave me a yellow scarf, then tracked me and saw me tie it to a tree. Last night the scarf was on a post out front." The story sounded as lame as I knew it would.

"Where's the scarf now?"

"It's gone. I threw it…" *at the forest while quoting Shakespeare…*"into the wind and it blew away."

The young man spread his hand across his eyes to rub his temples. He was already weary from the insanity of the day but remained courteous. "I'll take a look outside," he offered, and escaped through the front door. I closed it with my back and focused down the hall at the partition of the tiny bathroom that jutted into the kitchen. *If not George… then who? The hateful Indian woman? Maybe she sneaked up here from the trailer court and left her car on the highway. Then she trailed me all day until evening and tied the scarf on my porch.*

I dismissed the thought with a snort. George, with all his theatrical talents, still made the most likely suspect.

The cop knocked and I opened the door to see him holding a wad of yellow streaked with grime, Zeus at his side. I widened the door in a gesture of welcome. "That's the scarf," I affirmed, "and my dog." Zeus moved to me and I rubbed his ear to show appreciation for his loyalty.

"If you'd like," the officer said, "I'll track Mr. Murdock down and ask him a few questions. We pretend we don't know that he's panning for gold---"

"Sheeping for gold," I inserted.

Dave smiled. "We figure he's not hurting anybody." He realized he had just discounted my accusation. "I mean," he modified, "since there's usually nobody to bother." I vacillated between dropping the whole topic or discovering the truth. Truth won. "Please talk to Mr. Murdock. I'd like to learn what's going on."

Dave got in his car and dropped down on the winding path leading to the main road, which meant George wasn't within convenient walking distance. I returned to the parlor desk, where my work of the previous day sat neatly organized, ready for the next paragraph. Switching on the power, I typed, "...terminologies between 'ceramic' and 'pottery' have specific differences that must..." Two hours later a knock on the front door stopped me. I found the policeman standing stoically, his face glued into a non-committal expression. Policemen probably get special training to hide what they really feel.

"George says," the cop began, "that he didn't know you were in the old Hathenbruck place. He suggested that I show you where his cabin is. If you have any trouble, he's got a ham radio to call for help." He allowed himself the slightest hint of a smile. "My opinion is, it would be faster to drive into town than go to George's cabin. This year, it's a ways up."

I caught my cue. "You're probably right. Thank you for coming and putting my fears to rest."

The nice young man left, no doubt with a smirk on his face. I imagined the story he'd tell at the Kamas Cop Station about poor George and the lunatic lady. But I knew somebody had followed me through the forest and watched me tie the yellow material above the buried cannon. The scarf on my porch announced that I was being watched.

That night, the soft quilt settled around my neck and feet, keeping warmth in and breezes out. I had slipped into the relaxed awareness of an Alpha Wave state, when suddenly the "relaxed" part blew itself to bits and the awareness part warned me someone was in the room.

CHAPTER EIGHT

Heart hammering against its cage, I peeked through a slit in one eye, hoping the intruder would think I was asleep and postpone the attack. The only thing I could make out in the dark was the shape of the trunk. A wavering energy lifted from its round top, like heat radiating off a desert asphalt road. Both eyes opened to see a soft haze of light gradually congealing to the size of a baseball. It hovered over the trunk, glowing brightly enough to show details carved in the silver. Then the orb flashed from the room so fast I heard the 'whoosh' sound accompany it.

Thirty seconds later, the crash of a hundred glass prisms sounded downstairs. I jumped to my feet and met Zeus in the hall, poking his nose from his bedroom door. It was good to know both of us had heard the crash. The crystal chandelier must have loosened from the ceiling and plummeted to the top of the dining room table, like a scene from *Phantom of the Opera*. Ordering Zeus to stay and protect his paws, I ran back to my room to slip on shoes rather than tramp barefoot into a million shards of glass. Reaching the dining room, I flipped the light switch and gaped at the ceiling where the chandelier still hung. There was no glass on the floor.

On my way back to bed, I checked Zeus who had already crawled under his crib and snored softly, unaffected by the bizarre event. Turning on the ceiling bulb in my room, I touched the raised design on the trunk, expecting heat but feeling none. Its firm wood sides, reinforced with metal, were rock-solid. I circled the thing, kicked at it, and crawled back into bed. But I kept the light on and slept facing the trunk. It seemed more prudent than turning my back on it.

Morning light sifted through the room's dirty window. I don't clean second story windows and refuse to feel guilty about it. Daybreak brought sanity and I reasoned the whole episode of last night had been hallucinatory, brought on by exhaustion and emotional turmoil. The thought seemed logical until I rolled from bed and stood facing the trunk. I squared my shoulders, folded my arms and sternly spoke to the thing. "You don't scare me." I threatened the chest. "I'm gonna break you wide open and sort through your guts to find the heaviest skeleton in history. I'll sell it to the highest bidder and rip you off the floor with a crowbar." A wave of fear dampened my brave words and I looked away, the first to break eye contact, a show of cowardice. I laughed at myself. It was a bunch of wood and metal.

Old pictures topping the chest of drawers caught my attention. I'd dusted them the first day, only noticing they were small prints of the same man whose picture hung downstairs over the fireplace. Now, because I was a distant Hathenbruck relative, the collection of photographs held interest: a young man wearing a tux and tie, sporting a full head of dark hair, a mustache and goatee surrounding his lips. Two pictures of Germany, one titled *Hamburg*, the other a photo of the Imperial Palace in Berlin. A framed certificate, written in German, had a drawing of the Last Supper at the top. Established: Hathenbruck had ties to Germany.

An oval picture showed a lovely 1800s mother holding a child; There was a family group showing Hathenbruck as an older man with a matronly woman at his side; several photos depicted Hathenbruck at various ages standing by cabins and wagons. A group shot included a handful of men with guns, had handwritten names identifying Butch, Elzy Lay, Matt Warner... names from the gang of Butch Cassidy and the Sundance Kid. "So, Mr. Hathenbruck," I addressed the pictures on the dresser, "what were you doing with a bunch of outlaws?" Another photo caught my attention, a group of five Indians grimly posing for the daguerreotype camera. It reminded me of Chief Tabby at the top of the stairs. What had Jack Jamison said? *"Hathenbruck was a true friend of the Indians."*

The mysterious FWC Hathenbruck was a German man who built a house against a cliff in the Uinta mountains, flat on the ground, with a concealed doorway in the hall and a heavy trunk in the main bedroom. I glanced at the trunk again, half expecting it to move toward me. But it stayed in the middle of the room and I gathered my wits to prepare for the day. I was determined to relocate the buried cannon.

My medium-size backpack accommodated food, water, a small bowl for Zeus, a light sweater and sunglasses, and the new folding shovel in the rear flap. I slipped a whistle on the leather cord holding my compass, planning to blow it if I ran into a bear, not sure if such a tactic would save me. It was better than nothing, 'nothing' being my giant, worthless dog. On impulse, I threw a little penlight into the pack, not knowing why I might need it…maybe to blind the bear.

With a leash around Zeus' neck and the compass-whistle around mine, we stepped out the kitchen door, strode from the porch, and began the journey to find the buried cannon.

We followed the cliff on our left, using fractures and crevices as handholds to pull us over rough spots. Zeus tugged on his leash to get to flat terrain, but I needed to inspect the cliff for landmarks pointing toward the cannon's grave. We clambered around fallen boulders for half an hour until I recognized a large fissure in the rock face. Two days ago I had considered it the clue to strike out into the forest, but now I hated to leave the mountain wall. As a child I remember clinging to the side of a swimming pool, moving hand over hand to the deep end, waiting for courage to let go and splash my way to the other side. Now, as then, I didn't want to lose my only security, the cliff that led to my house. But if I wanted the cannon, I had to leave the mountain. Facing the forest, I jiggled my compass east and stepped into my symbolic deep water.

A stand of Aspens, the zebra of trees, offered a friendly welcome on our route until we hit the Pines. Aspens are polite trees that allow room for passage between trunks. But the bushy, two-needled Lodgepoles stood close together, barring the way. Checking the compass, I maneuvered around the square-patterned, reddish bark and continued east. We hiked through the forest, pushing limbs out of the way, scanning all directions for a barren, ragged circle of dirt covering a Spanish cannon. Suddenly, the trees dropped away to reveal a long open meadow at my left and the edge of a mountain to my right, thick grey smoke rising from its base. Where there's smoke there's fire. I moved quickly through the grass toward the white plume, hoping to prevent a disaster. As I got close, I realized the smoke came from a campfire in a circle of rocks, fueled by twigs and branches. A dozen potatoes ringed the circumference, cooking and spitting nicely over red coals. More potatoes waited at the side for their turn in the fire.

"Hello, again." George Murdock's voice sounded behind me. I turned to see him exiting the trees, loaded with firewood, wearing the same garish costume without the yellow scarf. "I understand you think I followed you home."

His blatant beginning deserved a barefaced response from me. "Did you?"

He smiled broadly. "Lady, I don't mean to be insulting, but if I was gonna stalk a woman, there's better specimens in town. Nothing personal. You seem like a nice person. Plus, you know Shakespeare." He dropped his load of wood next to the fire, still grinning amiably.

What could I say to such honesty? "It's true," I admitted. "Not many men would follow me home." I added a barb of my own. "I thought you were a serial killer."

He ignored the remark and bent to check his potatoes. "I hear you lost my scarf."

"My scarf," I corrected. "You gave it to me."

He stood, his tone accusing me of wanton neglect. "You tied it to a tree."

I threw caution to the wind, the way I'd thrown his filmy material into the air, and jumped straight to the cannon. "I used it to mark a Spanish cannon buried in the forest. Did you know about the cannon?"

I expected surprise, but he didn't react with even a raised eyebrow. "I haven't come across any that are buried," he said, "but there are still a few on the higher promontories." His head gestured toward the mountains in the background.

I tried to match his nonchalance. "What are cannons doing there?"

"They're proving that the Spanish came this far north looking for Montezuma's treasure." He prodded a potato with a stick. "These are about done."

"That's quite a feast you've got."

"Not for eating," he shook his head. "There's quicksilver inside."

Quicksilver, an old name for… "Mercury? Why would you fill potatoes with a poisonous liquid? You said you didn't like to use mercury or cyanide in your gold panning."

He turned the potatoes carefully. "Hathenbruck's journals talk about making an amalgam of gold and quicksilver---"

"Isn't an amalgam what dentists use for fillings?"

He added a few sticks to the coals. "Yes, except dentists combine silver with mercury, which, by the way, leaches poison into people. Don't let your dentist do that to you." He stood and surveyed the fire. "Hathenbruck dissolved gold flakes in quicksilver, put it inside a small hollow in a potato, and baked the poison into the potato meat. He said it left gold nuggets behind." He stood and gazed into the fire pit that had calmed itself into hot coals, then glanced at me. "I was curious to see if it worked. You can be my first witness." George rolled a potato from the fire pit.

"You have Hathenbruck's journals?" I asked.

"No one has the journals," he explained, lifting the potato with tongs to a flat board. "I have anecdotes. He was an educated man, a doctor and a geologist, but nobody knew his background."

"German?" I added.

"Could be. He sure didn't match common folks around here." George lifted another potato from the coals. "The Indians loved him. He gave them free medical care."

My interest zoned in on the hot potatoes. "So there's a gold nugget inside?"

"I followed directions, dissolved gold flakes from my sheepskin with quicksilver, the heat will evaporate the mercury into the potato, and what should be left is..." he stretched his arms and hands out toward the still steaming tubers, "...solid gold." George addressed me rather kindly, probably to repent from the insult moments before. "I have to wait for these to cool off. If you're interested in seeing some old Spanish signs, there's a trail up this mountain going north. You'll find symbols cut into the rock. By law, Spanish miners had to mark the trail so the King could locate his gold in case everybody got killed. The Mexicans didn't carve markings for the King after they won independence in 1821, so the symbols on the trail predate that time. Come down in thirty minutes and I'll open a spud for you." He put more wood on the fire to ready the coals for the next batch of potatoes, and I faced north to walk the Old Spanish Trail.

The steep, almost invisible track was defined by the precipice of the mountain on the right, reigning over rocks and scrub brush balanced on the brink. My eyes searched for unusual markings in the stone, something resembling Spanish symbols. Funny thing about a quest, if you look too hard you miss everything. It wasn't until a large, iridescent dragonfly diverted my attention that I saw the upside down cross, pecked into the side of the mountain, weathered almost to oblivion. I tried to remember what the symbol meant, something about the beginning of a path or route, leading to the next pointer. George was right, of course. Old Spanish law required trail markers every 1200 feet, to guarantee that the King of Spain could always locate his mines and keep the gold rolling in. I estimated distance and hoped the next symbol would jump out at me.

The view alone was worth the climb and required superlatives like matchless, unparalleled, and supreme for description. The meadow, spread with purple flowers, stretched itself from the forest like a quiet lake. I spotted my land with its stream shining in the distance and wondered if George had a fleece stealing gold from its waters. The track steepened with the terrain, forcing Zeus and I to huff our way onto a flat landing for a quick rest. Three large boulders crowded themselves onto the area and I leaned against one at the rim of the precipice, facing the western landscape below. A shadowing at the middle of the stone caught my eye.

"Well, lookie here," I said to Zeus. "Somebody has done some scratching."

Carved into the side of the five-foot boulder was a cross inside a circle about the size of a man's hand. I ran my fingers along its deep incision, then moved upward to the top of the rock. A groove had been dug along its length, running east and west, a V-shaped notch at each end. "Somebody," I verbalized to the dog, "did a lot of work to create an observation stone." I bent to peer through the groove, similar to a gun sight. At the end of the furrow, like a picture with an 'X' on it, was a cliff barely above the tree line. It was on my mountain range, the one I would follow to find my house again. Raising my head to do a naked eye check of the landscape, I lifted the compass bauble into my hand and oriented it toward the spot, west and slightly south, barely inside the edge of the forest. "That place is important," I told my dog. "Someone wanted to find it again." Zeus snapped at a dragonfly and I realized I had wasted my breath, which, at this altitude, couldn't be frittered away. Studying the landscape for a marker to identify the spot, I admitted my inadequate compass was the only way to find the spot.

I turned from the rock and headed back down the faint trail, Zeus hauling me from the other end of his leash. Ten minutes later we found the campfire, a new batch of potatoes roasting inside with George watching over them, rotating each like a chef in the finest restaurant.

"Glad you're here," he said. "These have cooled." He pointed to a pile of russets on a board, rolled one away, cut it lengthwise, and let it fall open. A tube at the end led to a hollow in the center, which held a gold blob about the size of my fingernail.

George nearly sang his triumph. "It worked! The old prospectors were right!"

I squinted my eyes to see the shiny spot in the center of the darkened potato. "It's pretty small for all that trouble," I commented.

My insult didn't dampen his enthusiasm. "If I'd found something big like hallmarked gold bullion or minted coins, the IRS would pounce with both claws. They'd want to know when I found it and tax it as income before I even sold it."

I added what I'd told poor little Candy about her bar of black silver. "The Antiquities Department wouldn't be far behind."

"But this," George held the potato out with both hands, "*this* tiny little thing isn't worth declaring. It's a raw nugget…all mine, a trinket to be exchanged when I need the money."

We stood, silently contemplating the power of taxation, until I changed the direction of conversation. "I need a lesson in reading a compass," I said, and lifted the leather string around my neck to display my compass sphere and whistle.

He guffawed. "That's a cute little piece of jewelry you're sporting there. I hope you don't expect it to get you home."

"It's all I've got," I spoke with sarcasm.

"You'll get lost if you use that toy. I'll give you solid directions to the Hathenbruck house." He waved a hand west. "If you go to the stream, you can turn south and---"

"Actually, I want to head west."

George stood straight, his eyes boring into mine. He folded his arms over his chest. "You've seen the sighting stone." It was a statement of fact.

"You know about it?" I allowed a little excitement to seep out. "Do you know what it's pointing to?"

"I've never checked it out." He returned to another cold potato, cut it in half, and extracted a yellow nugget. "You're asking for trouble."

"Well," I countered, "that's where I'm heading. I'll let you know what the mystery's all about." I faced west and rotated the little round toy.

"Alright," he reluctantly said. "You'd better borrow my compass."

I turned around as he handed me a transparent rectangular instrument with an arrow etched into one end, a flat, rotating circle embedded opposite it. Putting his foot on a rock, he rested the compass on his thigh. "The red arrow" he explained, "points to magnetic north. You want to go west and a little south." I caught the fact that George already knew the direction. He dialed the compass like a combination lock and talked about declination, compass lines, and grid lines. "Just keep this against your chest" he finally instructed, "and follow the arrow. Look ahead for a landmark to guide you. When you reach it, choose another landmark and follow the arrow again."

For a second I wondered if the complicated routine was a joke and considered singing *Follow the Yellow Brick Road*. But George looked sincere. Handing one of his petite pieces of gold to me, he said, "Take this for luck."

I expressed thanks and dropped it in my pocket. "Another gift of yellow. Must be a lucky color for you."

"The yellow scarf," he said, "was a talisman to attract gold. Maybe that nugget will bring something good."

I looked at my feet and shook my head. "Sorry about losing the scarf," I apologized.

"Don't think twice," he said. "They're a buck each in town."

I smiled and started the hike, jamming the compass to my sternum, keeping the red line pointing north. With Zeus leashed at my left, we tromped ahead in the direction of the arrow, away from George and his campfire full of miniscule, potato-produced gold nuggets.

The thirty-minute hike was easy until we reached the stream that crossed the meadow at an angle. With a deep breath and an apology to Zeus, we forded the gentle flow, water to my waist, Zeus' head barely above the surface. At the other side, Zeus did a doggy shake, his short hair like small pins standing straight in his pincushion skin. I sloshed onto the bank carrying enough water to irrigate the whole meadow.

Lining up the arrow with a tall pine, I oozed forward again, leaving pockets of water in the knee-high grass. When we reached the designated tree, George's compass took us into the deep green forest. In thirty seconds I was lost. The place was a malicious funhouse of mirrors, the same tree reflecting itself to surround me. I was a blind pilot in a fog, slavishly following the arrow jutting from my torso.

Without warning, thunder rumbled above us. There was no gentle hint of showers. A squall dropped like an attack of thieves in an ambush. The surprising suddenness reminded me of the words the desk cop had uttered: *"The weather in these mountains can be sunny one minute and pouring rain the next. There's been hail in July, ya'know."* I needed to get to the cliff for cover before the hail hit, but was only vaguely aware of a western direction.

"C'mon, Zeus," I yelled to the dog, "this way." We rushed past trees, the pack bouncing against my spine. *West. West for shelter and home. Go West young woman.* The tree zebras opened wide. I saw the mountain cliff ahead and put on speed. Letting go of Zeus' leash, I used both hands to pull myself to a protruding shelf. I crawled beneath, leaned against my backpack, and scrunched my already soaked legs against my chest. The deluge hit the shelf and formed a waterfall around us.

Us? Where was the rest of us?

Zeus hadn't stayed with me. The rain beat at my shelter while my disobedient dog was out there, whimpering for the mistress who took care of him. By now the short-haired Zeus would be shivering. I poked my head from the refuge and yelled his name. Water hit the bill of my cap, forcing it over my eyes. I withdrew, adjusted the hat, and poked my head out to yell again. "Zeus!"

I don't swear as a habit, believing it's evidence that a person doesn't have command of the language and can't think of a word to express himself. This time, "Stupid dog" didn't do the job. I entered the maelstrom yelling at the top of my power, "Zeus, you ba…" The noise of rain pounding against trees, leaves, and rocks took my frustrated words and threw them into the air, drowning them like little alphabet rats.

Tripping on slick rock, losing my footing, I grabbed a boulder almost as tall as me and hugged it, pushing my face into a hollow. Arrows of water pierced my pack with enough force to be felt against my shoulders. The giant rock had settled on a shelf and I shifted carefully to get to the other side, water cascading from the walls.

A piece of rope snaked from behind the boulder and I focused closer. It was a braided leash with a handle. Zeus must be on the other end. Three more cautious steps took me around the rock and I reached down to grab the leash, but the closeness of the rock against the wall made it impossible for anything as big as Zeus to hide behind it. Warily, I peered around the boulder, expecting to see Zeus smashed like road kill against the cliff, but the leash disappeared into a crevice partially hidden by the rock, curiously concave in the back. I dropped to my knees in slick mud and examined the slit of opening.

"Zeus?"

A doggy grunt replied, resembling a breathy "woof," but not a whimper. Zeus had found superior shelter. I crawled between the boulder and mountain wall, following the leash that passed through a three-foot hole, entering the dark mountain abyss.

CHAPTER NINE

There was enough headroom in the gloomy cave to kneel upright, and I tracked the leash until I touched Zeus' neck. He sat with his nose toward the back of the cave, his body stiff and alert.

"Zeus," I said, patting his head. "I like your place better than mine." I put my arm around his neck, the reeking wet-dog smell assaulting my nose, and wrestled him to my left side to face the cave opening. The boulder outside muffled the sound of rain. Removing my pack, I rummaged for food, water, and a bowl for Zeus. He accepted a dog biscuit, still turning his head to look behind us. It occurred to me that he had an unusual interest in something at the back of the cave. A bear? I twisted to face the rear and slowly pulled my pack toward me, whispering to the dog, "Come, boy. We're leaving."

Zeus turned his back on me and stared into the cave's gloom. A little slow on the uptake, I realized a bear couldn't get through the tiny slit we used. Maybe there was another entrance, but the fact was, the dog showed interest, not fear. I slipped my hand in the pack and rustled through food and clothing to find the round penlight I'd added that morning. The push button on the bottom shed a miniature beam of light on Zeus' brown behind. My hand guided the light to his head and over his ears before the dark gobbled it up. Moving the penlight left, it illuminated a ceiling four feet above the floor, and a triangle-shaped room on a slight incline that might be ten feet wide. I couldn't see far enough to determine length, but no bear growled. I joined Zeus's side and pointed the light directly in front, where three boulders blocked the area. To our right, I followed the wall down to the floor. Uniformly rectangular rocks were stacked on top of each other, rows of them against the wall. I shifted the light to the floor on the opposite wall and saw the same kind of rocks piled in rows halfway to the ceiling.

"Those aren't rocks," I said aloud. The cave ate my words the way it devoured the light, making them flat, one-dimensional. Putting the penlight between my teeth, I crawled left to check out what wasn't rocks. My hands touched a stiff material on the floor, which cracked under the weight. I picked it up to catch a beam from the tiny flashlight and felt flakes drop through my fingers, like old leather. It was a bag with a flap held by a buckle, a knapsack to fit a saddle. I carefully replaced it on the floor and continued crawling to the stacks, the small ray of light shining from my mouth hitting only part of the middle rock.

The wall was covered two feet high and deep with a collection of bars, eight inches long, one and a half inches square. Setting my flashlight on top of the stack, its beam shot into the back of the cave where it wasted into nothing.

I wished for a candle. Flickering firelight on the floor could banish enough blackness to see my surroundings, including any danger. Next time, I'd include a candle and matches in my pack to supplement the flashlight.

I attempted to pick up a bar with one hand but could only scoot it slightly. Using both hands I brought it up against my chest for support and estimated its weight at twenty pounds. In a déjà vu moment, I remembered the same action six days ago in a cave with rattlesnakes and a snippy girl named Candy. But this bar was half the size and heavier than the silver bar I had dragged out of the Kanab cave. A useless fact dribbled from my subconscious mind: the specific gravity of silver is 10.26, where gold is 19.29, a strange thing to remember in a...

"Zeus," I crowed, "This is---"

"Put it back."

I squealed like a little girl and dropped the heavy bar on top of its roommates. For the briefest instant I thought Zeus had spoken the words, but in that same frozen second I recognized a young male voice. Seizing my miniscule light and twisting toward the sound, I reduced my tone to its lowest register to show authority. "Who's there?" I shot the light around the cave.

"You can't stay here," the voice declared.

"I beg to differ," I countered. "This is my land and, whoever you are, young man, you're trespassing." I added the young man part so he'd know I didn't consider him a threat.

"It isn't your land yet." *Yet?* The kid knew about the inheritance. His disembodied words came from the boulders at the back of the room. "Leave now."

A crack of lightning sounded outside. "My dog and I are staying," I announced. There was no movement among the boulders so I added, "We've got food and water we'll share with you."

The boy's reply was quick. "I have my own."

"Good," I countered, handing Zeus another biscuit. "We'll have a picnic. It looks like you've already met my dog."

I waited. A few pebbles tumbled over each other as a pair of long Levi's emerged into view, followed closely by a shirt. I kept the light to the ground when the boy's head appeared, shoulder-length hair hanging in his face as he crab-walked across the floor, stopping a few feet away from us. The inadequate light cast his features in shadow, but his high chiseled cheekbones had smooth, dark skin stretched across them. The kid was Indian.

I spoke with a friendly tone. "My name is Dr. Matt---"

"We know your name."

"---Howard," I finished, catching his word *"we,"* the same word the Indian woman in town had used. Ignoring his interruption, I introduced my dog. "This is Zeus. And your name is…?"

He stayed silently sitting, legs bent, arms resting on his knees. The three of us played the waiting game, sounds of rushing water outside filling the calm of the cave. "Look, kid," I finally said, "we're stuck here until the rain stops. I'd like to know your name."

He shifted, curving his back. "Pope," he said.

"Nice to meet you, Mr. Pope. Do you have a first name?"

"That *is* my first name."

I kept the light pointing away from us and hoped he couldn't see my disbelief. His mother should be committed. "It's an unusual name. Are you Catholic?"

He straightened his back to sit upright. "I'm named after the great warrior Pope, who saved Indians from slavery in Colorado, Utah, California, and New Mexico." He waited for a reaction but I didn't recognize who he was talking about.

"Sorry," I said. "I don't think I've heard of Pope."

His disgust reached my ears in a short hiss through his teeth. "Of course not," he said. "Indian history isn't taught in white schools. But your people never had a smarter or braver commander in any of *your* wars."

Zeus changed position from butt to belly and I reached over to scratch under his wet collar while he stared at the boy. The rest of the dog was dry. My mud-encrusted pants would drip for days. "You're right, Pope, I never learned the story. I'd like to hear it."

Pope said nothing. I was tempted to shine my light on his face to read his expression, if he had one. Instead, I prodded, "Rainstorms are a good time for telling tales."

Pope began a matter-of-fact, unembellished, simple narrative. "In the early 1500s, troops of Spanish soldiers headed north from Mexico looking for Montezuma's gold."

May the gods preserve me, I thought, *it's Montezuma's treasure again.*

The boy continued his story. "They tortured Arizona Indians to get directions to the Seven Cities of Cibola. The Navajos made up phony stories to get rid of them."

"I know this history," I added. "The search for the Seven Cities covered 190,000 miles in America's Great Basin. Historians say they didn't get this far north."

"Your people are always wrong," the boy said. "The Spanish were here with their guns and swords and armor, but they didn't find Montezuma's treasure. Instead they discovered gold and silver streaked through the mountains and they started mining. The Spanish King demanded 20% of all the gold they found. It was dangerous work, and they needed slaves. In 1519, King Ferdinand---"

"You're pretty good at dates. You probably ace your tests."

"There aren't any tests. This is the history of my people. I learned it at the campfires. We remember everything so it won't happen again." He stopped talking. I waited patiently. Finally he resumed the story. "In 1519, King Ferdinand proclaimed war against all Indians from Mexico to the northern Rockies so that Spain could legally have slaves to work their mines. Before every attack, the military commander would read from an official paper saying that if the Indians fought back..." Pope raised his arm like a proclamation as he spoke the lines, "...*death and loss which shall accrue are your fault and not that of His Highness.*" He lowered his arm.

"You've memorized that part of the document?"

"I know the whole thing," Pope shot back. "My people didn't understand one word of the war paper and couldn't fight Spanish weapons anyway. They didn't understand why men, women, and even children were chained together and marched off to die in Spanish mines." His voice became lethal. "And they call *us* savages."

"Pope, I'm sorry. I've never heard this history."

I felt the boy stiffen, his controlled anger traveled through the air. "African slaves were lucky," he said. "We're jealous of them. We were lowered into pits seven hundred feet deep, never seeing the sun's light, breathing poisoned air. If our people fought back, they were nailed to the ground and burned gradually from their feet to their heads until the pain killed them. They were strung from gallows where their toes could touch the ground, so death was slow. Those who were given mercy had their hands cut off and sent into the desert to die."

The boy stopped. I couldn't think of anything to say that would make the story less hideous, so I kept quiet. The hard floor of the cave pushed its way through my wet pants into a bone. I transferred my weight and Pope picked up his gruesome tale. "Nine-year-old girls had to crawl into small places to bring out ore. By law, the boys had to be ten."

"Why the difference between boys and girls?"

"I don't know. None of them lived long, so it doesn't matter. Our slavery lasted three hundred years." His eyes flashed with hate in the weak light. I'd seen similar dark eyes in a grocery store two days ago. "And then," his voice increased with pride, "an Indian shaman from New Mexico rose up. His name was Pope. The spirit of Montezuma and the God Quetzalcoatl sent him to lead us. We don't know how he got word to all our people from the Rio Grande to California, but at dawn on August 10, 1680, all Indians revolted and killed the Spanish. Every last miner, trader, merchant, and priest was dead in one day. Their bodies were thrown into the mines they'd forced us to dig. They were tossed in like garbage, with their gold and silver bars, and their weapons and armor. The mines were filled in with dirt and hidden so no one could open them again."

I did some remedial math with his dates. 1500 to 1680 gave a hundred and eighty years in slavery. "Pope," I questioned, "how do you get three hundred years from---"

"They came back. After twenty or thirty years, the yellow rock was stronger than the fear of death. We banded with our old enemies, the Navajos, to keep the Spanish away. We fought hard, but they won. The old ones and medicine men knew where the mines used to be, but they didn't tell, even with torture." Pope shrugged. "The Spanish dug new mines, their priests built new missions."

"So your people were slaves again until...?"

"1810. That's when Mexico rebelled against Spain. Spanish soldiers got pulled away to fight. With the soldiers gone, my people attacked the mines and missions and forced everybody to run. The miners hid their gold and silver bars until they could come back."

"But they never came back," I inserted. "Mexico won its independence in 1821, so you were free after that. Right?"

"Wrong." Pope's head shook slowly. "Mexicans followed the Spanish trail to find the gold mines. But they figured out that slaves were worth as much as gold. They took our children. Traitor Indians stole children from other tribes to sell to the Mexicans."

I rubbed Zeus' head. "Didn't you guys get any breaks?"

"We made our own breaks. In 1844, the Utes had another rebellion like Pope's. We killed the Mexican miners and slave traders in these mountains. We threw their bodies in the mines, along with their gold, silver, and tools. We burned their cabins and tore down their missions." I felt his eyes on me when he said, "We still guard the hiding places so no one can find them." Pope shifted his legs into a sitting Indian position, knees sticking out to point toward his arms. The rain sounded softer outside. There hadn't been a crash of lightning for a long time.

I envisioned Spanish and Mexican miners fleeing for their lives, concealing their treasures, planning to return, and the truth dawned. "This cave is one of the hiding places for Spanish or Mexican gold bars." I ran my flashlight beam across the stacks against the walls. "Pope," I laughed, "Do your people realize how much these are worth?"

"We know exactly how much they're worth," he quietly said. "They represent uncounted Indian lives. Our people were forced to use fire, lime, and black powder to break the ore inside those pits. They made torches of grass and tallow pounded together, wrapped with cedar bark. My ancestors climbed up chicken ladders, carrying solid rock on their backs in cowhide sacks."

"Chicken ladders?"

"Trees tied together with steps carved into them. If a man tripped, he'd fall to the bottom of the pit. His body would be rolled out of the way and left there to rot while another man lifted the bag and climbed the chicken ladder. At the top, children pounded the rocks into pebbles and dust. It was put on a screen and the dirt washed away so only heavy gold was left. Then it was melted and poured into molds to make bars, all done by Indian slaves."

"It seems to me," I said, "this gold should belong to your people. Why don't they use it to improve their lives?"

Pope's voice turned brittle. "The white man's money rock will never improve Indian life. Towats has cursed it. There will come a time when Towats will purify the treasure and use it for the good of all. If anyone tries to open the mines before then, we will bury him and everything he has, just like we did the Spanish and Mexicans, until all their evil is covered. We will never retreat. This time, we win or we die."

I found my tongue. "Did your people bury any brass cannons?" I had to ask.

Pope leaned forward. "The rain has stopped. Leave now. Don't come back."

I pressured him. "Did Indians bury Spanish brass cannons?"

The boy straightened. "Listen to me, Dr. Howard. You seem like a nice lady so I'm asking you…telling you… don't try to find any cannons, don't take even one gold bar from this cave, and, for your own good, don't inherit the Hathenbruck house."

Dirt from the cave floor had cemented itself to my wet pants. I was heavy with grime and stiff from sitting on the hard ground. At that moment, a hot shower was worth a cave full of gold. It was time to withdraw from this battle and fight the war another day.

CHAPTER TEN

I said good-bye to Pope, who made no reply, and left the cave pushing Zeus in front as we crawled into a warm, late afternoon sun. The air was bursting with birdcalls announcing an end to the storm. Small creatures rustled from their burrows to test the truth of the song. Even the trees stretched higher after hunkering in the onslaught of rain. My every miserable step squished water between my toes from cotton socks and wet canvas shoes.

We chose to hike directly home on the relative comfort of flat ground. The brass cannon had waited a couple hundred years, it could remain in the ground another day. With the mountain on the right, we hurried over level land through trees that dripped water on us like leftover tears from the downpour.

My subconscious told me an item was missing. Zeus was accounted for, sniffing at undergrowth from the leash in my left hand. *Check.* My backpack still dug into a middle vertebrae. *Check.* The folding shovel sat in the outside sleaze. *Check.* Still, something wasn't there. I stopped and gripped the leash on Zeus, who leaped like a puppy in the fresh washed air. My right hand arranged itself against the center of my chest, as if remembering that position, fingers curved to hold something rectangular. I looked down to recall an arrow…George Murdock's compass. I'd left it under the ledge where I'd taken refuge and lost the dog.

Frustrated and angry, I did an abrupt about-face and stomped across the rocks, retracing my steps to find…I spoke the words aloud, "…a borrowed compass that has to be returned." Zeus balked at the change in direction and I yanked on his tether while scanning for the boulder concealing Pope's cave. The shelter would be slightly beyond it. Each fissure and crack merged into a collage of meaningless marks. Large rocks and stones blended together, giving no clue to the ledge I had crawled under. We'd have to move closer to the mountain and inspect every possibility. I reluctantly faced the mountain cliff.

"Are you looking for something?" Pope's voice hung in the air behind me. I whirled to see him standing next to a tree I'd passed ten seconds ago. His existence outside the cave registered in force. He stood a slender six feet tall, maybe twenty years old, straight black hair almost to his shoulders, parted in the middle. Black eyes introduced high cheekbones and hawk nose that are typically Indian. He could have posed for a close-up shot from a John Wayne movie where the Indians finally won.

Pope was dressed in dark blue Levis topped by a mottled shirt in camouflage colors with long sleeves, a blousy thing that wouldn't be worn by a proper teenager. Its baggy sleeves were gathered by elastic at the wrists, the front placket tied with heavy twine threaded through grommets. Part of a hood rested crookedly over his shoulder as if he had hastily removed it from his head before speaking to me. A fist-size brown buckskin bag rested against his chest, held by a leather cord around his neck. The old mountain men had called it a 'possibles bag' because it held supplies for every possible emergency. Whatever Pope's sack carried, it held enough bumps to catch my curiosity.

I forced my stare from the bag to his face and confronted him. "Where did *you* come from?"

"Where are *you* going?" He was good at avoiding questions.

My response was left over from a long-ago childhood: "I asked first."

"Are you looking for this?" He held the compass in his hand.

The sight shut me up for a second. "Where did you find it?"

"Where you left it, under a ledge."

I shifted from the compass to his eyes. "Wait a minute. How did you know I left it…"

Facts organized themselves into an uncomfortable suspicion. "How did my dog find your cave?"

"He followed me in."

"Followed?" Repetition solidified the new information. "You were outside and he saw you and followed you into the cave?"

The boy nodded and I assaulted him with yet another question. "What were you doing that close to us in the rain?"

A sly grin moved his mouth corners up. "Getting wet, like you."

I took two steps toward him, hands on hips. "Pope…" without his last name, my confrontation didn't have much power, "…have you been following me?"

"I'm a tracker." He shrugged one shoulder, adding, "The best."

"How long have you…" a new thought interrupted. "Did you watch me tie a yellow scarf above my buried cannon?"

"It's not your cannon."

My squinty Danish eyes locked into his large black Indian eyes. "It's on my property."

"It's not your property."

"This land comes with the house."

"It's not your---"

"Did you take my scarf off the tree?" I folded my arms to demand an answer.

"The scarf was yours and I returned it. I am also return-ing your compass." Pope held the rectangular instrument toward me and I grabbed it with indictment.

"Were you going to leave it on my porch, where you left the scarf?"

The kid showed no emotion. I'd caught him fair and square and he didn't even have the decency to lower his eyes. "I'm an honest man," he said. "I don't keep what isn't mine."

I noticed the implication that I, a dishonest woman, would keep what isn't hers. I reached boiling and spewed steam at him. "That scarf marked the place of a buried Spanish cannon. It is absolutely vital that I find it again.

The cannon has historical significance and should be studied. It proves the Spanish came this far north."

Pope stood taller. "We don't need proof."

I changed tactics to plead the case. "Scientists don't know your story." I waved my arms in the air. "How many Spanish cannons are in the Uinta Mountains? Where are they? They'll help us put together your history."

"We don't need your scientists to tell us our history." Sunlight sifted onto the boy's smooth face. "We already know it."

Zeus suffered the brunt of my irritation and I roughly reeled him to my hip while verbally attacking Pope. "Young man, stay off my property. If you play your tracking game with me again, I'll notify the law."

Pope spoke calmly. "Dr. Howard," he informed me, "you won't know if I'm behind you or at your side. You'll never see me or feel my presence unless I want you to."

"Zeus will warn me."

Pope huffed in scorn. "I've trailed you and your dog for three days. You don't understand his value *or* how to read him."

"You…" I spluttered, picturing this kid in his hooded camouflage blouse observing my every move. "You don't know me or my dog. Stay away from us."

Pope leaned forward, speaking deliberately. "Stay away from forbidden places."

I wanted to say a phrase that would flatten the kid, words to let him know that his veiled threat wouldn't work. But all my vocabulary hid themselves in the files of my brain and refused to come out. I finally swiveled around and stomped south, murmuring aggravated words to myself, the trees, the dog, the town, and my mother's cousin once removed who married a Hathenbruck and left me a house. "That cave has a fortune in gold," I mumbled, "and it's mine." Words I'd spoken to Candy filtered from my memory. *"You know, of course, about the Antiquities Act. The silver bars are artifacts and you'll have to report your discovery. An archaeologist will come and assess the place and you might get a small finder's fee."*

"It's mine, on my property," I said out loud. "I'm spending it all." My response to Candy now applied to me. *"When you try to sell it, the dealer will have to call the authorities and you'll be considered a thief. You might even go to jail. It's better to inform the state and be grateful for what they give you."*

"The state doesn't need it," I protested. "It isn't fair."

"Life isn't fair," I'd told Candy. *"Get over it."*

I stopped walking to open the pack and slip George's compass inside, thoughts roiling in my brain. *"Even after the Antiquities Department confiscates my gold as historical archaeology and the IRS gets its share, there's still plenty of money. The cannon is cream topping, worth a lot to a museum."* I waited for Zeus to untangle himself from a tree trunk. *"An abnormal teenager skulking around trees like a dog isn't going to keep me from taking what's mine."* I swung the pack over my shoulders, giddily singing the words, "I've got gold on my property." Pope's statement inserted itself into the private conversation I was having with myself: *"It's not your property."*

I assumed Pope was somewhere in the vicinity and spoke loudly enough for him to hear, twirling slowly to include all directions. "As soon as I sign the papers," I called into the pines, "the house and five acres will be mine. I'll dig where I want and take what I want." I increased the volume. "You are no longer in the Wild, Wild West where you can threaten people. This is a civilized, lawful place. You can't stop me." Then and there, with the trees as witness, I committed myself to ownership of the Hathenbruck Estate.

Zeus and I forged through the forest while gold bars and a buried cannon sparked a glow of anticipation in my innards. I didn't have to teach anymore. I could finance my own archaeology digs. I'd clear trees by the house for an airstrip and fly my private plane here when I needed isolation, but I'd have a beach house in La Jolla for the fun of it. I'd also need a high-rise condominium overlooking Central Park, to lounge in when I jetted to New York for Broadway plays. The smile on my face could have etched permanent dimples as I hiked toward home, fantasizing about a hot shower and chicken cordon blue with asparagus tips and white rolls with herb topping. What I would get was chicken noodle soup from a can. I made a mental note to hire a personal cook.

The clearing in front of the yellow brick house opened before us. We entered the front door and walked through the dining room to leave Zeus in the kitchen with filled dog bowls. I fished out the gold nugget George had given me and dropped it into a plastic sandwich bag. My target was the tiny bathroom where I stood under a lukewarm drizzle of water, counting imaginary money until the shower went cold.

Wrapped in a towel, I curved through the dining room to climb the stairs and scurry to my bedroom door. The menacing trunk sat in the center of the room. I squared my shoulders and walked around it, pretending nonchalance as I gathered clothes. Intellectually, I knew that last night's episode with the fallen chandelier was a simple nightmare, but for psychological reasons I hurried into Zeus' room to dress and consider options. The only bed in the house was in the trunk's room. No, it was not the trunk's room. It was *my* room and I wouldn't let a silly dream frighten me from a good night's sleep.

The dog's large foam mattress caught my eye and a solution formed. Struggling with the unwieldy material, I dragged Zeus' bed from under the crib and pulled it into the trunk's room to place it at my bedside so the evil chest would see I had protection. I laughed at myself and shook my head. The hallucination had been powerful enough to motivate childish actions, breaking the primal rule of dog ownership: if you let your dog sleep in your room, he'll soon take over everything, shedding hair on the bedspread and drooling on your pillow.

Zeus watched the moving of his mattress and stood at the door to investigate. His eyebrows created a rounded "M" over his large brown eyes. "I'm changing the rules," I told the dog, "which is my right under article twenty-seven of the dog owner's license." The animal studied my face and cocked his head, giving the impression of intent listening. "You can be here a few nights," I said, "but don't get used to it. When I return to sanity, you're banished to your place under the crib again." Zeus backed away from the door and stood in the hall, confused and bewildered, as if I were a stranger who only resembled his mistress.

That night I pulled on Zeus' collar to get him to the new sleeping arrangement. When I let go, he slinked back to the hall. A brief tussle forced him to obey, but the dog's trembling body and bowed head was evidence of his submission to the old rules. I cradled his giant head in my hands, scratching the base of his ears, speaking soothing words of encouragement as I led him to his dog mattress. Walking back to the door, I closed it until I heard a solid 'click', insuring that only someone with hands could leave the room. As I flipped down the protruding light switch on the wall, I stared at the trunk. There was no glowing orb hovering over it.

Early next morning, before driving into town to sign inheritance papers, I worked in the parlor on the pottery textbook. The picture of Hathenbruck watched me from above the fireplace and I couldn't concentrate. I finally went over to stare back. Behind the receding hairline of his head, black waves of hair burst forth to fall past his ear lobes. The eyes were expressionless, seeing beyond the painting to an unknown future. His heavy goatee, topped by an upturned handlebar mustache, hid any hint of a smile he might have had, but some quality in the face showed compassion. The shirt had a double row of brass buttons down the front, like an army uniform, but fringe along the sleeves didn't fit the military image. A bulge inside his shirt reminded me of Napoleon's right hand resting in his uniform, but Hathenbruck's right arm was missing, the sleeve fabric hanging at his side. Jack-the-Real-Estate-Man had mentioned a watch. The gold chain curving into his shirt was evidence of a watch, but I couldn't imagine a timepiece as large as a man's palm.

"Mr. Hathenbruck," I addressed the painting, "your great-grandson's wife has given me your estate. I intend to find out who you were and why you didn't live in this house you built. Who covered up the closet in the hall? What's in the trunk? Are there buried cannons in the front yard?

Did you know there was a cave filled with gold bars? Why did you die a pauper?"

It's never wise to talk to inanimate objects. They tend to communicate back, like the trunk upstairs that bullied me into needing my dog for security. Hathenbruck's picture sent a gentle but distinct mental message.

"Go home."

CHAPTER ELEVEN

Extra money for trips to town was getting rare, due to the high price of gas at $1.13 a gallon. My main supply of cash, hidden in the underwear drawer, had to last another three weeks. I searched hidden flaps of my wallet and turned the pockets of clothing inside out to find coins among the lint. The treasure hunt gathered enough to put gas in the car. Remembering George's gold nugget, I put it in my pack in case Kamas had a coin or pawnshop that would buy the little bauble. The Shove-It kicked into animation and I guided it off the edge of the meadow toward the main road to town. Zeus was left behind under the table to meditate on his existence.

Jack Jamison sat at his desk, poring over papers. Today's T-shirt said, *The Early Bird Gets the Worm, But the Second Mouse Gets the Cheese.* No reputable business would carry the T-shirts Jamison wore. He probably ordered them from a catalogue delivered to his house in plain brown paper. I short-circuited greetings and went straight for the jugular.

"I'm here to sign the inheritance papers."

He removed his glasses, folded them, and set them carefully on the desk. "Aren't you being hasty? You might want to consider your decision a little longer."

"Consider it considered," I quipped. "I like the house. I'll take it."

"Alllll-right," Jack drew the word out slowly. "I'll send the request tomorrow."

"I need those papers today. I'll pay you to fax it."

He rolled his chair to the file behind his desk and rummaged in a drawer, pulling out an 8x10 document. "You should read the rules of inheritance first."

"Can you get the papers here within the hour?"

Jack studied me a moment, the booklet in his hands. "Probably. You'll need a Notary Public."

"I noticed a little notary sign painted on your window," I pointed out. He produced a sheepish grin. I resisted shriveling him with accusations. "Mr. Jamison," I sat in the chair across from him. "Level with me. Why don't you want me to have the Hathenbruck Estate?"

The guy scooted back to his desk, still exhibiting his embarrassed smile. "I'd rather sell the place. I'm sure you understand."

"I'd rather inherit it," I pleasantly replied. "I'm sure *you* understand."

He held the booklet out to me. "I suggest you read over the legal ramifications."

I took the document and headed out the door, quoting a line from Arnold Swartzenegger, minus the accent. "I'll be back."

Instinct warned that Jack would get nosy if I asked about pawnshops. Instead, I drove to the Chamber of Commerce, which I'd passed during trips to town. The door led to a room smaller than the real estate agency. A lumpy older woman sat at a desk surrounded by brochures and pamphlets. Her midriff under a light blue blouse stretched the material between buttons and rolled over a belt. She was topped like an ice cream cone with bluish white hair cut in the style of elderly women: short and ratted to cover bald spots. Her surprise at seeing me made me think that tourists rarely made it to town. She recovered and smiled broadly.

"Welcome," she effused. "Help yourself to everything. No charge." I chose a brochure about bears in the Uinta Mountains. She noticed my choice. "You have to watch out for bears," she volunteered. "A few weeks ago a family was attacked in their tent by a bear. The thing tore the canvas to shreds and hurt one of the kids."

"Was it looking for food?"

"They thought it was a rogue bear, out for blood." She cocked her head to ask, "Are you camping up there?"

"Yes, but I'm in a brick house."

Comprehension rose in her face. "You must be the one in the Hathenbruck house. Darn spooky place, I hear. Nobody will stay in it."

I ignored the fact that she knew who I was. "Who else has been up there?"

"Another lady a few years back didn't make it through the night. She came down lickety-split before the sun was up and hired Jack to sell the place for her."

So, I had out-lasted cousin Hilda. "I've been there a week," I informed the blue lady, "without a problem." The mysteries of the house slithered forward, but I added an untruth, "It's a lovely home, very peaceful."

She nodded and kept smiling, but her eyes said she thought I was lying.

I pulled myself together for my original purpose. "Is there a coin or pawnshop in town?"

We both relaxed at the change of topic. *"Harvey's Hoard,"* she offered. "North of the Grocery store on the main highway. You can't miss it."

She was right. I couldn't miss it. It had a dozen large, metal wind-catchers shaped like sunflowers, all moving in time to the breeze, catching light from the sun. Pansies poured from the sides of aging wheelbarrows. Four cracked wagon wheels leaned against the unpainted sideboards of an elongated shack. Hand lettering above the door proclaimed, Welcome to Harvey's Hoard. A bell rang when I entered and a man's voice said he'd be with me in a minute. I spent the time peering at jewelry and pistols under locked glass cases. The cash register sat on top of a glass display of silver and gold coins. I'd come to the right place.

A big man with two rolls of chin and four of belly maneuvered his way down a skinny aisle. I expected to see him bump into something and send it sprawling to the floor. But he moved in a practiced dance, twisting to avoid the shelves, raising his arms for tighter squeezes.

When he reached me, his tone was deep and reassuring. "I guarantee I've got what you're looking for. What's your pleasure?"

"If you're Harvey, I came to sell you some gold."

His smile faded. "Look around," he said. "As you can see, I don't need to add anything to these shelves."

I held out my nugget. "It's just a little thing."

An intrigued Harvey put out his giant hand and I deposited the potato nugget into it. He fingered the irregular circle, moving it to see all sides. "I've never seen one shaped like a big kernel of corn before. Where'd you get it?"

I fudged a little, "On the ground near a campfire. What's it worth?" I wasn't up on current 1992 gold prices.

Harvey tested its weight by tossing it lightly into the air, letting it fall back into his massive hand. "It's less than half an ounce. I can give you eighty dollars."

I was astounded at that much money and blurted, "Eighty?" I'd hoped for maybe half that.

Harvey misinterpreted my shock, thinking it was disgust at the low offer. "All right," he shook his head, "ninety, but that's as high as I can go for novelty gold." The fat man was cheating me, but both of us were satisfied and the transaction was completed like a magician's hands moving faster than the eye can see. Harvey examined the spot of yellow, half hidden in the creases of his palm. "Are there any more of these things?"

A vision of two dozen potatoes sizzling on the fire had me calculating their worth, wondering if George knew how much he had casually given me. If I offered to help with the tedious routine, maybe I could wrangle a few more kernels. On second thought, I had a cave full of the real thing and didn't need bright little nuggets that resembled large chicken feed. "That's the only one I have," I told Harvey. "If I find more, I'll bring them to you."

Harvey ended up with the gold and I walked out of his hovel with four twenties and one ten, a fortune to supplement the dwindling wad of cash in my underwear drawer.

I breezed into Jack Jamison's Real Estate Office. The promised paperwork sat on his desk. I signed them with a flourish. Jack notarized reluctantly. Glancing at my watch, I realized I still had all afternoon to locate my golden cave and remove one bar to finance the beginnings of my very bright future.

All the way up the canyon, my heart sang joy in three-part harmony.

Zeus lounged under the dining room table and I let him stay there while I put new money with old in the dresser drawer. I packed only things vital to the mission: an umbrella, a hat, a candle with holder and matches. The rest of the bag would hold a twenty-pound bar of gold from my personal Fort Knox. I'd have to scrape off the identity markings to avoid antiquity rules, which I hated doing but…oh, well. The rest would be easy. I could say my dog uncovered this single specimen while we were camping, wear down the questioner with tedious explanations and details of the circumstances, and try to smile when I declared the gold as income on my IRS 1040. The plan was elegantly simple.

"We're off again," I said to Zeus. "Your job is to scare bears."

The trek to the cave was getting routine. At the large fissure in the rock face, I climbed the mountain, dragging Zeus behind, surveying all the boulders that fringed the cliff. Zeus hobbled miserably across pebbles and rocks, his head sagging toward the ground. Finally he sat, refusing to move, not responding to my threats of certain death. I looked to the heavens for help and saw the protruding shelf that had been my refuge during the storm. Serendipity, alive and well, had come to my rescue. We climbed to the shelf where I re-enacted my movements of the day before, searching for a boulder resting on a ledge.

The dog found it first and I followed his rear end into the passage behind the boulder. Above the cave entrance, a hand-sized circle with a cross inside was chiseled into the stone. I hadn't noticed it yesterday but now saw it was the same design on the Spanish Trail, carved into the sighting stone. This was the treasure cave someone had long ago pointed to from a notch on a rock. I entered eagerly.

Zeus stayed against the inside wall while I moved to the center of the cave. Fumbling for the candle and fitting it to its holder, I struck a match and lit the wick. A quick blaze of light dimmed into a gentle glow and I set it down. When my eyes adjusted to the flickering flame, I gazed around the room, pleased with the illumination my candle provided. A diffused light chased the dark to show the ceiling, three large rocks at the rear, the old leather pack on the floor, and no gold bars.

The cave was empty. Bare, cold and vacant.

I dove for the juncture of floor and wall, my fingers scattering dust, seeking a twenty-pound weight. Clambering to the back of the cave, I felt behind rocks, pushed by a desperate hope, finding nothing. "No, no, no…" my moaning bounced between cave walls, piercing the emptiness. Crawling to the opposite wall, I scratched along the floor but found nothing. The thought came that the cave was wrong and I checked the opening leading outside. Above the entrance my fingers touched the deeply etched circle and cross. There was no doubt this was the place that only yesterday sheltered hundreds of gold bars.

I pushed my body back inside. Flickering candlelight created moving shadows, like ghosts in a game of hide and seek, taunting me to make treasure out of dirt. The candle's illumination missed a far corner of the wall where Zeus waited. I moved quickly to explore the place, kicking the candle over, plunging the cave into yawning blackness. Zeus sighed and I heard him plop his big body to the ground. I leaned with my back against the wall, hands around my knees, head sagging on my arms. We stayed there a long time, the cave oppressive in its silence, Zeus on his stomach, me rocking back and forth in the dark.

The sun was behind the cliff when we staggered from the cave. A wispy place in my mind knew that Pope had somehow moved the heavy bars and now watched us, smirking in his victory. I wanted to curse his name loudly into the trees, but refused to give him the satisfaction of seeing me beaten and bloodied. Struggling to stand tall, I strode off into the forest. *"I've been infected with gold fever,"* I lectured myself, *"addicted like George with his sheepskin or Candy and her black silver bar. But I will overcome. I will survive."* Zeus led me off the cliff to flat ground. *"I'm a university professor, an archaeologist writing a textbook. True, I'm only adjunct on slave wages, but money isn't everything."*

My empty pack created a barely perceived caress against my back, a reminder that my anticipated wealth was as bare as the bag.

CHAPTER TWELVE

About five in the afternoon we reached home and stumbled through the meadow. I entered the fairy ring where the desiccated yard whispered at me to look closer. Squinting in the oblique light, I imagined four individual round spots outlined by a hint of short yellow weeds. I blinked, lost the vision, and the ground morphed into a vacuous mass again.

We continued to the cake-icing porch and entered the house. Dinner consisted of dog food for Zeus and leftover canned chicken noodle soup for me. Our diet variety was abysmal. I considered trading meals with Zeus, but he had better taste. There was no possibility now of hiring a private cook.

That night Zeus happily broke the former rules and settled into his spongy mattress on the floor of my room, but I closed the door anyway to guarantee his presence. The trunk sat serenely in the middle of the room without growing, ghouling, or glowing. Last night's powerful illusion faded in the logic of tonight and I slept in peace.

About midnight I woke to a violent wind whirling around the house, screaming against the cuts of the corners, sending tree branches banging into windows. The sound of glass shattering downstairs woke Zeus and he whimpered. Burrowing under my blankets, I groused about the bad timing. Since the house was now mine, I'd have to clean up the mess and pay for repairs.

In the morning, the house, porch, and yard showed no damage. The windows were intact and all branches hung from their trees. I'd experienced realistic dreams in the past, during illness or when taking medication, but this beat everything. I pushed the experience back into the dark places of my mind and directed attention to the fairy circle, determined to solve its mysterious reality. My new folding shovel scraped at the lifeless yard, which could have doubled for concrete. After digging until my hands were numb, my progress only measured a few inches.

I felt the Indian beside me and resisted the urge to look up.

"Hello, Pope," I said calmly, kicking the shovel to start a hole, "You're trespassing."

He spoke quietly. "You need to stop."

I remained at my work. "You said you were an honest man." A wheeze escaped my lungs when I jumped on top of the shovel and bounced off again. "You don't take things that don't belong to you."

Pope treated my words like fruit flies, not worth swatting. "Dr. Howard, you have no concept of what you're doing."

I threw the shovel to the ground with a hint of hysteria and spun around for an attack. "Who gives you authority to order people around with big words of warning?"

Pope looked down at me, his eyes serious. "What words will you listen to?"

I pulled myself together, my voice low and even. "It's time *you* listen to warnings." There was no loss of control. "Today I'm buying a pickaxe to loosen this dirt. While I'm in town, I'll visit the police and have you arrested for theft."

His mouth wrinkled in a slight grin. "Say 'hi' to Dave for me. Tell him you found a cave full of Spanish gold and I stole it." *Rats. He and the cop were friends.*

I did a sudden splash into curiosity. "How do you know they're Spanish?"

"They're marked with a 'V'," he explained, "showing that the Spanish King's twenty-percent tax had been paid."

"Are there any other markings?"

"They're stamped with Ano Dom 1675."

Now I got excited. "1675! Are you sure?" He stood like a wooden Indian in a frontier tobacco store. I begged shamelessly. "This changes history. You can't keep it a secret. All I need is one bar, for science." He shook his head. "C'mon," I pleaded, "You've had three hundred years of mining in these mountains with countless caches of Spanish and Mexican treasure. You can give me one little bar. I won't tell where it came from."

"You'll have to tell," he said, "to prove your claim."

He was right. I'm pretty sure my face fell off. "Who *are* you?"

"I am Pope Tabby-To-Kwanah. I'm 24 years old and a university law student. In the summer, I honor my family commitment to guard the sacred places against..." he considered his words and went on. "...against people like you. It doesn't matter whether the motive is treasure or science, hoards will come here looking for gold. We won't allow the mines to be opened again."

"Who's 'we'?"

"The priests of my tribe."

I considered Pope's last name, Tabby-To-something. "There's a picture of Chief Tabby at the top of my landing. Any relation?"

"Tabby-To-Kwanah, Chief of the Northern Ute tribe, my great-great grandfather." Pope's eyes twinkled with what looked like a sense of humor. "My family still has influence around here. For instance, I'm on the Town Council."

My throat hardened. "That was a clever way to say no one will believe me when I tell them you've stolen my gold."

"It isn't your---"

"It *is*." I interrupted. "I signed the papers yesterday."

He shrugged. "The transaction won't be legal for a few more days." Pope lowered his voice. "I thought I made it clear why you can't have the Towats treasure."

"Towats?" I moved to sarcasm. "I thought Montezuma's treasure was in the Towats temple. *My* cave had Spanish gold."

His face gave no hint of emotion. "All Spanish gold originates in the Uintas, where the Aztecs mined. Everything belongs to Towats."

Something important had just happened. I squinted my eyes in concentration, waiting for an answer to surface. "Did you transfer my gold to the Towats temple?"

"We're working on it. It'll take a few more days." He shook his head and grinned. "You've caused us a lot of trouble."

Pieces of information tumbled into my head, sending back waves of understanding. The temple of Towats was real. Aztec gold had been mined there, moved to Mexico, and returned during the Cortez conquest. The archaeologist in me had gone into hiding while I scrambled for treasure, but now she pushed her way out.

"Please, Pope," I groveled shamelessly, "I want to see the cavern. You owe it to me. I won't take anything or report it, but I have to see Montezuma's treasure. Please."

"No one enters the temple, especially not— "

I raised my palm to stop him. "Don't say a white woman. George told me eight white men have seen the cavern."

"They had permission."

"How do I get permission?"

"Dr. Howard," Pope closed his eyes in a give-me-strength manner. "You'll never have permission."

"I'm an archaeologist, trained to examine ancient sites without destroying anything. That should be enough to get me an invitation."

The boy smiled. "Your science works against you. The men who saw the temple honored the Ute ways and understood our responsibility."

"I have great admiration for native American traditions."

"Dr. Howard," I detected an ounce of pity, "give it up."

He had pushed me to a precipice. I picked up the shovel and marched toward the house. Pope spoke to my retreating back. "Do not dig in this spot."

I faced him at the porch. "Why not? Did your ancestors bury sacred cannons here?"

"They're not sacred."

Pope had thrown another curve ball, this one answering the mystery of what was beneath my dead front yard. I scanned the barren ground. "So," I nodded, repeating the new revelation, "old Spanish cannons are buried in my yard and poisoning it."

"Don't uncover them, for your own good." Pope was on a recorded loop.

"Are you threatening me? What will you do if I disobey your orders?"

He hesitated. "I've guarded treasure caches since the age of thirteen. I have never yet had to kill."

The word "yet" had an ominous ring. I put the shovel against the porch railing and leaned into the wood column, arms folded, one leg crossed over the other in a position that reeked confidence. "I'm not scared, Pope." I was, but threw caution to my faulty instincts about people. Pope didn't strike me as a murderer. George, maybe, but not Pope.

He took a short breath, making a quick, seemingly desperate decision. "I'll show you the buried cannon in the forest, the one you found."

"Thanks anyway, young man. I've got better possibilities under my feet. Besides," I added, "it will be easier to dig here."

He slowly shook his head. I stood away from the porch column and made a stab at reason, spreading my hands toward the fairy ring. "If there are multiple cannons under this dirt, one hole will loosen the others and simplify excavation."

"You cannot—"

"This debate is over," I announced. Head held high, I moved to the front door, sending a message over my shoulder. "When the estate transaction is legal, I'm hiring a backhoe."

Pope's next offer traveled fast. "We'll help you dig out the cannon in the forest."

His sudden willingness to cooperate and include the infamous 'we' made me suspicious.

Facing him, my hand still on the door, I asked, "Why should the cannon in the forest be better than the ones in front of the house?"

"It doesn't carry the curse."

A single word found its way outside my astonished mouth. "Curse?"

Pope's dark eyes hardened. "You don't want to know how these evil cannons were used."

I let go of the door and faced him squarely. "Give it a try. 'Evil' is too heavy a word for brass cannons probably used to defend the mines and missions."

His dark eyes studied me. Slowly, deliberately, he began his description. "The Spanish forced Indian slaves to stand front to back in a line. Bets were made on how accurately the cannons could be fired from a distance, and how many bodies one cannon ball could rip through before it stopped. Indian men were blown into such tiny pieces, the bodies couldn't be gathered for burial."

There's a childhood game called "statues." You swing a friend by the arms in a circle and let go. They tumble across the grass and freeze where they stop. The game involves guessing what the position represents. Pope had swung me with violence and I landed in shock with a stunned face, mouth gaping, hands loose at my sides.

"You're right, Pope. I didn't want to hear that."

"Answer this for me." He paused before making his request. "Does the house seem strange?"

This was not the time for true confessions. "Not really," I lied. "It's an old house. Moans and rattles are natural." He nodded, but not in agreement. It was more like he heard what I wasn't saying. I amended the statement. "Not moans and rattles like ghosts in chains or anything." I was the one getting rattled. "Just old noises, you know, creaks—"

"And sometimes wind?" He maneuvered me into a trap.

I refused to cooperate. "No wind to speak of."

"How about a cold spot, say, in the hall?"

I cocked my head to get a bead on his motivation. Was he goading me into confessions or just letting me know he was aware of the house's spooky nature? I kept a straight face when I said, "I don't know what you're talking about."

He let it drop. "I'll be back in four days with men to shovel out the cannon under the trees. An extra pickaxe would come in handy if you want to bring one. Meantime, let the dog guide you." He began walking away but turned to add, "Promise you won't dig in the yard."

I smiled at him. "Why would I do hard labor by myself when you're bringing a crew to give me what I want?"

"Promise," he insisted.

"On my honor," I said, raising my hand in the Boy Scout oath, two fingers forming a 'V' like the stamp on Spanish gold bars.

Pope bowed slightly and walked toward the east pines. I stood on the porch sorely tempted to follow him. *"He's going to the Towats Temple,"* I thought, vaguely aware that I was crossing the patch of bare ground in front of the porch. *"The stream, the Spanish Trail, and George's gold-gathering hobbies are north. Pope is going East."* My feet hurried through the meadow. *"The western cliffs were used to hide a cave full of ancient gold bars…"* I picked up speed and sprinted into a run, *"…which are now being deposited East in the caverns of Towats."*

The forest edge stopped me and I glanced back at the house, somehow surprised to see it half a football field away. A miniature Zeus peered from the dining room window, his paws on the sill lifting him higher to watch me. I felt guilty leaving him behind but didn't have time to go back. Pope already had a two-minute head start. The connection between thought and action vanished. I plunged into tree shadows, hoping for a glimpse of faded Levi's leading to the temple.

Without water, a watch, or even a compass around my neck, I knew the attempt to follow Pope was foolish, but the opportunity to see Montezuma's Treasure wouldn't come again. Thick forest wrapped around me, fingernail branches scraping at my face. I did a western square dance of do-si-do with the pines, my palm feeling the rough bark while I hunted a human trail: a freshly broken branch, footprints on soft ground, the phlegm of spit dripping from a leaf. Pope wouldn't leave a blatant trail like that, but it was all I knew. Girl Guide leaders didn't teach tracking in my day. I'd have to wing it.

Time fades in a place where sunlight filters in but the source can't be seen. I judged a ten-minute lapse and reviewed my path, memorizing landmarks behind me.

Pushing forward again, an odd arrangement of trees captured my interest. Five living pines supported the remains of a dead tree at the center, its lower trunk rotted away, the bark nearly gone. There was an image of something etched into the cambium layer. I approached slowly, as if it might hold a danger I couldn't see. The picture of a turtle came into focus, probably carved when the tree was alive. The bark had been removed to give the turtle a white background that could be seen from a distance.

In the parlance of Spanish trail symbolism, everything is up for interpretation: circles, crosses, hearts, cactus...everything except a turtle. A turtle always means treasure. I looked east, the direction the head faced, and noticed a dry streambed several yards away, perfect for easier traveling. Another turtle, again facing east, had been carved into a boulder. Apparently, the stream was the treasure trail.

The ten-foot-wide course moved toward steep cliffs with bushes growing from cracks in the rock. The waterless stream had frothy weeds bending on the banks with taller, darker pines in the background. I walked over flat stones polished by running water, grateful to have found a better path, continuing to watch for more markers giving directions to a sacred cavern. A heart shape in the shaded cliffs was the next clue that this was the trail. The meaning of the heart might have come from a supposed conversation between Montezuma and Cortez:

Montezuma: Why do you so much desire gold?"

Cortez: Because we Spaniards have a disease of the heart which is only cured by gold.

A shaft of light broke through the trees, touching the earth in a yellow-white glow. I paused under it like a shower, soaking in the warmth, lifting my face to the sky. On the cliff five feet above me were three lines of writing carved into the rock face.

Cuidado
Maldicion Espanol
Los muertos no habla

Spanish was required during my Arizona high school days. I had tried to cheat my way through, but it was easier to learn the language, and I knew "habla" should have been "hablan." The message was:

Beware
the Spanish curse
The dead do not talk.

A dry branch snapped ahead of me. Judging by the sound, the branch was big, broken by something bigger. Abject fear restricted my heart, immobilized by the fight or flight response. I riveted my sight for signs of movement beyond the streambed, then sensed something behind me and stiffened. Squeezing my eyes shut against the dread, I turned slowly, expecting the feel of sharp claws across my face. I rarely use a female-type Hollywood shriek, but years of unused yells heaved into my throat. I opened my eyes and screamed.

CHAPTER THIRTEEN

My screech rumbled through the forest and ricocheted down the canyon as Zeus slumped into the sand, head buried under his paws. With my heart still thumping, I didn't know whether to be angry or relieved that the monster behind me was my dog.

"Zeus!" My tone caused the animal to shrink further into the rubble. The sight evoked pity and I bent to pat his light brown head. "Hey, fella, how did you get here?" He struggled to stand and I saw a leash wrapped loosely around his neck, clipped to his collar. It was a neon advertisement that either Zeus was a genius dog that could open doors and fit himself with a leash, or someone had brought him to me.

I glared back at the trail and yelled with force, "Pope! I know you're there," then addressed Zeus in a gentle voice, "Which way did he go?" The dog stood straight with ears lowered to half-mast. I reached for the leash and he stepped back two steps. I moved forward and he continued in reverse, taking a playful stance, body lowered with angled front legs ready to leap away in a game of tag. I lunged and missed as he bounded a few feet down the streambed, taunting me.

"C'mon Zeus, don't do this." I swear the dog laughed as he ambled along the dry river, obliging me to pursue him. The "here, boy" commands and "good dog" coaxing didn't reach his pointed ears. There was little choice but to follow the animal. Habit forced me to repeatedly look on my left wrist for a watch that wasn't there. Not knowing the time is a psychological disadvantage that fills the spaces in your head with thoughts contaminated by the phrase, "What time is it?"

After following the course for what seemed a long time, Zeus bounded over the bank and waited for me. Weary of the chase, I slowly climbed the short bank to watch Zeus enter the trees, facing me again, checking to be sure I followed. He led me in a zig-zag pattern around the pines until tree groupings thinned, allowing rays of sun to penetrate thick vegetation on the ground. Shadows diluted to gauzy wraiths in the power of light. Zeus casually trotted ahead, never getting beyond my sight. There was no doubt the dog was forcing me home.

Eventually, evergreen branches parted like a curtain to introduce the open field with the sun above my yellow brick house at the opposite end of the meadow, making the time about three or four in the afternoon. I had spent most of the day in the forest. Zeus broke into a run for home. I stumbled and fell to my knees. Already depressed, I stayed among the grassy weeds in defeat. I couldn't even run across a meadow without falling. My effort to track Pope to the cave of Towats had failed and, even worse, while I wandered aimlessly, Pope had circled back and brought my dog to lead me home. He must have seen me thrashing through the forest and decided to save me from my own incompetence.

I rolled from a hands and knees position to sit, back bent above stretched-out legs. In a lethargic head move, I noticed an upright stone with another next to it, and several after that, forming the beginning of a circle. I grunted to a standing position, gazing through grassy growth at a ten-foot ring, flat stones fitted inside to make a floor. An occasional upright rock delineated the boundary, and I knew I'd found the ruins of an arrastra, a crude but effective mechanism designed for crushing quartz to loosen gold. Ore was broken into small chunks with a sledgehammer and poured into the circular milling area. A draft animal tied to a wooden shaft, held in place with 'T' supports, dragged three heavy stones in a circle over the ore. Five hundred pounds of quartz could be ground in three or four hours by mule. Arrastras were common among the Phoenicians and introduced to the New World by the Spanish. If the arrastra in my meadow was Spanish, I had a feeling human slaves did the labor.

A milling operation confirmed a gold mine in the vicinity. I wandered slowly towards home, crisscrossing the grass in search of clues. A second arrastra showed signs of fire. Perhaps Indians burned the wooden supports and shafts, blackening the flat flooring stones. The mining operation must have been big if it needed two arrastras. My eyes swept the area for likely signs of mining, probably against the cliff. When I reached the porch, I viewed the meadow again, imagining a large camp with tents, fires, sluices, and constant work in the mills. The Kamas museum diorama had shown total destruction of the landscape. There would have been no meadow here at that time, only choking dust and dirt holes.

Zeus waited patiently by the front door, which was his only choice as a dog. I scratched the bridge of his nose and he followed me inside. The invisible ghost barrier stretching across the hall was more effective than a yellow tape printed with "Crime Scene" repeated along its length. We avoided the hall as usual and turned left through the dining room.

We ate an early dinner. I typed some pages of my book. We ate a late dinner. I proofed the pages.

At ten o'clock the dog and I scaled the stairs to the landing and turned right. I paused to say good-night to Chief Tabby. "You'd be proud of your great-grandson," I told the photograph. "Today, he knew I'd be in trouble if I followed him, and went out of his way to help me. You did the same for your friend, Hathenbruck. Pope is a good man…like you." I half expected the corners of Tabby's mustached mouth to lift slightly, but he remained a stoic Indian inside his frame.

We passed the second bedroom and entered the larger third room. Everything was the way it should be, with pictures crowded on the dresser and the trunk in the center of the floor. All was right with the room. Zeus wiggled into his foam mattress, groaning in comfort. I shut the door, turned off the light, and fell into bed with my own noises of gratitude. Soon, Zeus and I ruptured the silence with our personal brands of snoring.

Awareness of a soft, agonized moan intruded into my hearing. Enough moonlight sifted through the window to allow me to sit up and check Zeus, whose breathing presented its normal noise level. The moan came from downstairs and I rolled out of bed to walk to the door, planning to check the source of the sound, maybe air in a pipe. I put my hand on the doorknob when the moan grew louder, registering a pain past physical suffering into an anguish of soul that makes you bury your head in your hands. It was the grief you experience if you drive over a little boy on his tricycle and feel the car lift against something small. You've killed the child, you can see his bent trike under your wheels. But you can't force yourself out of the car, terrified of what you'll find. Instead, you bury your face in your hands. The misery downstairs held that kind of hopeless pain.

The wail settled into wrenching sobs. I stood with my fingers still on the doorknob, hesitant to enter the nightmare below. A woman's prolonged scream knocked me away from the door and sent me leaping back to bed, brushing into Zeus standing by his mattress, staring at the door. We were both having the same nightmare that increased to a chorus of howls. The sounds of weeping women wafted between the shrieks of men. I bolted to a sitting position at the cries of children. Echos of mourning filled the main floor and rose to lean against my closed bedroom door. Tears welled into my eyes at the suffering I heard. My normal senses shut down, conscious only of the tormented cries. I covered my ears with my hands, waiting for an end. It had to end. All things end.

It came unexpected. The swirling, tortured voices simply stopped, leaving nothing behind. Not a single resonance of sound floated in the air. The house was quiet. Zeus padded to the side of my bed for reassurance. I rested my hand on his head. "It was just a dream, Zeus."

We both knew it wasn't.

Morning arrived without further interruption and the light encouraged me into near normalcy. We had slept later than usual, exhausted from the night's terror. I dressed slowly, hesitantly walked to the door, and placed my hand on the knob, envisioning some unspeakable horror waiting in the hall: a body hanging from a rope by the neck, its eyes bulging, tongue dangling from a mouth dripping with blood; A blue-skinned ghoul grinning at me, teeth sharpened to a point. I inched the door wide enough to peek through a slit. Zeus rose to a sitting position for any necessary quick action.

There was nothing there. I breathed in relief, Zeus stayed alert, and we entered the landing, cautiously moving down the stairs. The house was calm and, once in the kitchen, we relaxed and discussed breakfast plans. I ate cold cereal, Zeus agreed to a bowl of lukewarm Kibbles. The day began.

In the parlor, I wrote two pages of the pottery textbook, aware of Mr. Hathenbruck watching me from his gilded frame suspended over the fireplace. I swiveled in my chair to face him. "I'm staying," I told him. "I don't believe in ghosts." I reconsidered the words. "Okay, something eerie is happening here, but there's a scientific explanation. Your cheap amusement park ride through a haunted house isn't going to run me off." The man's kindly eyes looked beyond me into some blue sky of his own. "You look like a nice guy," I said. "But you're not. The artist must have painted you on a good day."

I turned back to my electric typewriter and wrote my best chapter yet, titled, "Looking for a Lithic Date Mate." It was a play on words, mate and date. Maybe not. I changed the title to standard boring and wrote the rest of the morning.

In the afternoon, Zeus and I clambered into the Shove-it and rolled over the edge of our meadow on the path to the main road. Thirty minutes found us in front of the Jamison Real Estate Office. I allowed Zeus to follow me in. Jack sat at his desk. Today's T-shirt read, *Without Geography, You're Nowhere.*

"Hello, Dr. Howard." His eyes transferred to Zeus. "So this is your famous dog."

"He's famous?"

"He's big. That makes him worth a few sentences of gossip."

"Don't people around here talk about the weather?"

"The weather comes ahead of your dog."

It rankled me that everybody in small towns knew everything. Curious, I asked, "So, Jack, what gets said about me and the Hathenbruck house?"

Jack leaned back in his chair. "Today, the word will be that the house is yours. The official papers will be here within the week. I assume you've read the inheritance rules I gave you."

"I didn't have time."

Jack stared at my dog before returning attention to me. "Just remember, *you* made the decision."

I got an itchy feeling at the words, like I'd forgotten to put on underwear or lost my wallet. Finally, I nodded wisely as if I knew something he couldn't possibly understand and exited the office.

Next stop was the grocery/hardware store. Zeus languished in the car while I stood in front of a bewildering supply of pickaxes, long and short handled, garden, fork spade… I chose one I could lift and journeyed to the checkout when I stopped at a rack of sledgehammers. An advertisement at the top said, "A Sledgehammer applies more impulse than other hammers and distributes force over a wide area for destruction work." It resembled the weapon used by the Norse god Thor. I envisioned its use to break ore for crushing in my arrastra.

You don't need a sledgehammer, I told myself and walked away, then did an unexpected U-turn back to the strangely-shaped tool. I chose one with a ten-pound metal head and dropped it next to the pickaxe. The wheels creaked against the weight.

The man at the checkout counter was chatty. "Looks like you're doing some prospecting."

I laughed. "I just want flowers in a place that's too hard to dig."

"That explains the pickaxe," he grinned, entering numbers on the cash register. "Are you planning to kill gophers with the sledgehammer?"

I ducked my head, pretending not to hear as I searched my backpack for cash. "How much do I owe you?"

He told me, took the money, and rang up the purchase. "Are you the one in the Hathenbruck place?"

I took a deep breath before answering. "That would be me."

He gave me the change. "Is it true the place is haunted?"

I veiled my surprise by struggling with the cart. "Not that I've noticed." I pushed the cart away, banging it through the doors to get outside into the sunshine.

On impulse, I drove back to Jack's office and caught him leaving. He stopped by my car to say, "I'm on the way to an appointment. Can I help you first?"

"You said a lot of people have looked at the Hathenbruck house, but nobody bought it." I leaned toward the window. "Why?"

He shrugged. "Not everybody wants an isolated house in the mountains."

I hit him with uncushioned words. "People in town are asking me if the place is haunted."

Jack produced barely enough smile to wrinkle his eyes. "You've been there longer than anybody. You tell me."

I put my elbow out the window. "I don't believe in ghosts, but something is strange about the house. Noises happen in the middle of the night: high winds, glass breaking, moaning and screaming. It stops suddenly." The description sounded like a children's ghost story, effective only in the dark with squealing Girl Scouts.

"That's sort of disappointing," Jack said. "Noises in an old house don't make it haunted. No apparitions or smells? Nothing tangible?"

I grinned apologetically under the influence of a bright sun. "That's pretty much it," I said. "It sure ruins a good night's sleep." I took the offensive, which is good procedure when you're feeling silly. "Why didn't you warn me?"

"Warn you about what?" Jack sidestepped my procedure. "I don't believe in ghosts, either. If you didn't like the house, why did you agree to inherit it?"

I couldn't tell the real estate agent I'd found and lost a fortune in Spanish gold on the property. Half the truth would do the job. "Nothing happened until I became the owner."

He stood straight. "That's a first," he almost spoke to himself. "Most people don't make it through the cold part of the hall." He leaned down again. "But your cousin still could have sold the house if she hadn't allowed potential buyers to stay the night. Hilda was a good woman and insisted on honesty. No one made it through…" Jack raised one eyebrow, "…except you. Why is that?"

"I told you. Nothing happened until I accepted ownership of the house."

He paused a moment, as if debating whether to speak his next thought, then glanced at his watch. "Gotta run. I'm sure you'll find a logical explanation for the noises. Nice talking to you." He headed toward his real estate car.

I put my head out the window to bellow at him. "Is it too late to change my mind?"

He smiled and saluted before opening the car door. "In a few days you'll have the official papers to the Hathenbruck Estate." He got in and hauled himself out again. "By the way, five years is all I care to handle the house. If you decide to sell, you'll need to use another agent. Good luck with that."

CHAPTER FOURTEEN

I leaned against the warm car seat and closed my eyes to review the facts. I owned a haunted house in the Uinta Mountains, seven hundred miles from where I worked and resided. Selling or renting was unlikely, given the spooky ambiance of the place. Harsh reality slapped me up the side of the head when I realized I'd have to pay property taxes on a five-acre estate when I could barely keep up with my little Scottsdale home. The purpose for this adventure had been the promise of wealth flowing in, not hemorrhaging out.

"Matt," I chided myself, "why didn't you consider the costs and taxes before you took the house?" "Because," I angrily replied, "I found a fortune in a cave." I threw some nasty thoughts through the air at Pope, Chief Tabby, and the entire Ute nation for donating my gold bars to the temple of Towats. My dreary future now included foreclosure of the Hathenbruck Estate, the forced sale of my Arizona home, and relocation to a trailer court.

A few insults were hurled at cousin Hilda for saddling me with a house she couldn't stay in for one night. "May you and the entire Hathenbruck family spend eternity in…" There was no point finishing the curse. In spite of what they'd done to me, they were nice people, no doubt already settled in Heaven, which was more than I could expect for myself. I ground the Shove-it's gears into reverse and backed out of the strip mall. "Let's go home," I said to the dog sprawled in the middle seat, "and figure out how to change our fate."

On the drive I studied the surroundings with new focus, the main thought being: "How can I unload the albatross?" Houses in the gully were pleasant and well maintained, the road paved, utilities available, good advertising for house buyers. I could describe the trail winding to my property as a "scenic drive" rather than "a skinny dirt path requiring four-wheel drive." When we rounded the top of the lane I let the car idle while I drank in the legitimate beauty of my house at the end of the meadow. "Turn of the century charming" and "enchanting" would be descriptors.

I knew I could sell the house because, unlike cousin Hilda, poverty was my motivator. I had to trick someone into buying it. A heater behind the wall would warm the cold spot. I'd have to muffle any moans and screams with background music. No one would be allowed to spend the night until they'd paid for the house. Flowers in large half-barrels, strategically placed in the dead yard, would add a note of welcome. The bedroom trunk could be hidden under a table covered with a floor-length cloth.

Was that nice? I was honest enough to know it wasn't. I was even sorry about it. But desperation trumps guilt.

When Zeus and I entered the kitchen, resurrected hope convinced me I could still come out of my monetary mess smelling good.

Plan A began when I stared down the hall toward the front door, arms folded. *"Defeat the hall,"* I commanded myself. There was no plan B. I stepped into the forbidden area and waited. Nothing. Two steps to analyze the feeling. Still nothing. Three strides in a game of Mother-May-I, sneaking to the goal before getting caught. A chill registered against my right side. Gathering courage, I riveted to face the wall, mentally pushing at it, attacking with logic, exploring possible answers. A frigid blast struck me and I backed to the opposite wall. The sensation was like dry ice in my brain, sticking to the tissue, peeling it away. My nerve endings prickled and I scurried back to the kitchen.

After dinner I made a surprise attack on the passageway by galloping through the cold spot to the parlor. The hall barely had time to register its malevolence against my skin and I considered that I had won a partial victory. Psychology classes teach the motivation of "Fear" and "Reward." Last night's haunting had frozen me in a terror that curled me into a protective ball. Tonight, the reward of money from the sale of my property would catapult me into action. Whatever resided in Hathenbruck House was in for a fight. I would not retreat when the moans and groans began. I vowed to find the source of the cries, which I suspected would come from the hall.

The electric typewriter clicked as I pounded its keys, fleshing notes into a textbook while Zeus padded through the dining room to settle on my feet. At ten o'clock, words finally refused to surface. I shut everything down and climbed upstairs, Zeus at my heels. When I shut the bedroom door, it closed tightly with a distinct click. Satisfied, I switched out the light and crawled into bed. I waited tensely for the first sob of human misery, but the night was quiet and I drowsed into that netherworld which is neither here nor there.

An abrasive sound yanked at me. I rolled my head toward the origin at the center of the room. The noise stopped. The trunk threw its dark shadow against the night. Reassuring myself that lack of sleep had tricked me into delusion, I closed my eyes again. Minutes later the sluggish grate of something heavy moved across the floor, jerking me to a sitting position.

Experience with the house prompted me out of bed to turn on the light. The trunk seemed closer to the door. Determined to watch the ornate chest for movement, I left the light on and slid down the door, wrapping my elbows around my knees. Ultimately, even with the light on, my head twitched, nodded, and fell on my arms.

A harsh, prolonged scraping on the floorboards jolted me awake and I realized the trunk was on a course to block the door and trap us in the room. Adrenaline lifted me to my feet. Zeus was at my side, statue-stiff, his throat producing a low, sustained growl directed at the piece of now silent furniture. I placed my hand on the dog's bristling back, his muscles rigid against the strain of tension. In a sudden frenzy of action and piercing barks, he jumped toward the trunk, bounded away, then sprang forward again in a series of feints and attacks.

While Zeus kept the trunk busy, I backed from the battle and opened the door for a quick retreat, thinking whatever was on the other side couldn't be as threatening as the trunk. I was wrong.

A thick, writhing energy rolled through the door and oiled itself around me. The room darkened as if a storm cloud covered the ceiling bulb. Zeus' fierce barks changed to whimpers and he tore through the door. Dread pounded through the arteries in my neck. I heard Pope's advice in my head, *"Let the dog guide you."*

I left the door open, clawing through dense air, like a nightmare where you try to run but only move in slow motion. I found Zeus cowering in the second bedroom under the baby crib. I dropped to my hands and knees to crawl next to him. We wiggled around each other, his head in my lap, my arms around his neck, watching a black substance ooze across the floor, searching for us. The baby crib offered safe haven. I did not consider sauntering out to find the source of the dark energy, even though I had promised myself I would. The psychology of fear succeeded over reward.

Zeus and I finished out the night with the crib above us, guarded by the painting of a lop-sided angel with one eye larger than the other. By early morning my hips had turned to stone and were cemented to the floor. Zeus, already awake, had stayed in place as my pillow. I patted his head, figuring he was worth more than the four hundred dollars he had cost, and we struggled from our shelter to cautiously descend the staircase.

The house was its usual charming self, like an abusing husband who begs forgiveness with promises to change, until his pilot light explodes into violence again. In the Hathenbruck house, the pilot light was in the hall, always on, ready to blast foulness into the night.

At the bottom of the stairs, determined to defy the hall, I hurried briskly past the center, bracing for its cold assault. "Shut up," I said with pretended bravery, and quickly finished the journey to the kitchen. While eating cold cereal I decided to destroy the trunk. The question was how? When the answer came, I grinned and thanked the Norse god Thor.

Zeus accompanied me outside, watching with interest as I pulled the heavy sledgehammer from the car. He trotted next to me, his concerned face lifted to mine when I shifted the load and grunted. Back in the house, he stayed in the kitchen when I dragged the hammer down the hall, telling the cold spot to "drop dead," pleased with my clever irony. Zeus ran through the dining room to meet me at the stairs and I hefted the hammer up each rise to the bedroom where the trunk and I faced each other.

"Meet the new and improved Matt Howard," I announced. Hefting the weapon of Thor in an arc over my head, I brought it squarely down on the silver top of the trunk. A dent in the design brought a glimmer of regret at vandalizing the beautiful antique, but once begun there was no stopping the rhythm needed to continue. It required two hands and a swinging torso to accomplish full power. I rounded the weapon behind my back and over my head to strike repeatedly, again and again. The crashing force fractured the top, sending wooden missiles into the room. I was Mickey Mouse in *The Sorcerer's Apprentice*, hacking an enchanted broom to pieces. Somewhere in a deep corner cupboard of my mind, I had a memory that Mickey Mouse's broom continued to live, each piece forming a new broom. I stopped swinging and watched the trunk with suspicion. Shattered wood lay inert, hardly worth gathering for kindling.

Exhaustion loosened my hold on the hammer and it thudded to the floor. The weapon used by a mythological god had conquered one of the Hathenbruck ghosts. I sat on the floor and closed my eyes against the carnage around me. Zeus curled his large body on my feet and we rested until I was ready to assess the damage. Three sheets of mangled metal lay on the floor, the pressed pattern visible on both sides. I could take the ruined silver to *Harvey's Hoard*. Maybe he would buy it.

Wood shards surrounded the trunk, remnants of the oak arches that had fastened the silver sections to the rounded top. The lid's disfigured frame met at the lock, now smashed like a tin can, its bolt snapped and twisted in random directions. The box of the trunk, however, was still intact. I boosted from the floor, steeling myself for something out of an Alfred Hitchcock movie, expecting black beetles scurrying through human skulls, devouring the remaining flesh.

I wrenched the top off. The lid fell backward, hanging by one hinge. I peered into the trunk to see its contents.

CHAPTER FIFTEEN

B ooks.
Books of various sizes, in disarray from the pounding
they'd received. I lifted a thin 6x9 volume from the top of
the pile, brushed wood slivers from the leather cover, and
opened it. The words were German, hand-written in black
ink with swirls embellishing the letters. In my undergradu-
ate days I had substituted German for a math class and recognized fundamental words:

Vater: Father, Frederick the Third. *The third of what?*

Mutter: Mother, Louisa Hudinburgh,

Palastdienerin: a palace servant. After a few more pages,
I read, "… *eine Tante en Homburg…geistliche Unterweisung.…
Englische Schule.* Frederick lived with an Aunt in Germany
and received religious training. His family had the money
to educate him in England.

A birth certificate, lodged between the pages, showed
the name *Frederick Wilhelm Claude, 30 November, 1852,* born in
England. I walked to the dresser and compared the name to

the framed confirmation I had noticed the first day in the house: *Frederick Wilhelm Claude, 20 May 1866.* The boy was fourteen at his confirmation in the local German church. Strange that neither document used the Hathenbruck surname.

The word *Opa* caught my attention, a familiar term for grandfather, followed by William the First Hohenzollern, Emperor of Germany. *Emperor?* Clues snapped themselves together like magnets. F.W.C. Hathenbruck was the illegitimate son of Frederick the Third Hohenzollern, crown prince of Germany. His mother was a palace servant. I did a quick intake of breath at the revelation. Since a bastard son of royalty could not receive his father's name, the surname "Hathenbruck" must be an anglicized version of his mother's name, Hudinburgh.

I laughed out loud. In my wildest hopes I hadn't expected such treasure. The haunted trunk held Hathenbruck's lost journals, his secrets, and my answers. Sitting amid the rubble, I scanned the book for any elementary German I could understand: *Musik, Literatur, Kunst, Krieg, Fiend, Meinen besten Freund.* The boy had an education befitting the ward of the royal household. He studied music, literature, and art. His friends were from upper class families with titles.

War was mentioned, but young Hathenbruck identified his personal enemy as William II, his younger half-brother, legitimate heir to the throne. Then these words: "*Ich wurde sowohl von meinem Vater als auch von meinem Grossvater meinem Bruder vorgezogen.*" According to Hathenbruck, both his father and grandfather liked him better than his brother. If the preference was blatant, family politics could be hazardous for Hathenbruck.

The German journal offered bits and pieces of the story. When Hathenbruck was sixteen, his friend Karl blurted at a palace gathering *(Palastversammlung)* that Hathenbruck was really the son of Crown Prince Frederick. I couldn't decipher the paragraphs leading to the event, but scandal and threats were clear. "*Ich habe um mein Leben gefurchtet.*" The boy was afraid for his life. A few pages later, *Amerika* showed up. Hathenbruck left Germany with loose-lipped Karl and a cousin named Wilhelm to explore the American West until things cooled down at home.

My morning segued into noon. I fed Zeus, took him out, brought him in again, and returned to the bedroom. The trunk yawned open and I picked up another volume, this one written in English. Delighted with the find, I rifled the trunk for more. My fingers plowed through German textbooks on physiology, anatomy, pharmacology, geology, mineralogy, and three more journals in English. My aching tailbone cried for a better seating arrangement and I took the books downstairs to the parlor. Hathenbruck's portrait stared past my head into the distance.

"Good afternoon, Fred." I used the nickname for Frederick to show my disregard of his royal status. "Thanks for writing these journals in English." He sat quietly on his log, the rifle resting against his left arm. I goaded him with my victory. "I'm going to learn why you locked your life up in a trunk, and why you haunt this house." He didn't fight back. I chose one of the soft chairs with red velvet cushions and settled down to probe the man's life, from royalty to American immigrant.

1869 Frederick is seventeen years old in the uncivilized American West. Guided by Jim Bridger, he and his friends hunt Bison in Kansas and big horn sheep in Wyoming. At Fort Bridger, Karl and Wilhelm go home. Frederick stays behind, unsure of his safety in Germany. He gets a job as a topographer with the Denver and Rio Grande Railroad. He is fascinated with the Indian tribes he encounters and keeps notes on their languages and customs.

1871 On June 8, Frederick marries Rozilla Saunsecie, daughter of a half-blood Cherokee. He is nineteen, she is sixteen. They start their life together in a small town at the base of the Rocky Mountains. Not long after, Frederick receives a letter from German relatives inviting him to finish his education at the University of Heidelburg. He accepts, graduates with honors in medicine and mineralogy, but finds himself in the middle of political intrigues. He is still preferred over his half brother, which will either make him the Emperor of Germany or leave him assassinated. He renounces his royal heritage and returns to Rozilla and their growing family.

The next decade finds him in a variety of careers.

- Physician, U.S. Cavalry. Signed death certificate of General George Custer in 1876.
- Minerologist for a mining company. While cleaning the augers of a machine, it switches on, mangling his right arm. Efforts to release him fail. He sends for his medical bag and amputates his own arm.
- The handicapped doctor opens a Mercantile Store, setting up additional trading posts on the borders of the Ute Reservation.
- He learns the Ute language and becomes an interpreter.

1888 *"I have received word that my father is dead. My half brother is now the Emperor of Germany, but my father has left an annuity which will be a blessing to me and my family."* A few pages later he writes: *"Wilhelm has canceled my annuity."*

The mercantile store isn't profitable. Hathenbruck tends to give things to those who can't afford to pay, and actually donates and delivers supplies to the Indians.

1894 *"A man named Caleb Rhoades has presented me with the offer of a partnership to develop a Spanish gold mine. His father once discovered a gruesome massacre of Mexicans and found a map showing the location of three Spanish mines. Rhoades has located one, but it is within the boundaries of the Ute Reservation. He hopes I can use my influence with the Indians to gain legal access and title to the mine. Rhoades is under oath not to take anything from the sacred mine, but the Spanish mines and caches are not sacred. Nevertheless, the Indians are dangerous."*

October 15: *"The entrance is low, almost at the base of the cliff, and very small. It shows signs of once having been much larger, but someone has filled it with slag rock and dirt until the only access is by a small aperture at the top of the heap. It is close to a reddish colored ledge, indicating the presence of iron ore. This may have been the source of the iron used by the Spanish. Mr. Rhoades assures me there are several old kilns in the vicinity."*

1895 Winter prevents the men from prospecting until spring. *"We took great care not to be seen and traveled to the mine under darkness. There are old pieces of broken harness, buckles and buttons from decaying Spanish uniforms in the tunnel entrance. The pay streak is from three inches to three feet wide where it disappears into the roof of the tunnel. Presumably it expands to even greater width beyond where the Spaniards ceased their excavation."*

July 23: *"The vein is of the purest gold in such concentration as I have never before seen in my experience. I took assay samples only from an exterior vein, nothing from the main vein. To reveal the existence and value of the main vein would be the cause of a Klondike rush to the region which would destroy any plans for development."*

The assay report showed that Hathenbruck, at the age of forty-two, had indeed found a bonanza in excess of $27,000 to a ton of ore, at a time when gold was $16 an ounce. He and Rhoades carefully planned the steps to develop their enormous wealth.

1896   Early in the year, Hathenbruck camps on the reservation among the Indians, gaining their support for the lease and development of the mine to the benefit of all. But word about the mine leaks to the press. Headlines announce a new Klondike has been discovered. Hathenbruck writes in his journal: *"There is dirty work afoot to prevent me from securing my lease. I've been shot at a number of times. I hold my life to be in danger all the time. I've made an agreement with Matt Warner, gunfighter and member of Butch Cassidy's Wild Bunch, to protect me and my interests."*

August: *"Matt and his boys were ambushed, took refuge behind some trees, and fired back. Matt has been arrested for murder. Butch and seventy-five men in his gang gathered to break Matt out of jail, but Matt said he'd rather have a good lawyer. So Butch and the Wild Bunch robbed a bank to raise the money, but they aren't available to work for us anymore."*

Four months later, Hathenbruck writes: *"I won. I got the consent of all 980 Indians on the reservation and then called them together in open council to sign the lease, which is required by law to make the lease legal. Old Chief Tabby wasn't among them and the Indians wouldn't sign without him. I suggested that we send for Chief Tabby and bring him in. None of the Indians would go. Some Indian Agents were there, but I could get no white man to make the trip. Finally I said, 'I will go myself.'*

I took my nephew and we went forty-five miles into the mountains in the dead of winter to Chief Tabby's camp. We found the chief sick and it did not seem as though he could live. He might have been ninety at the time. I doctored him for a week until he was well enough to travel. We put him into a lumber wagon and went three or four miles in the warmest part of the day, then stopped for the night, built up a great fire, and filled Chief Tabby with herbs and coffee to thaw him out.

I sent runners ahead to notify the agents that we were coming and to keep the Indians from straying off. When we reached the council every Indian was enjoying a good hot meal. Old Chief Tabby got up on the spring seat of the wagon and made them a speech telling them to sign my lease. This was December 18, 1897. The council closed with a barbecue."

I placed the journal in my lap and rested my head against the red velvet of the chair. My eyes wandered to the ornate, pressed-tin tiles covering the ceiling. I studied the pattern, thinking of the joy Hathenbruck must have felt at his success. Too bad he couldn't see ahead to his future. Born to wealth, he would end his life as a one-armed door-to-door salesman. I avoided looking at his portrait over the fireplace wishing I could warn the man, but I didn't know where he had gone wrong. In the next decade of journal entries, Hathenbruck wrote down his life. It was like reading about a runaway train wreck.

1898-1905

- *"Caleb Rhoades has met with an accident. The roof of his cabin collapsed on him. He is partially paralyzed. I assured him we are still full partners and friends."*
- *"I have made application to the Department of the Interior for a grant of four miles square in the desired locality. If it is successful, we can inaugurate a mining enterprise on a gigantic scale."*
- *"My troubles are by no means over. I have people to deal with more uncertain than the Indians. I won on the reservation, but that is only part of the battle. Before we can strike a pick on the property or ship a pound of ore, we are obliged to secure permission of the government to ratify the lease."*
- *"We know someone high in government is blocking our efforts to have the Indian lease ratified. But I have a card up my sleeve: the Emperor of Germany. For the sake of the mine, we can pretend brotherly love."*
- *"The U.S. wants Germany as an ally. I have written to Wilhelm about my gold mine and difficulty in getting Congress to ratify the lease. I suggested he petition Congress in an exchange for his loyalty: a land grant of 100,000 acres which would include the wealthiest gold mine in the world."*
- *"I have maintained correspondence with the Senators in Washington and assured them that even after the Kaiser acquires his share of the gold, there will be enough to pay off the national debt of the United States and stock the treasury with gold."*

June 2, 1905. *"Caleb Rhoades is dead."*

Hathenbruck continues the battle alone, writing hundreds of letters to Washington, neglecting his mercantile store and other businesses. Unscrupulous politicians bar his way.

"I have never had nor could get any justice from here to Washington. Several Congressmen have formed the Florence Mining Company. They have filed a restraining order against me."

The First World War ends his dream of a deal with his half-brother. Germany becomes a Republic, Wilhelm flees to Holland, and the land grant is rescinded.

In 1916 Hathenbruck blames himself for his son's death from mercury poisoning. Only two months earlier his daughter Susan had died. He had already experienced the loss of four children in infancy. The pain of these events darken his life. *"I have only the memories of flowers now withered. The path of my life is strewn with ashes."*

By 1920 Hathenbruck, now sixty-eight years old, is the only living person who knows where the mine is, but his lease has never been ratified by Congress. If he shows anyone the location, the mine could legally be stolen from him.

- *"If I had ever gone directly to the mine, I have no doubt that my bones would be there to this day."*
- *"People ask if I am worried that professional geologists will find the mine. I tell them I have no concern. It is in the least likely place they would ever expect to find it. They could stand on top of it and never see it."*

In 1927 his wife died. His daughter Joanna had died the year before. He was weary of the world.

At six that afternoon I read the last page.

"Tonight I am sad. Memories of the past come hounding through my mind, telling me of my might-have-been's and my shouldn't have been's. Around my feet are the wrecks of perished ideals, the broken vases of hope."

I slowly closed the back cover. With my head turned toward the enigmatic portrait of Frederick Wilhelm Claude Hathenbruck, I spoke aloud. "You were a good man who got a raw deal. No wonder you haunt this house. I'm sorry, Fred."

One name imprinted itself over my mind. "Frank," the thought said.

His friends called him Frank.

CHAPTER SIXTEEN

I made excuses to stay downstairs that evening. I cleaned the miniscule refrigerator, scrubbed the tiny toilet and shower, and mopped floors, anything to keep from walking through the hall and going upstairs to the bedroom. I even went outside to check the propane tank and generator, from which all blessings flowed. But time hastens when you're on death row. Ten o'clock rolled over me and there was nothing to do but face the night.

With a breath for bravery, I shivered through the hall and up the stairs, where my feet slowly crossed the landing. I played the scary game where you leave a light on, move forward to turn on the next one, then back up to switch off the first. The bedroom door had been left open, inviting me into the disorder I'd left that morning. Under the light of the ceiling, piles of books covered the floor and my bed, plus Zeus's foam mattress. Zeus joined me as I hesitantly walked to the trunk, kicking aside wood and debris. Behind the trunk I searched the floorboards for scratch and dent marks, which would prove movement. None were visible. On my knees, I cleaned the area with my hands, trying to feel any gouges. Nothing.

The trunk sat in the exact center of the floor, the outer casing trashed, its innards spread about the room. "The trunk didn't move," I told Zeus. "Last night never happened." I peered inside to see one last book on top of a pile of clothing. Titled "De Re Metallica" by Agricola, the book printed in English had chapters for prospecting, mining, milling, and smelting. Also included were the topics of dowsing, dip needles, and pendulums. With all of Hathenbruck's formal training, he apparently still liked old magic. I grinned when I saw the chapter "Amalgam Mixtures" and visualized the baked potatoes in George's fire, each with a small nugget of gold inside. Hathenbruck had used the technique.

I placed the book on the floor and reached into the trunk to hold up a woman's white dress, cut to a small waist, tucks in the bodice, probably Rozilla's wedding dress. Beneath it were long baby dresses meant for either a boy or girl. I shifted fabric to uncover a man's dark blue uniform, a double row of brass buttons down the front, the same worn by Hathenbruck in his parlor portrait. I tried to pull the uniform from the trunk but it was too heavy.

I gently unfolded it, exposing part of a yellow rock coming to light for the first time in eighty years. I carefully reached between the folds of the old uniform to touch the object: round, rough, the size of a small hen's egg. It took both hands to lift the heavy item from the fabric. First I gawked, then laughed in delight. It was Hathenbruck's watch, set into a gold nugget, the chain still attached. I cradled the item, estimating a three or four pound weight.

My first instinct was joy at owning such a treasure. It was mine. It came with the house. I thought of its monetary value, then admitted I didn't have the heart to melt the artifact down. I returned the golden watch fob to its place between the folds of the blue uniform, checking underneath for any additional treasures. Two thick bolts fastened the bottom planks to the floor. The mystery of the immovable trunk was solved.

I spoke to my dog, pretending he understood. "I don't know what the house will do to us tonight," I said, "but I haven't had uninterrupted sleep for four days. I'm going to take my chances in the Shove-it." I snatched a pillow and stripped the quilt from the bed. Zeus wisely followed. When I shut off the light we were plunged in darkness and I quickly turned it on again, repeating the scared game to the bottom of the stairs.

"You win tonight, Frank," I called into the parlor, remembering his name preference. Facing the hall, I said, "You win, too." Zeus and I padded through the dining room to the kitchen where we turned off the light, locked the door, and walked across the porch toward the car. I leaned over the railing to touch the rock face of the cliff. Frank Hathenbruck may have had degrees in medicine and geology, but he was a rotten architect. Why would he build the house so close to the mountain? For now, like everything else in my bleary life, I'd quote Scarlett O'Hara and think about it tomorrow.

I settled in the car, fluffed blankets over the gearshift to soften it, and left the house to haunt itself. By morning I sat with my back against the passenger door, listening to Zeus snort. When the rising sun hit the east tree line, its radiance spread across my meadow like gold butter. I stumbled out of the car and turned toward the glory, remembering Ezra Snow conducting the sunrise. It was a good way to start the day.

Zeus and I entered the house, had breakfast, then took a look around. Nothing in the bedroom had moved. I picked up books and placed them carefully in what was left of the trunk, covering Hathenbruck's nugget watch, the only treasure I'd gotten from this adventure. A bitter laugh escaped me and I quoted somebody named Anonymous. "Adventure," he had said, "is just poor planning."

After a meager shower and change of clothes, I returned to the trunk's room with a broom and dustpan to sweep wood dust and splinters from the floor. I checked again for scratch marks. The planks were old and worn, but not marred.

Descending the stairs carrying Thor's hammer, I noticed Zeus at the stained glass window next to the front door, his stub of tail fiercely waving. I plunked the hammer down to rest against the banister and peered out the window over the dog's head. Pope stood beyond the dead circle, arms loose at his sides.

I cracked the door open and peeked out. "What are you doing?"

Pope stayed in position "Waiting for you."

"Why didn't you knock?"

"In my world, we stay outside until we're acknowledged."

"What if it's an emergency?"

"Then we knock."

I stepped onto the front porch and closed the door. "Consider yourself acknowledged. Now what?"

"Now, you come with me to meet the Elders." I must have looked blank because he added, "We're here to help you uncover the cannon in the forest."

I whooped with glee and opened the door to call my dog. "We're saved, Zeus. Get your lazy behind out here. We're going on an adventure."

I used "adventure" again. It was the worst possible choice of words.

Zeus slipped outside before I slammed and locked the door. We crossed the dead zone to join Pope in a walk toward the north forest and the buried cannon.

"How long," I asked, "were you waiting for me to notice you?"

He answered in his infuriating way, with a question. "Are you having trouble with the house?"

"No," I lied, never missing a step.

"Why did you sleep in your car?"

Now I missed a step. "How do you…did you…" the words flustered out, "have you been waiting since dawn?"

"We needed an early start. The work will take the day."

His long legs forced me to match his stride. "What if I hadn't seen you? Would you still be waiting?"

"No," he said. "I would have sent the dog to get you."

I noticed Zeus had slipped over to pad at Pope's side. "Are you telling me you can talk to my dog?"

"*He* talks to *me*," Pope said matter-of-factly.

The words produced a touch of anger in me. "What, exactly, does he say?"

Pope shook his head at my denseness. "He doesn't use words."

We traveled in silence while I mulled over the truth that my dog preferred strangers over his owner, who kept him fed and brushed…okay, not brushed, his short hair didn't need it. But I fed him and he ate a lot. Furthermore, I paid for his shots and had a giant pooper-scooper to clean up his droppings. For two seconds I considered leaving him with whoever would give me gas money home.

Pope broke through my negative thoughts. "You should know," he said, "that your dog searches for better communication with you, but you don't listen."

"In my defense," I retorted, "the dog doesn't say anything I can hear."

"But you *can* hear the house," Pope challenged, in a deft transition to the original topic.

I stopped walking to confront the young man. "Do you know the house is haunted?" He turned to face me and I rephrased the question to an accusation. "You *know* the house is haunted." He nodded once in agreement, showing no emotion at my indictment. I finished with the facts. "The dog and I are assaulted every night by something evil. We are both aware of it. But inheriting the house carries financial nightmares worse than ghosts."

Pope surprised me by saying, "There's no such thing as ghosts."

"You just admitted the house is haunted."

Pope began walking. "Not with ghosts."

I caught up. "What is it, then?"

"Vibrations." He said the word casually, as if I would recognize the meaning as soon as I heard it. I hated to admit I didn't understand, so we walked for a bit without talking.

I finally swatted my pride aside. "What do you mean by vibrations?"

"Dr. Howard," he emphasized the word *Doctor* and I caught the patronizing tone, "even your scientists understand that everything in the physical world vibrates. Every tree, each blade of grass, all life vibrates. What they don't know is that actions and even thoughts create vibrations, both good and bad. They last forever. Have you considered---"

Pope was moving into the tiresome subject of philosophy. His next question would probably be the old riddle: *If a tree falls in the forest, and no one is there to hear it, does it make a sound?* I decided to circumvent the discussion.

"If you're going to ask about the falling tree thing, I know that answer." I spoke as if I were way ahead of him. "When a tree falls, the sound is just vibrations in the air until it hits an ear. The ear translates the vibration into sound." I waved my hand, sweeping away the whole vibration discussion. "What I know is, my house is haunted and I need to fix it. I have to sell the thing and salvage my life…" I spoke the next words carefully, "…unless you can return my gold bars."

Pope, perhaps offended that I didn't play his philosophy game, stopped walking, still facing north. "The gold does not belong to you."

"The cave is on my---"

Pope walked again, increasing the size of his steps. "There are legal complications you're not aware of. You'd have to find some crook on the black market who would buy the bars cheap and melt them down into bullion. I don't think you have it in you to destroy ancient artifacts."

I hurried to catch up, reaching his side to say, "Don't overestimate me. Yesterday I hacked an antique chest out of existence." I said the words proudly, but I wasn't proud.

He didn't respond at first, seeming to think about the statement as we passed a stand of Poplars. "Why?" he finally asked.

"Because," I spoke rapidly, "it was moving toward the door so it could trap us in the room. It planned to kill us." I waited for his response to the creepy little story.

Pope looked down at the weeds he tramped under his feet. "Did you find anything in the old chest that would help you with your money problems?"

"No." It was an honest answer. I couldn't melt down the gold watch fob.

I felt Pope glance at me. "Will the cannon make a difference?"

"The historical value is important enough to sell to a museum and make money, even after the IRS grabs its share." I softened. Pope and his people were trying to help me and I showed ingratitude. "I appreciate everything you're doing for me. I couldn't dig out the cannon by myself."

I remembered the pickaxe in the car and hunched over in an apology. "I forgot the pick axe." I began a trot to my house. "It will only take a minute." I looked at my dog and decided to test his loyalty. "Come Zeus." He hesitated, looked at Pope, then ran to my side, matching my pitiful jogging speed that proves I'm a thinker, not a runner. I spoke to Zeus harshly, "Good choice, dog. You were about to get left here forever."

At the edge of my meadow, Zeus growled. He stood in his tracks, turned his head back toward the trees, and growled louder. I threw out a few words of irritation, created by five nights without sleep and a disobedient dog. "Get over here, Zeus," I commanded. The animal ignored me, changed the growl to a howl, and charged back through the trees. I chased after him, yelling orders, but his legs at full run outdistanced me.

The noise of his baying bounced into echoes that grew thunderous, a collection of growls, howls, and roars. I didn't know Zeus could roar. Hidden under the noise I thought I heard a scream. Several trees ahead swayed as if a strong wind were captured in the branches and fought to get out. A snatch of brown moved behind the scene. It rose, fell, then lifted again amid the sounds of battle. A massive head appeared and disappeared followed by an undulating hump with silver threaded through long, course black hair. Zeus had attacked a large bear.

The dog was dwarfed by the snarling giant. Immobilized, I helplessly watched as Zeus was tossed through the curtain of green branches. He leaped to his feet and charged at the monster again, teeth bared, barking furiously. The fight might have lasted a few seconds or several minutes, my own shock interfered with a sense of time. Eventually, the two combatants crashed through the forest, taking the clamor with them. I took a few steps in pursuit, but decided I shouldn't follow the action.

A soft moan reached me and I carefully walked toward it, considering that a wounded animal could be dangerous. Spatters of red dotted the bushes and a groan quickened my steps. At the edge of a mashed clearing of weeds lay a human form on its right side, curled into a fetal position with arms over the head, covered in blood. I recognized the clothing, levis with a loose shirt, matted hair the color of coal. The ball of blood was Pope.

I kneeled at his side assessing the wounds, deep claw marks across his left arm, shreds of flesh tangled with his shirt. There were puncture wounds in his side. The blood flowed rather than pumped in spurts. I thought that meant something, but couldn't remember. What I *did* remember was the brochure I'd picked up a few days ago, the one titled, "You Are in Bear Country." The leaflet had pointed out that wounds from a bear attack could bleed out in three to six minutes. I ripped off my cotton shirt, buttons flying, tore the long sleeves out, and wrapped them tightly around the largest bleeders. More bandages were needed and I used the whole shirt. It wasn't enough. A thought came from a thread out of nowhere.

"Give me ten minutes," I begged Pope. "Do not die. You cannot die."

I rushed from the forest toward my house, running like a track star, aware of the breeze against my bare skin. At the house I fumbled for the key, dropped it, picked it up with trembling fingers, and nearly ripped the door apart getting it open. I sprinted down the hall to the bathroom, wrenched open the cupboard under the sink, and grabbed an entire package of Kotex Maxi-pads. I searched a kitchen drawer for duct tape, picked up a shirt from the top of the laundry basket, and sailed out of the house without locking it, my thirty-ish body fueled by adrenaline.

The forest loomed ahead, getting bigger as if I were the zoom lens on a camera. I kept sending the message, *"be alive"* ahead of me while I bumped into branches and hurtled over bushes. By the time I saw the body I had nearly run past it and circled back to drop to my knees. I ripped open the extra thick nighttime sanitary napkins and duct-taped them tightly everywhere that bled, which was everywhere. I didn't have the strength to roll the big Indian over to check for wounds on his right side. It worried me that he didn't groan anymore and I searched for a pulse, finding a weak one in the artery of his neck. Finally, there was nothing more to do but put on my other shirt, which turned out to be a light blue silky pajama top. Pope's people were at the forest cannon, but I didn't think I could find the place. Hopefully, they would look for us. I slumped, exhausted, next to Pope's quiet body and put my hand on his head, the matted hair sticky with wet blood.

I felt their presence before I heard the grass rustle. Four large men kneeled to check Pope. They said nothing and I moved out of their way as they placed their arms into some kind of formation under the body and lifted it smoothly from the ground. I broke the silence. "I have a car to take him into town." One of the men nodded and they began a rapid walk toward my house. They knew the way and I trailed behind until we reached the Shove-it. While I got the keys they wrapped Pope with the blankets I'd used the night before, gently settling him in the back. One man sat in front with me, directing me to the closest hospital in as few words as possible.

We bypassed Kamas, driving an extra thirty minutes to a small but modern facility in another mountain town. Once inside, the air turned tense with loud words in a medical language I had never learned. I was in the way and sat on a folding chair to watch as Pope was transferred to a bed, hooked up to tubes and wires, and tested for blood type.

Someone on a phone called for life flight to a larger facility. It was like watching a TV show. I wanted to change the channel but was under a spell and too involved to get up.

The Indian man who had directed the drive stood above me. "You're Dr. Howard, aren't you." It was a statement and I nodded, waiting for him to make his point. "Pope wants you." Dreamlike, I followed the man to the concrete pad where the helicopter was preparing to land. Pope lay on a gurney. I located his face behind a mask and half a dozen plastic tubes full of fluids. His words could barely be heard through the droning of the rotor blades. "Dr. Howard," he whispered. "The vibrations are real, but you are the ear."

CHAPTER SEVENTEEN

The helicopter twirled above us and swerved northwest in a steep slant that should have caused it to fall from the sky. The four Native American men slowly walked away. I lingered to see the sun's rays bounce off the metallic machine. I guessed the time at four-thirty in the afternoon, not a bad estimate. My watch announced it as five. When I reached the Shove-it, the Indians sat waiting for me, one in the driver's seat. I gratefully entered the passenger side and closed the door, handing the keys over. Considering the trauma we had experienced together, I should have known what to call him, but I felt uneasy saying, "*So, what's your name?*" We remained silent as the man brought the car to life and moved it forward.

I leaned my head against the car window, aware of scenery passing by, farms nestled against hills, cows grazing in fields. A variety of fences marked private land with barbed wire changing to rough-bark logs, replaced by split rail posts. I was aware, but not attentive. Instead, I studied the man driving my car, a classic Indian with a Jewish profile. Pockmarks scarred his tawny skin, perhaps the result of a childhood disease or a bad case of acne as a teen. I examined the scars closer. No doubt about it, chicken pox. His eye, the one I could see, peered behind a slit pressed down by a heavy brow. The dark hair peppered with gray, covered by a baseball cap, showed a standard white-man cut, like stubble on a day-old beard.

An hour's drive took us past Kamas onto a dirt road bordered by trees. We stopped and a man in back got out, his nose a long exclamation point in the middle of his face. I watched him from the side-view mirror as he disappeared into the trees. Maybe he had a cabin in the woods. Another five minutes up the road, the remaining two men got out. The one with a scar on his cheek followed a wide trail into the forest. The other, one eye squinted, walked across the road to his destination. My driver turned the car around to retrace our route and spoke to me.

"Are you okay?" It was a deep voice.

"No," I answered truthfully. "Will you let me know how Pope is when you find out?"

He nodded. "Pope owes his life to you."

I shook my head. "My dog chased the bear off. If you hadn't come, Pope and I would still be sitting in the weeds. I couldn't have dragged that boy to my car."

His nod of agreement became the end of our conversation. When we got south of town, he parked at the same trailer court I had seen the first day. This time there were no women selling trinkets, no children playing under the card table. I walked around the car. "Thanks for driving. It gave me time to think." Once behind the wheel I did a

U-turn back to town and he vanished between the trailer court's tin houses that replaced teepees.

The sun had already dropped behind the mountains. It would be too dark when I reached my meadow. I couldn't face the burden of spending another night of horror in the house. The Shove-it drove itself to Motel Three-and-a Half where I signed for a cubicle, collided with a mattress, and didn't move until my eyes opened of their own accord.

When I pulled aside the rubber-backed curtains, light filled the room and I checked my watch. Twelve delicious, sleep-filled hours had passed, purchased with a crumpled bill in the bottom of my backpack and a flotsam of loose change. A long, hot shower prepared me to face the day. I expected Zeus would be waiting for me on the porch and felt the tiniest regret that he hadn't been able to curl into his foam bed. I laughed at my concern. He was a dog. He could sleep anywhere.

The car clock showed nine a.m. when I parked on the south side of the house and took the small step to the porch, expecting Zeus to leap up and greet me, but the area was empty of any dog-like creatures. I entered the back door into the kitchen with worry at the edges of my thoughts.

Knock.

One knock coming from the hall. The wretched house was haunting me in broad daylight.

Another knock.

I walked to the edge of the hall and waited, tense with anticipation. A third knock came from the front door. I laughed in relief and walked through the passage to open the door. On the porch stood the chicken-pox Indian who lived in the trailer court. Behind him were the other three men holding shovels and picks. It was bad timing. I wasn't up to a trek through the forest to dig for buried cannon.

My eyes focused on a large bundle at their feet, light brown, short hair, a collar...I pushed past the big man and ran across the no-grow zone to kneel by my dog in the grass.

"Zeus?" I placed my hand on the giant muscle of his shoulder. It felt cold, like the hall. I shook him gently, then harder. "Zeus," I commanded. "Wake up." The men made no move, but the words of their spokesman drifted down to me. "We found him this morning."

I spoke what, to me, was an obvious fact. "He isn't dead." I checked the body. "There aren't any marks on him."

"The wounds are on the other side. The bear clawed him across the whole of his body, the cuts are---"

I held my hand up. "Don't," I said quietly.

"We came to help you bury him."

I stood with a calm that surprised me. "He can't be dead." I caught pity in the eyes of the men and looked down at the dog, certain I saw his sides lift slightly with air. "Look! He's breathing." My knees hit the ground again, hands caressing the side I could see, the one that seemed alive and normal. "C'mon, Zeus, get up." His stub of a tail didn't greet my voice.

"We will wait," the Indian said, "until you're ready." They walked outside my vision to the north end of the house. The dull scrape of metal through dirt vaguely reached my ears. They were digging a grave. My hand followed the contours of Zeus' back leg, the muscles of his thigh designed for power. I drifted my fingers to his neck, slipping my other hand under the head to stabilize it. My palm fell into a gap and felt something hard…a bone, sinews. I cried out and quickly withdrew my hand, covered with a dark, tacky substance. Zeus had left his life soaking into the hard ground of the Uinta Mountains.

My tears splashed on the dog's nose for a long time until the men finally squatted, waiting to raise the animal from the grass. I nodded consent and they lifted Zeus away from me. "Wait a minute," I told them, stumbling toward the house. "He needs…one last thing." I climbed the stairs to my…our…room and stood above Zeus' foam mattress. I could almost hear his sigh of comfort when he wiggled into it. With all the strength I could collect, I dragged the mattress through the landing, letting it bump noisily down the stairs. One of the men waited by the door and helped me carry the bed to the deep hole waiting for us. We flattened the foam to fit the bottom and sides of the grave and they laid Zeus on top. My voice cracked. "It looks like he's sleeping." When they dropped the first shovel of dirt on the body, I had to leave.

Wandering aimlessly over the meadow, I repeated the phrase, *"stupid dog,"* words I had always used to describe Zeus. If he had obeyed my orders and stayed by my side, he'd still be alive. If I had left the animal in the house instead of inviting him to come, he'd be meandering the meadow with me. *If…if…if.* Another voice pushed under my thoughts. *Pope would have died.* Zeus had become the sacrifice that saved a man.

I smeared tears across my face and raised my head to see the four men, holding their shovels, walking toward the north forest. "Wait," I called. When I caught up, I spoke as if there were rocks in my mouth, formed from grief. "Thank you. I couldn't have..." The big man bowed his head once and they continued their trek through the trees.

The grave was flat, distinguished only by disturbed dirt. Next year, new growth would cover it. I wanted a headstone with words of praise. "Here lies man's best friend." Dumb, but something like that. "Here lies woman's best friend." I shook my head, remembering my last angry words to Zeus: *"You were about to get left here forever."* My own mouth had made the prophecy.

A flashback of his body, cold and stiff...no...when I first touched Zeus, he wasn't yet stiff. His death had been recent. He had lived through the night while I slept in a motel bed. He had whimpered for help and I wasn't there. I crumbled on his grave as the remainder of the day's tears flowed. Tomorrow there would be more, and a new supply ready the day after. There would be plenty of tears. I cried until all that remained was remorse.

At three o'clock I left the grave and shuffled into the house. I placed a bowl of cold cereal and milk on the table and stared at the small blobs floating in a white background, then pushed it aside. Hoping to escape the pain by working on the textbook, I made my way to the parlor through the hall. The usual chill hit my right side, nothing extraordinary, but my reaction spun into violence. Whether from the frustration of the house itself or the great sorrow of losing a friend, anger propelled me to the stairs where the sledgehammer still rested. I seized it and returned to the cold spot.

"No more," I yelled my war cry and buried the hammer sideways into the wall. The blow created a hole large enough for a man's fist and I rounded the hammer behind my back, shrieking defiance. The head-on collision nearly took me through the wall with the heavy head of the hammer. The closet door had been replaced with a thin piece of wood for smooth camouflage.

I wrestled the hammer from the rupture in the wall. Three more strikes accompanied by Ninja cries opened a cavity the size of a man's upper torso. I struck a blow at the bottom and the hammer slipped from my sweating hands to thud against the inside of the hidden closet, falling onto something firm. The house had been built directly on the ground, but the closet floor sounded like wood. I used my hands to tear out pieces of the lightweight door and, breathing hard, stepped back to examine the opening. Blackness surged from the closet in an increase of cold, creating the same panic that had chased me under the baby's crib two nights ago. The exact fear, the same oily energy.

"The vibrations are real, but you are the ear."

My intense anger must have insulated me during the destruction of the door. But now my mind was free to interpret the vibrations behind the wall. It created terror. I fought my mental decode with the truth: none of the hauntings had happened. The storm, the voices, the trunk scraping across the floor, all of it an interpretation of vibrations left behind. What kind of thoughts and deeds had been done in the Hathenbruck house to create such evil ambiance? I yelled defiance and kicked at the remaining thin wood that split into pieces and fell inside the closet.

Even in my current state of mutiny, I knew better than to enter a black hole without light. I searched the house for options. The pantry held a glass lantern with a thick candle. My daypack still carried matches, another candle, a small

Boy Scout knife, and the tiny penlight. Thus equipped, I marched back to the hall closet.

Lighting the candle, I held the lantern inside the opening, its glass prisms illuminating the gloom. The floor looked solid and I played the fool, entering where angels fear to tread. Placing the lantern on the floor, I inspected the closet, starting from the right, where large nails held antique miner's equipment from the mid 1800s. A hat resembling a baseball cap made of a thick felt material was fitted with a metal plate attached to the front with rivets. Hanging next to it, a candle holder had a hook that fit into the hat to make a headlamp. The efficient design left hands free for digging.

An oblong metal bucket hung by a wire handle on a heavy nail. A tin cup fastened to the top identified the bucket as a Cornish lunch box. It would have three sections, the bottom for tea that the miner could heat with his candle. The middle would have carried meat, potatoes, and vegetables wrapped in pastry. The top third might store bread, crackers, perhaps a dessert. I smiled at the thought of viewing the remains of a hundred-year-old lunch.

Stepping forward to inspect the lunchbox, I was distracted by a change of pitch under my shoes, a hollow sound instead of a thud. I kicked at the dust to uncover a door on the ground almost the length of the closet. A large metal ring was bolted to the edge nearest me. I grasped it, struggled to lift the heavy door, and pushed it up to rest against the wall. The trap hid a square hole with a dirt ramp disappearing beneath the floor. Worn steps were carved in the hard dirt, its slope steeper than a normal stairway.

I held my lantern over the abyss to determine the length of the ramp, but dark reached up to steal the light. I pulled the mini-flashlight from my fanny pack, switched it on, and rolled it down the stairs. It bounced beyond my vision, hidden by the closet floor. Holding the lantern with one hand, I sat on the precipice of the first worn step and bumped carefully to the second, then the third. Confidence encouraged me to move faster and I slid into an uncontrolled plummet before my heels found purchase. I had traveled past the opening and was now underground. The lantern swung in my hand and I waited for stability.

Cold crawled up my legs. I shook it off and concentrated on the next stair, with a niggling concern about how I would climb the ramp on my return. The tiny penlight beam spread across the dirt floor at the bottom of the stairs. After perhaps twenty feet, the ramp leveled and I was able to stand in a tunnel almost six feet tall. Raising the lantern high, I was surrounded with gentle yellow light and stepped into the passage.

I estimated myself to be twenty feet under the kitchen. The tunnel had been hewn from the rock, but was strangely free of rubble, as if a housekeeper had swept it clean. My candle burned brightly, evidence that oxygen entered the lantern. I smugly smiled at my wise use of candles, superior to flashlights, and continued my pace.

A sparkle on the wall at my right distracted me. A three-inch vein of yellow ran along the wall beyond my beam of light. A few more steps saw an increase in size to six inches, then eight. I put the lantern on the floor, removed the Boy Scout knife from my pack, and shaved its edge against the yellow streak. Raw gold is the most malleable of the metals.

I dug the point of the knife into the yellow vein and a chunk the size of a quarter fell into my hands. I put both knife and gold piece in my bag.

With the lantern held high, I ran the fingers of my right hand over the vein, hastening my steps, all my attention on the widening line of gold. Hathenbruck had described this vein in his journal, saying it had reached a size of three feet before disappearing beyond the ceiling. Fifty steps or so later I decided I must be inside the mountain behind the house.

My foot kicked an item on the floor which rolled a few feet away. The lantern shone on something round, brassy, and familiar. I stooped to pick it up. A button with an X in the center, a scroll design around the border. The brass buttons in the Mason jar in my room had come from the tunnel. I stood, the button still in my hand.

Sudden awareness of something white loomed directly in front of me, a gaping mouth, empty eye sockets. I shrieked involuntarily, then bowed my head against the sight. Reminding myself I was a scientist, I stiffened in preparation to look.

The skeleton hung against the wall, its jaw open in a silent scream. A metal brace around its neck had been screwed into the rock of the tunnel. Narrow pubic bones indicated a male, his feet firmly on the floor, no sign of ancient shoes around it, no shreds of clothing. He had been... I couldn't think it...he had been fastened here to die. This vile act alone would be enough to haunt the house forever.

I turned my head away from the skeleton and saw what the man guarded: a wooden door constructed into the mouth of the tunnel, resting on massive leather hinges now dry with age. An iron padlock had once kept the door secure, but now the wood hung crookedly into the tunnel, revealing a twelve-inch gap between the door and wall with rock rubble at the bottom.

The candle still burned, showing there was oxygen in the room beyond. I rolled rocks from the base of the door and, hoping it wouldn't fall, gripped the open edge and tugged outward. A dusting of debris collected at my feet and I debated between survival and curiosity, common sense arguing in favor of survival. But the gap had widened like an invitation to enter.

My hands reached for the door again and pulled until the crevice was big enough to fit my head. The rest of me could be compacted, molded, and fitted sideways into the next room. I took off the fanny pack, dropped it to the floor, and pushed the lantern ahead. Regretting a lifetime of chocolate consumption, the big squeeze began.

I moved sideways through the door and stepped on something that cracked. My foot jerked in a reflexive action, kicking an item that clanged as it rolled away. I held my foot in the air and considered what might be on the other side of the door. Slowly, I worked my foot through a few bumpy places before I felt the floor and finished compressing myself into the room.

The candle revealed a skeleton under my feet. I had broken its femur. Not far away was a metal helmet with a typical Spanish lip around the edge and a ridge on top. I lifted my lamp as high as my arm would reach and the song *Tiptoe Through the Tulips* ran through my mind, a gut response to the gruesome scene that lay before me.

CHAPTER EIGHTEEN

The large room, its ceiling lost in the dark, was a gold mine turned into an open grave. Skeletons mingled their body parts together, gray bones covered with scraps of uniforms. Spanish helmets, swords, and antique pistols salted themselves over the bodies as far as my light would reach. Countless leather bags, bumpy with probable gold ore, were poking from the collection of arms and legs in every possible position. A cruel branding iron was stuck at an angle into the bones. My feet stood by a skull with the remains of an arrow embedded in it.

At the far end of the room, piled skeletons made a seven-foot hill, shreds of mummified skin still attached to their dry carcasses. Two large tree trunks, stripped of branches, randomly rested on the mound of remains, as if they'd been dropped on the bodies from above. Crude steps carved into the trees identified them as chicken ladders, used by slaves to climb into the pit and out again with ore on their backs.

I looked up into the cavern as far as my neck would bend, but needed stronger light to see the top. Calculating the length of the chicken ladders at thirty feet, the two lashed together would reach sixty feet to the mountaintop entrance. Many slaves must have fallen to their deaths from the top of the mine shaft, their bones now beneath the Spanish soldiers.

I kept to the edge of the wall where the bodies were shallow, wading carefully through the carnage, but couldn't avoid the sickening crunch of bones, like walking on dead Arizona cockroaches. Surveying the room, my lamp acted as witness to a three hundred year old rebellion of Indian slaves against their Spanish masters. The Utes had thrown the dead soldiers down the shaft, along with their possessions, and hidden the entrance.

My shoulder ached from the lantern's weight held high above my head. Its light revealed spots of gold still in the walls, and several door-sized dark blemishes on the walls. I plotted a course across open-mouthed skulls to investigate. During the macabre trek I lost control and was suddenly freezing, my skin prickling. A bundle ahead of me shifted. One bony hand lifted from the heap and reached for my ankle. I couldn't allow even a brief moment of panic. My own mind could kill me down here.

"I don't think so," I said aloud. I stepped on the hand, heard the crack, and concentrated on the dark section ahead.

The Spanish typically had two entrances to their mines. The tunnel under the house must have been one. If the vein I followed had continued getting bigger, as Hathenbruck described, this room had been gouged out in a massive gold retrieval. Ore had been taken from this mine and processed in the Spanish arrastras in the meadow. It was crushed, separated, and melted into bars, one-fifth sent to Spain in taxes. The rest was cached in the cave where I'd met Pope, its entrance hidden by the hollowed boulder.

I held my eyes on the black opening ahead, hoping for a continuation of the main vein. When I reached it, however, the excavation slanted up, leveling after several yards, then dead-ended without a sign of gold. I tried another channel which also went up before it ended, this time showing gold at the edge of its ceiling. The massacre must have occurred before the Spanish widened the tunnel to follow the deposit.

Suddenly, the candle dimmed. It had burned itself to the bottom of the wick with only a small amount of liquid wax floating around it. I remembered with horror that I'd left the spare candle in my fanny pack on the other side of the door. My feet kicked and plowed through dead Spanish soldiers that blocked my way to the exit, their clattering bones producing background music for a Halloween cartoon. Hurling insults at my stupidity, I forced my fat cells through the tiny opening and fell to my knees as the candle sputtered out.

A profound absence of light enveloped me. Crawling on all fours, I located my small pack and fumbled through two zippers before finding a candle, which I put in my lap. When I touched the oblong matchbox, I explored the ends of the wood stick to determine where to strike. A blaze of fire blinded me and I dropped the match. A second try succeeded long enough to find the lantern. It didn't occur to me to light the new candle on my knees. I was losing logic.

When the third match fizzled, a thick force fell over me like a net, heavy enough to prevent movement. I positioned my fingers in front of my face, but wasn't sure I had raised my arm to perform the action. Disembodied, no longer existing in a reality I recognized, panic replaced reason. *"You're losin' it, Matt,"* I thought. *"Pull it together."*

The penlight! I encouraged myself in the knowledge that even my small penlight, when I found it, would bring me back to sanity. My fingers frantically searched the pack. A protein bar rattled its paper and I reveled over a familiar noise in this forsaken place where sound seemed as impossible as sight.

A soft moan behind the door, barely audible, was followed by the whimper of a child far away in another world. Muffled voices began to gather from a departed past. I couldn't find the flashlight and began bouncing my fingers along the floor until they hit the matchbox. I struck a match that blazed brightly in a moment of victory, but a force of wind blew it out. There could be no wind in this underground prison.

Voices, louder now, pushed at the door behind my back and flowed through the opening. I felt them surge like frigid water on the floor to cover my bent knees, rising to my thighs. The bones of a skeleton foot lightly kicked my arm. It was the man shackled to the wall. Full speed adrenaline coursed through my veins. I leaped to my feet and ran, leaving everything behind. I crashed into the tunnel wall, veered to the other side with hands out, colliding against the hard rock. Chased by voices of agony, I became a frightened doe darting without purpose to hit against rock walls, desperately escaping an unseen hunter.

Something hissed at my left and struck at me. It missed my face but grazed the back of my neck. A scream, probably mine, reverberated down the tunnel. In the far distance, my mind produced the memory of a point of light and what it once looked like, a tiny white thread of a lazer cutting through nothingness. I struggled to stay on my feet and hurried toward it.

The light grew slightly larger and hope burst into my throat. It was my insignificant penlight still shining at the bottom of the ramp, a yellow beam in a backwash of gray night from the open trap door behind and above it. I dove for the little stick as if it were a fluorescent raft on the open sea and tripped on the staircase, falling on my face. Spinning to my side, I aimed the light on the tunnel behind me. "Get back," I yelled at whatever rolled from the dark. "You don't exist." *Like the dark itself, where nothing exists.*

I scooted myself backwards up the worn stairs, the little light held in my teeth pointed toward the tunnel. With arms and legs pushing my body up the ramp, I made slow progress in a birth toward the opening. When my head cleared the top of the ramp into a dark night, I crawled to my feet and slammed the heavy trap door onto the dirt of the closet floor. It made an explosive crash, dust rising to cover me as I crawled through the demolished wall and limped to the kitchen.

The penlight dimmed and died, its valiant batteries spent, but the moon and stars provided light like welcome sunshine compared to the blackness of the mine. My oblong table appeared as an outline against shadows, the bowl of cereal still where I had pushed it. The white refrigerator became a ghost in the gloom. My little washing machine sat silhouetted against the wall next to the kitchen door on the left, bordered on the right by the bathroom partition Hilda had added. I dimly identified the light switch on the wall and flipped it up, closing my eyes to protect them against the intensity, slowly emerging to bask in glorious light and life.

I gratefully dropped to a chair at the table, resting my forehead on intertwined fingers held up by arms designed to accomplish such miracles. A stream of blood trickled to the table and I followed its source. My hands were cut and bleeding. A gash on my forehead added red color to the pool forming around my elbows. With blood dripping in thin rivulets down my arms, I breathed deeply the joy of living. The cells of my body filled with gratitude over the evidence of life splashing on my table. I would never go to the mine under the house again, not for all the gold in the Uinta Mountains.

In some far distant future, when Towats removed the curse, other archaeologists might follow the tunnel to its decrepit door, surely fallen to the floor by then. Underneath, they would find the remains of my lantern, an unused candle a short distance away where it had rolled when I stood and ran. My fanny pack would still carry a protein bar, reduced to dust, and there would be a chunk of gold topped by a Boy Scout knife, both flattened by the fall of the door. It would present a great mystery. Scientists might even find my four blackened matches on the floor. Conferences would be held to develop a thesis about who had been to the ancient Spanish mine and left 20th century artifacts behind. I laughed at them. I had gone into hell and survived. My cuts would heal, unlike the wounds of...

Zeus…who lay forever at the north side of the house, his great hulking body fated to become only bones like the ones I had crushed in the mine. Tear ducts in my eyes formed a new supply of salt water to blend with the blood on my kitchen table. Blood and tears, a good name for a Rock Band, the title of a novel, a Grade B movie. Blood and tears and dirt, the mixture of life.

I stood from the table to act out the rituals of existence: a shower to wash off dirt from the bowels of the earth, a little first aid on the deeper cuts, some cold cereal topped with milk just barely turning sour, a new blanket for the night because the one in the car was soaked in Pope's blood. I couldn't find another quilt and ended up wearing several layers of clean clothes before I tucked myself between the sheets.

I knew it was a dream even while it seemed real.

I am on the hill watching Ezra Snow conduct the sunrise. When he finishes, he smiles at me, turning deep wrinkles of his dry skin to gullies.

"Hello, Ezra," I greet him. "I inherited a house."

"Sorry ta' hear that," he says. "The house will be nuthin' but trouble. Ya' better sell it."

"I can't," I explain. "It has ghosts."

Ezra clears phlegm from his throat and spits the yellow wad on the grass before saying, "There ain't no sech thing as ghosts."

"You and I know that," I reply, "but when people feel cold and hear screams, they won't buy the house. The worst part is, I almost had a fortune that would have solved my problems."

"Almost?"

"The Indians took it and gave it to Towats."

"Yep," *Ezra says, nodding his head knowingly.* "Injuns tend to do that."

"What would you suggest, Ezra?"

The old geezer looks at me with blue eyes hidden behind puffed bags of skin. "If'n it wuz me," *he drawls,* "I'd give it all away...th' house, th' gold mine, ever'thing."

I figure Ezra wants the gold for himself, but I ask anyway. "Who would you give it to?"

"I'd give it all ta' th' Injuns," he says. *"That's who it belongs to."*

I woke, suddenly alert to a change in the room. The old ruined trunk glowed. Its gentle light formed into a base-ball-size orb and leisurely floated to the side of the bed. It lifted to my eye level, lingering twelve inches from my vision, emanating comfort for the loss of Zeus. There were no words, just peace.

I watched with curiosity before reaching my fingers out to touch it. The image drifted through my hand like the 3D effect of a movie at Disneyland. I briefly wondered if my conscious mind had the power to change vibrations from evil to neutral. Maybe if I went back down to the mine and willed the evil to dissolve, I could gather enough raw gold to…

Nope.

I shifted toward the wall and slept soundly until morning.

CHAPTER NINETEEN

I ate guilt for breakfast. It burped its way back into my throat and I swallowed it again like a bitter pill, bile burning at my conscience. I had behaved shamefully toward Zeus and he returned the treatment with affection, anxious to please, to respond, to love.

He had died alone.

I pushed from the table and went out the kitchen door. Leaning over the porch railing, I touched the face of the cliff. Beyond my hand, inside the massive mountain, was a rich gold mine. In my past life I would have climbed above the cliff to search for the deep shaft used by slaves to enter the mine. Today, I didn't care. The Indians would have hidden it well, anyway. The second entrance beneath the Hathenbruck house had been hideous. A sixty-foot drop ending in an open graveyard where dead Spanish soldiers were pushed into the pit, followed by their possessions and the gold they had mined. Someone else could dig through the pile of bones and pick out treasures. It wouldn't be me.

Walking north along the porch, I stepped to the ground and headed toward my magnificent dog's grave. I noticed a single purple flower the size of my fingernail growing among the weeds and kneeled to ponder its fragile existence, alone, without companions.

A male voice interrupted my thoughts about tiny flowers. "And, when he shall die, take him and cut him out in little stars…" I twisted my head to see George, who continued his quote. "And he will make the face of heaven so fine that all the world will be in love with night and pay no worship to the garish sun."

I stood, brushing dirt and weeds from my knees. "Romeo and Juliet, Act Three."

George stared at me, his face wearing shock. "Did you tumble off a mountain or something?"

"You mean the black eye, band-aids, and bruises?" He nodded and I answered in a face made for poker. "You should see the other guy."

He grinned, then grew serious. "I'm sorry to hear about your dog. He was a splendid animal."

"Thank you. I'm afraid I didn't appreciate him."

George nodded solemnly. "The bitterest tears shed over graves are for words left unsaid and deeds left undone."

I thought for a minute. "Is that Shakespeare?"

"No," he said. "Harriet Beecher Stowe." George held out a small burlap bag with bumps in its bottom. "I believe it's customary for neighbors to bring food to the grieving family."

I took the bag and opened it to see four potatoes inside, still warm. It seemed like a strange gift, but I was gracious. "Thank you, George. This is very thoughtful."

"You know, of course, not to eat them." I waited for an explanation, which he promptly gave. "Quicksilver is poison. Use gloves when you open them up. Don't let animals get into it. I'll collect the bag later to recycle the mercury."

In an intake of breath, I said, "George, are you giving me," I counted the potatoes again, "four gold nuggets?"

"I heard you acquired the Hathenbruck house…big mistake by the way…and could use some cash."

"This is too generous." I was giddy with joy.

"I've had a good season," he shrugged. "I can afford a few potatoes."

"The guy at Harvey's Hoard will give me ninety bucks for each nugget."

George shook his head. "He's cheating you. Gold this year is $360 an ounce, up from last year's $333. You should get at least $150 for a single trinket."

My gold experience was limited to ancient artifacts with historical value. "Where," I asked, "do you cash yours in?"

"I take my collection to different places in the cities. I never sell here in town. People would talk. I prefer to have them think I'm an eccentric who likes to spend summers in the mountains. They have no idea I'm making more than I earn as a teacher. You're the only one who knows the system to my madness."

"I'm honored and promise not to tell."

George gestured to the sack in my hands. "That's a gift, not a bribe, but I'd appreciate your silence."

"You have it," I agreed. "As a matter of fact, I can return the favor. Wait here." I dropped the potatoes, ran into my room, and unloaded the trunk until I found the volume *De Re Metallica* by Agricola. When I returned to George, he was standing at the grave, head bowed. I handed him the book. "This is from FWC Hathenbruck. He'd want you to have it."

George looked at the cover, flipped through the pages, and smiled broadly, "It's the Spanish Miner's Bible, first published in Germany in 1556. This has more value to me than a whole summer of potato nuggets." He held the book in the air and launched into a quote from Twelfth Night, "I can no other answer make, but thanks, and thanks."

I picked up the heavy bag of potatoes and cocked my head to the side in a sign of gratitude. "And thanks, and thanks," I repeated.

"I've got to get back to work," George announced. "Wear gloves when you open those spuds. I'll come back in a couple of days to collect the leftovers. I'm sorry about your dog." He turned to leave.

"George," I stopped him. "Why do you think it was a mistake to inherit the Hathenbruck place?"

I expected him to talk about isolation or wild animals. Instead he said, "The inheritance tax will kill you."

He had caught me without a clue. "Thanks, again," I said vacantly, and stared at George's back as he walked toward the northeast trees. I had inherited my parents' house without paying a tax and didn't consider there might be a penalty attached to the Hathenbruck Estate. There had been warnings, however: the renunciation paper from Hutchins, Eyring, and Lowe; the cryptic statements from Pope; even the real estate agent had offered a booklet which I didn't read. All my attention had been riveted on wealth, the cave of gold bars blinded me. I shook my head to clear it. How much would an inheritance tax be? I muttered words from

Hamlet over my dog's grave. "When trouble comes, they come not in single spies but in battalions."

In the kitchen, I dropped the burlap bag in the sink before heading for the parlor to find the inheritance book. The demolished wall in the hall gaped open on my right. Its jagged edges, like devouring teeth, brought me to a halt. The dark closet held shadowed outlines of mining gear still on their pegs. Fierce cold seeped under my skin and I quickened my steps to the parlor.

Hathenbruck's portrait beckoned. "It was very clever," I said aloud, "to build a house over the gold mine you wanted to hide and develop later. No wonder your enemies never found it. But why didn't you sneak down there and bring out bags of gold nuggets instead of living in poverty?" I waited for Hathenbruck to send a mental message but he remained silent in his gilded frame. His journals made it clear he knew where the mine was but his lease had never been made legal. Anyone could steal it from him. *"If I had ever gone directly to the mine,"* he had written, *"my bones would have been left there to this day."*

The inheritance booklet was under the pages of my pottery textbook. I sat at the kitchen table to avoid the distraction of Hathenbruck's picture and studied the rules of inheritance. After the introduction, which explained why an inheritance tax was good for everybody, especially the government, I chewed on the meat of the law. Property valued at $600,000 or more was taxed at 30-50%, great news since my property at the time of Hilda's death was worth $500,000. I naively thought I had squeezed past the law.

The next page explained that furniture and improvements were included in the value. The antiques and improvements in the house brought the property beyond the taxable bracket. I dropped my head to the table and moaned. With luck, the IRS would only demand $200,000 and give me nine months to pay the bill. I stretched my neck across the table in a guillotine position, balancing my chin on the surface, ready for the axe to fall, remembering that the only guarantees in life are death and taxes. At that moment, death was the lesser evil.

I stood and exited the house to drive thirty frantic minutes to Kamas, screeching the tires into the strip mall where Jamison's Real Estate Office was sandwiched between the day old bread store and video rental. Jack sat behind his desk, his T-shirt slogan for the day titled, "Whatever Hits the Fan Won't Be Evenly Distributed." I took the statement as a personal taunt and placed the inheritance booklet on his desk. He nodded knowingly before saying, "I guess you finally got around to reading it." The man reached inside a filing cabinet to hand me a sheaf of documents. "The paperwork came," he said. "You own the house." He caught sight of my mangled face and added, "Did you fall down the stairs?"

I didn't waste time. "I have to sell the house," I said, leaning on his desk for emphasis.

He shook his head. "The house should sell, but it doesn't. Is the place really haunted?"

"No," I replied with honesty. "There's no such thing as ghosts." *There are worse things, like your own mind.* "Please," I was reduced to begging, "put the house back on the market. I have to pay the IRS a minimum of $200,000 in nine months."

He weighed my words and came to a conclusion. "Five years with that property is my limit."

Desperation motivated me to divulge Hathenbruck's secret. "When you write the advertisement," I told Jack, "you can say the house is built over a lost gold mine." The man's eyebrows shot up and I punctuated my statement by adding, "Really."

He molded his face back to normal. "I don't think that ruse will work," he said. "It's a poor town around here that doesn't have a lost gold mine or two. Everybody's cousin has a treasure map found on the body of a massacred Mexican. When the Indians get talkative, they say the Lost Rhoades Mine is under a little meadow, which is impossible. Nobody takes it seriously." He looked at me curiously. "If you have gold on your property, why don't you work it yourself?"

I didn't have the energy to fight his lack of belief. Instead, I pleaded. "The place is destroying me. I can't sell it and can't pay the taxes. Tell me what to do."

He put his pen down and leaned back in his chair. "There might be a way to unload the property. Find someone who's willing to lift it off your back *and* pay the tax. Then you can sign a quit-claim deed."

"Where will I find someone like that?"

Jack avoided my worn, drained face and turned to the contracts on his desk. "I don't know." He said. "I'm sorry, but there's nothing I can do."

I dragged myself out of his office. There was no place to go but home. I drove slowly, languishing my way up the canyon to my hill, arriving at the meadow about one in the afternoon. The sun overhead cast a blinding light that blurred the landscape, but I detected movement coming toward me from the north forest. I squinted to make out five figures on horseback…five people, six horses.

I parked the Shove-it by the south side of the house and returned to the front porch where the figures were large enough to be identified as my four Indians. A woman rode with them, middle-aged, dressed in a long full velvet skirt topped by a billowing blouse. Her ebony hair, pulled back into a braid, rested over her shoulder. It was the woman who hated me, the one I'd encountered at the trailer court and grocery store.

I stood behind the porch railing as they lined themselves in front of me. On the left were the three Indians I had never spoken to. The pockmarked man under his baseball cap sat next to them. A small, riderless pony fidgeted on his left, the reins held by the woman who was mounted on a large grey horse. As usual, the big Indian was the spokesman.

"Pope will live," he solemnly said.

I smiled at the news. "Thank you for coming to tell me."

"Can you ride a horse?"

The statement was unexpected. I reacted with my usual defense and lied. "Of course I can. I'm from Arizona." *I haven't seen a horse since I was ten years old, when my folks took me to a Dude Ranch.*

"We wish to honor you and the memory of your dog by allowing you to ride with us."

He spoke as if they had invited me to a sacred ceremony. I followed his lead. "Thank you. When do we leave?"

"Now."

It took an effort not to be startled. "Do I need to bring anything?"

The big man didn't crack the smallest smile when he said, "You won't need anything."

I figured, what the heck, I could handle a horse for an hour. I clicked into scenes from old cowboy movies and approached the honey colored pony from my right, jammed my left foot into the stirrup, and struggled to haul my body up. I threw my right leg over the horse, crashed into the saddle, and proudly straightened to breathe from my belly. It was good to be young and agile.

The woman snorted when she handed me the reins.

Six of us rode single file into the east woods, the pox-faced man leading the way, followed by the three male Indians, myself, and Hateful-Woman at the rear. My back itched knowing she was behind me. The clop of her horse against the dirt increased its pace and she caught up to me. "It looks like somebody beat you up," she said. Her voice was soft and strangely feminine for a person who could express loathing so expertly.

"How nice," I thought. *"She wants to be friendly."* I twisted in the saddle to face her with a smile. "I was running and tripped on some stairs." I laughed slightly in an effort to ingratiate myself.

"Too bad," she replied. "I wanted to congratulate the person who did it."

I was stunned into speechlessness. She held her horse back as mine plodded forward, and took her position again at the end of the line. I steamed in my own juices for not having an immediate come-back. For the next thirty minutes, while my bottom hit the saddle in a rhythmic bounce, my mind boiled up retorts I wish I'd said, insults I should have thrown, slurs I might have used. *"What's your problem?"* I could have answered. *"Did you eat a brain tumor for breakfast?"* We wove around a stand of poplars and I remembered a good insult. *"Your outfit will never go out of style. It will look ridiculous year after year."* My own style sense, of course, is limited to jeans and long sleeve cotton shirts. Bib overalls are my first choice.

We swerved right to follow a dry streambed and I thought of another affront: *You are a shiver looking for a spine to run up."* A stand of trees looked familiar, holding a dead, gray trunk in the center. I didn't study the grouping because another cutting remark occurred to me: *"Your mind is so narrow, your earrings bang together when you walk."*

The landscape stirred a forgotten recess in my memory, but I was busy concocting rudeness to use on the witch-woman. Someone ahead called a halt and the group dismounted, each removing a small hand shovel poking from the maze of horse straps. Everyone wandered behind the trees. In an epiphany of understanding, I recognized the universal call of nature and gratefully located my little shovel to dig a private hole in the forest. Toilet paper grew everywhere and I chose a variety that was soft and furry.

With the holes filled and covered, the journey continued and I remembered another insult for my enemy: *"I wish I'd known you when you were alive."* I giggled over that one and vowed to use it at the first opportunity. The laugh caught in my throat as we approached a dark, narrow canyon bordered by tall cliffs. I recognized the Spanish words carved in the rock face.

Cuidado
Maldicion Espanol
Los Muertos No Habla

I'd seen it when I tried to follow Pope to the Temple of Towats.

Beware the Spanish curse.
The dead do not talk.

CHAPTER TWENTY

W e entered the twisted canyon, sunlight thwarted by
sheer walls, and followed the dry stream. Stones under horse hooves rattled through the canyon like maracas
shaking in diverse rhythms. No birds added music to the
percussion. No one broke the somber silence as we followed
the winding path single file. The steep canyon produced a
feeling of vulnerability with no escape. I focused my mind
on the geology of the cliffs, the scarcity of vegetation, the
lack of water...*my* lack of water.

"Excuse me," I finally called ahead, "is there something
to drink?"

Without slowing, a ripple of movement came from
the front as a two-liter plastic bottle was tossed between
the four men ahead of me, the last holding it out behind
his back, waiting for me to trot close enough to grab it.
I kicked slightly at the horse's ribs and rocked forward
in the saddle. "Giddy-up" I gave the childish command,
without results. The sound of horse hooves from the rear

advanced to my side. I shuddered when the devil woman passed me, her braid swinging smoothly as she rode to the man ahead and took the water. She lingered in place until my horse caught up, then flung the canteen at my chest. I grunted at the impact, fumbling with the half-full container to prevent dropping it to the ground. The words "Thank you" fell from my mouth and I hated myself for groveling in gratitude instead of using one of my well-planned insults. She returned to the back of the line and I greedily drank the remaining water before stuffing the empty flask between two straps on the horse. We treaded wearily on for another half hour before I decided I'd had enough honor.

"Hey," I yelled out. "Thanks for the trip but I have to get home now."

No response. I tried again. "Really, guys, it's been two hours."

Nothing. I stopped my horse, pulling on his reins so hard he backed up and whinnied. "I have to turn around now. I can find my own way home. Thanks for the nice... experience."

The line of horses halted as if on command, though no words were said. The lead man dismounted and leisurely ambled back to me. "Dr. Howard," he said kindly, "we have a long journey ahead."

The bones on my bottom bit through the flesh. "How much time do you need?"

"Until tomorrow night."

I leaned forward with a disbelieving stare. "You're kidding."

The big man removed his baseball cap to run his fingers through short, salt and pepper hair. "This is what Pope asked us to give you. He wanted it to be a surprise."

Incredulous, I said, "Pope wants me to have…" I counted two days out, two days back, "…a four day horseback ride?" No doubt about it, the kid wanted me dead.

The man with chicken pox scars was tall enough to see nearly straight into my eyes as I sat on my small horse. He waited a few seconds before uttering the whammy. "Pope said you wanted to see the treasure of Towats."

I felt my brows lift, making room for the eyes to widen. "You're going to take me to the caverns? And let me go inside?" Both hands moved involuntarily against my heart.

My enthusiasm forced a smile to his lips. "In two days, if you want."

It's a funny thing how a journey that exhausted my patience moments earlier had dramatically transformed into a quest. The Temple of Towats called like a siren song, promising the sight of Montezuma's treasure. Even hunger pangs didn't dampen the thrill. I patted my horse's rump with affection and announced, "I'm right behind you."

Like ants in a line, we resumed the monotonous beat of plodding hoofs reverberating against steep cliffs. Since my Indian companions hadn't introduced themselves, I dubbed them with unofficial monikers based on the physical appearance of their faces. Pox rode at the front followed by Longnose, Squinteye, and Scar. The horse plodding under me became "Blackfoot" because his front leg was black against his honey-colored coat. The woman behind me remained nameless except for derogatory terms that surfaced as needed.

A bag of hard peppermints passed down the line, casually tossed and caught with skill. The man in front of me, nicknamed Scar, turned in his saddle to carefully do an underhand throw, ensuring that I didn't fumble the package to the dirt. I took four candies, two to eat and two to hide, before hurling the prize at the witch-woman behind. I didn't watch to see if she caught it. She didn't pelt me with rocks so I assumed she intercepted the sweet prize. After that solitary bit of excitement, I drifted into a catatonic state and waited for a motive to return to life. It came when we reached the end of the gorge.

A valley spread itself before us like a banquet in myriad colors of green, speckled with turquoise lakes, bordered by snow-capped mountains. The expedition traversed its way down and crossed a wide stream that tumbled in layers to end in a lake. The group stopped at a flat clearing without discussion. They must have made previous camps in the area. To the north, two small mountains close together had rounded crests, one bald, the other covered in trees. They were conspicuous because they resembled …there's no other way to describe them…a woman's breasts, creating a memorable landmark.

Everyone, even rotten-woman, slid easily from the horses. I had transformed to stone and tried not to whimper when I lifted my right leg off the animal and crumbled to the ground. The Indians pretended not to notice the humiliating dismount, but they could hardly miss my hands and knees crawl to the nearest rock. I became aware of dark colors in front of me, maroon, navy blue, deep green. A heavy skirt undulated in the breeze. What's-her-name dropped a brush and hobbles on the ground, then pointed toward my horse, her callous way of indicating no one was coming to help me. So much for guest status.

I returned to my pony and studied the load on his back. The saddlebag came off the animal without much effort, as did the bedroll. But the saddle itself required a struggle with complicated loops and ties. I jumped back when it slid to dangle under the horse's belly, pulling a multihued blanket with it. I undid the last loop and it fell to the ground where I shoved it into an upright position before contemplating the piece of metal in the horse's mouth. Gingerly, I reached into the wetness to remove the bit and bridle, expecting to lose a few fingers. My hand emerged soggy but intact.

In a monkey see, monkey do imitation of the Indians, I brushed, watered, and hobbled Blackfoot, leaving him to graze in the lush grass before preparing my bedroll, consisting of a ground cover and one wool blanket. I isolated my camp several feet away from the others, feeling uncomfortable at the thought of an evening with strangers. I gathered dead wood for the small fire Squinteye created for the group, its border defined by ragged stones. The Indians added smooth rocks to the inside edge, maybe a Ute religious superstition. I didn't know these people well enough to probe into the deeper meanings of their culture.

Longnose wove willows into a crude basket that he secured in the tumbling stream to catch dinner. The Fish and Game Department would not approve, but we were on the reservation where the Indians lived their own rules. Before the sun hid behind the mountains, fish sizzled over coals and unleavened bread baked on white ashes. During the day's long ride of silence, I had searched my pockets for anything edible and found four lint encrusted M&M's trapped in a seam. I had allowed each one to melt under my tongue and thought it was heaven until now, when I feasted on burned fish without salt, pepper, or tartar sauce. I brushed white dust and cinders off the hot bread, made without yeast, no butter, and felt like a queen dining under a silk canopy sprinkled with diamonds.

There were no songs or stories around the campfire. When the meal was finished, the five Indians settled on the ground around the fire to sleep and I walked to my little camp, rolling myself into the wool blanket. After a few hours, I was shivering. Even with shoes on, my feet burned with cold. I stood, wrapped in my inadequate cocoon, and moved to Blackfoot's saddle on the ground where I tugged the blanket out. Using the saddle as a raised cot under my shoulders, I arranged the horse blanket around me and curled into the fetal position.

Events of the last two days seeped into me like the frigid air: Zeus' death, the tunnel leading to a gold mine, a grave-yard of murdered men, IRS property and inheritance taxes I didn't have, and the gentle kindness of the ghost in the trunk. I waited for the miserable night to pass.

The smell of fish and ashcakes pushed me awake. After breakfast, I took two leftover ash cakes, aware that Scar watched me. He appeared to be in his late twenties, his hair bluntly cut past his ears, a gray scar over his cheekbone. I brandished the biscuits for him to see. "Insurance," I said with a smile. The man quickly looked away and I figured I had committed yet another social faux pas and could add an additional enemy to my collection. But later, while I wrestled with the saddle, he took it from me and swung it over the horse, tying and cinching the straps, fitting the bridle and reins, his fingers quick and practiced.

I should have been quietly grateful but felt the need to defend myself. "It's been a long time since I rode a horse," I said, "and these mountains are different than the Arizona desert." The words wilted on the ground between us. The man recognized an excuse when he heard one.

He spoke with a trace of humor behind his dark eyes. "It's also been a long time since you camped." He lightly tossed the saddlebag over Blackfoot's rear while explaining, "Food is on this side, water on the other." Then Scar added a final straw to my disgrace while he tied my bedroll in place. "Tonight, I'll teach you how to stay warm. You can start by joining us around the fire."

I dropped my head and mumbled thanks. He nodded politely and left while I peeked in the saddlebag to find dehydrated fruit, nuts, jerky, and dried bread. I had spent the first day hungry, too proud to ask questions, while my hosts acted on the lies I gave them and didn't insult me by explaining the obvious.

The Indians made the camp disappear like Las Vegas magicians with mirrors. Even black coals from the campfire became invisible. We mounted the horses and directed our march toward the two round-topped mountains, but regardless of how far we rode, they seemed to slide further into the distance.

The terrain reminded me of the painted panoramas we created as kids on long paper rolled between two sticks, placed in a box with a cutout square like a television. The pictures slowly moved through the box, giving the impression we were riding ponies, though we knew we stood still.

Now, I swayed on top of Blackfoot as Pines changed to Aspen that transformed to grassland, all moving past me on a roll of paper in a cardboard box.

We traveled through a patch of sagebrush and I noticed a ten-foot circle of rocks with a smaller circle in the center. A configuration like that doesn't occur in nature. The Uinta Mountains shouldn't have man-made concentric rings in its sagebrush.

I called to the front of the line. "I'd like to stop and get a closer look at those rocks." To my surprise, the travelers halted and I hurried to get off the horse and scamper to the area before someone said it was forbidden. At the small circle's center sat a bronze bell, mottled pale orange and brown, pitted with age, about four inches high and three inches wide. I picked it up to see "1878" inscribed between two Maltese crosses. The faint letters *"saigneleceur fondeur"* were stamped around the rim. I looked closer and wondered if the first word could have ended in 'gier.' A presence invaded my musings. The four Indian men stood outside the circle. The woman had remained on her horse.

"Does anyone know what this is?" I indicated the rocks on the ground.

Pox answered. "It's an old gravesite of Spanish miners. Indians killed them but the burial isn't our work. Someone made this monument to honor their dead. We consider it sacred." *Translation: get out of the center circle.*

I ignored the hint and held up the bell. "The two Maltese crosses show that this bell came from a Spanish Mission. The letters indicate it was made outside America."

"My father," Scar volunteered, "was one of twelve men who knew the way to the sacred temple. He passed this burial many times and thought the words on the bell were a mix of Latin and French. He worked hard to understand the meaning. The bell says, '*It grieves me to the very heart.*'" Scar raised his head, proud of the interpretation his father had done. "My father said an important man lies here."

I checked the words on the rim again. I was pretty sure "*saignelegier*" was a town in Switzerland and "*fondeur*" was French for "*smelter of ore.*" The bronze bell was likely made at a foundry in Switzerland and no doubt ended at this spot with a murdered Jesuit Priest. Two weeks ago I would have argued my point, insisting that the words on the bell were simply a logo for the company that did the casting. Scientific fact should be more important than sentiment. But Scar had befriended me. It wouldn't be nice to belittle the opinion of his father. *Since when,*" I thought, "*have I been nice?*"

I gulped down the facts and said, "I agree with your father. Whoever made this burial was grieved to the heart."

We returned to the horses, each person clinging to his own truth.

CHAPTER TWENTY-ONE

At two in the afternoon we entered an area of abundant grass and dismounted for the horses to graze while we chewed on jerky and dried apples. I reached for my canteen, certain it was still half full of water, but now the container felt empty. I shook it to make sure, removed the lid and tipped the bottom up to produce nothing. The devil woman appeared in front of my vision.

"I can show you pure water very close," she quietly said, her voice silken. In a fleeting vision, I saw the wicked witch offering Snow White a poisoned apple.

I leaned into Blackfoot for protection. "I think I should stay with the horse."

The woman displayed a convincing smile. "I'm going for water now. I'll fill your canteen for you."

I suspected a trap and held tight to my canteen, obvious distrust in my action. Her eyes narrowed for a moment, but she still spoke sweetly. "You can follow at a distance if it makes you feel better." She turned to wade through calf-high grass without looking back to see if I tagged behind. I shook my empty canteen again and decided to take a chance. When I topped a small rise, I saw her standing by a slow stream that formed a small pool. She stood and waved, then walked several feet to my left. "I'll stay here while you get water."

The stream, barely two feet wide, moved in a lazy line. Keeping an eye on the enemy, I bent to fill my canteen. A deep voice startled me.

"Dr. Howard," it commanded, "stop." I stood to face Pox but he spoke to the woman. "What are you doing, Mary?"

Mary, the name of my nemesis, didn't flinch at his tone. "I wasn't going to let her drink it." She spoke petulantly, like a child caught doing something naughty. Pox stared at her, forcing the woman to justify herself. "It wouldn't have killed her." She shrugged, then added, "Yet." Mary turned her back to us, skirt swirling, and walked up the rise. The big Indian began to follow but I chased him to the foot of the hill.

"Wait a minute," I demanded. "What's wrong with the water?"

His reply was too casual. "It has quicksilver in it." A glance at my horrified face convinced him to assure me, "Mary's right, it wouldn't have killed you."

I quoted Mary's last word. "Yet," I said. "The tiny amount of mercury just in a flu shot stays in the body for weeks. What would a canteen of this water do to my kidneys?" Now I was angry. "This is dangerous stuff, some forms have a four hundred year half life. No treatment can reverse the damage. I should---"

Pox cut me off. "Mercury has to accumulate before it does damage. An old prospector drank this water every day for twenty years before it killed him."

I was quick on the offensive. "It must have destroyed his brain immediately or he wouldn't have stayed."

Pox sighed and lowered himself to sit on the edge of the hill, wordlessly inviting me to join him. "He stayed because he thought he'd found one of the lost Rhoades mines."

Lost Rhoades...famous...lots of gold..."Did he find it?" I settled against the knoll, planning to pull every shred of information from the big man.

"No," he said, "but he was close enough to keep trying. He knew Rhoades and Hathenbruck had worked here. He didn't know they washed mercury amalgam in this stream."

My mind suddenly zoomed back to his earlier reference of *one* of the lost Rhoades mines. "You said mines, plural. How many did they find?"

The Indian placed his arms over bent knees. "Thomas Rhoades, Caleb's father, found the bodies of some massacred Mexicans. A tin box in the middle of the slaughter had a map inside, showing the location of three mines. Thomas never found them, but his son Caleb located two called the Pine Mine and the Rhoades Mine."

Caleb Rhoades had been introduced to me in Hathenbruck's journals. I posed my problem. "If Caleb knew where the mines were, why did he need Hathenbruck as a partner?"

"Dr. Hathenbruck," he said, "was a true friend to the Indian. The mines were on our reservation. Caleb needed Indian permission for a lease and hoped Hathenbruck could get it."

"And he did," I said, remembering the story. "Chief Tabby even traveled through a storm to cast his vote."

The man narrowed his eyes, adding a few wrinkles. "But the Washington bureaucrats didn't ratify the lease. A few powerful Senators wanted the gold and formed a company to take it. Caleb and Frank fought those men for seven years, but lost." Pox chuckled. "In the end it didn't matter. Nobody ever found those mines again."

Hathenbruck had written in his journal: *"The mine is in the least likely place they would ever expect to find it. They could stand on top of it and never see it."* They could stand inside his house, I thought, in the hall to be exact, and never see it.

I was ready to ask harder questions. "Do you know where the mines are?"

He looked intently at some distance object. "Yes," he said.

I let my next question fall like an anvil. "Is one of them under my house?"

A roar of silence surrounded us, like earplugs under water. Even birdsong seemed to cease. Pox finally answered me. "How did you find it?"

"The vibrations led me to it."

The man didn't seem startled at the 'vibration' revelation. "How far did you get?"

"From the underground passage to the graveyard and into two tunnels before my light went out. I panicked and ran like a madwoman hitting walls, tripping on stairs, falling on my face."

I expected him to glance at my cuts and bruises, but he didn't twitch a muscle. "One of the tunnels," he said, "leads to a vein even richer than the main room, but my people didn't let the Spanish develop it." The scene flashed before my eyes of murdered Spanish soldiers thrown on top of dead slaves. The Utes had finally been pushed too far.

I chose to be blunt. "I found gold bars in a cave on my property. Was that gold mined from the large room where the Spanish skeletons are?"

Pox said nothing, which was the same as a resounding 'yes.'

My next words were an accusation. "Those bars were taken without my permission to the Temple of Towats." I was treading forbidden ground but I plowed through it anyway. "If you don't return some of the bars, the raw gold under my house can pay the inheritance tax." The statement, veiled in a smile, was designed as a threat.

The big man lowered his head, as if conquered, but when he raised it again his defiant expression let me know the defeat was mine. "Dr. Howard," he said, "Hathenbruck built his house on the Ute reservation."

I began a protest. "The land is no longer on---"

He didn't wait to hear it. "Congress can change the boundaries all they want. The gold mine still belongs to the Indians. Hathenbruck gave us perpetual mineral rights."

Perpetual…forever…Pope had told me the gold belonged to… "Why?" I couldn't fathom a reason for giving such wealth to the Indians rather than his family. I rested my forehead on my hand and covered my eyes. "Why would Hathenbruck do that?"

"He lived with us for a year, learned our language, served us, understood our history and respected our obligation to Towats. We knew he wouldn't search for the sacred temple, and gave him permission to take gold from the Rhoades mine."

So," I guessed, "when the Senators stopped Hathenbruck from developing the mine…"

The big man shrugged. "It was the will of Towats. After Caleb died, Hathenbruck was legally stopped from working the mine, and he promised us he would keep the gold hidden from anyone else."

"People figured that Hathenbruck knew where the mine was," I inserted, "but didn't think he'd build a house over the entrance."

"Hathenbruck was a good man," Pox said. "Towats tested him with poverty in his final days, but he refused to break his promise to us. He wouldn't go to the mine and take a chance that someone might follow him."

"And maybe kill him," I added.

Malicious Mary's words at the grocery store floated to the top of my memory and finally made sense: *You will break the promise.* She feared I would discover the mine and start a new gold rush.

I let half a minute pass before asking, "What part does Mary have?"

"Mary?" His tone seemed confused by the sudden topic change.

"The one that hates me," I explained. "The one who tried to poison me a few minutes ago. She's been vicious from the minute I drove into town. How does she fit into Spanish gold mines and the Treasure of Towats?"

It was his turn to let thirty seconds pass. "You represent a great loss to her." I cocked my head with interest and he proceeded. "Her family took care of the house when Hathenbruck was alive and still maintains it as part of the promise. Mary's the housekeeper and tells us of any repairs that need doing."

I groaned at the revelation. "The first time I entered the house, I knew someone was taking care of it. Did Mary live there?" *My coming must have forced her into the trailer court. No wonder she hates me.*

Pox shook his head. "The house is her duty, not her home. Foul deeds of the past still haunt the place. Vibrations of good and evil can be controlled in our minds, but none of us want to live there. It isn't worth the energy. We prefer to live with peace."

I reviewed my experience with the house. I had spent six nights there before the violent storm. "Why did the house take so long to start haunting me?"

"You're a scientist and might not have listened at first. But it's like mercury," he smiled, "where the full force collects over time."

I nodded in understanding. After the storm, the hauntings became graphic and violent until they finally chased us out. "I understand why nobody wants to live there. Does Mary's family keep their part of the agreement without compensation?"

"We all accept responsibility without pay, like Pope who takes his turn guarding the sites in the mountains."

I thought of Jack Jamison. "Does the real estate agent know that Mary cleans the house?"

"Jack's thinking is shallow," Pox said, "about the same level as his T-shirt slogans. We don't worry that he'll figure anything out." Pox directed his eyes at me, one brow higher than the other. "We've been concerned about what you'll do. Mary's work is vital. If the house deteriorates it could reveal the mine, which would be a disaster to the purpose of Towats."

I lost patience with Towats and his demands. "I would think Towats could protect his own gold mines."

The man's eyes sparked with irritation at my lack of reverence. "He does. That's why no one can find them."

I pursed my lips to keep the next words in, tried to force them down, to swallow them whole, but they slipped through my teeth in a challenge.

"I found one."

It was my final attack of the day. We sat very still as the friendly conversation between us shriveled. Pox lifted himself from the slanted hill to stand and I joined him. The walk back was done in silence until we reached Blackfoot. The horse was still tearing grass out in great clumps.

Pox put his hand on the pony's neck. "Right now, geologists don't believe there's gold in the Uinta Mountains and we want to keep it that way. If money rock is discovered again, Congress will change the reservation boundaries and white men can return with machines to tear out our mountains. They will steal our peace and search for all the treasures. We won't be able to frighten everyone who gets close to the temple."

I reached under Blackfoot for the reins. "I guess you can't just shoot people anymore."

The Indian's cheeks lifted slightly and I knew he was at least thinking of grinning when he said, "We miss the good old days." Then his eyes lost their sparkle and went flat. "Don't let Mary know you found the gold mine that her family has worked so hard to keep hidden."

"That's good advice," I said. Then, afraid of losing my great desire, I begged without shame. "Can I still see the Treasure?"

Pox grimaced. "That is Pope's wish and we agreed."

There was nothing more to say and we parted to mount our horses and take our positions in line, like children who slavishly keep the same desks in school. Ahead, the mountain's round bustline beckoned and we rode into the cleavage.

CHAPTER TWENTY-TWO

I dropped the fifth rock on top of my collection. "Are these good enough?"

Scar separated them with his foot to examine their quality. "You can't use anything that was in a riverbed. If there's water left in the rock, steam could explode it and kill somebody."

"They were all high and dry," I promised.

He picked up a six-inch specimen shaped like a tortilla and hefted its weight. "This one is too flat to hold the heat all night." The young man gave the rock a toss and bent to choose a thicker sample. "Two of these will keep you warm."

I shivered at the memory of my previous night. "Can I use them all?"

He shrugged. "If you don't mind sharing space with a bunch of hot rocks. Your wool blanket won't melt like a white man's sleeping bag, so you should be fine."

I hauled four smooth rocks to the fire and settled them at the inside edge, smiling at my idiocy of yesterday in thinking the rocks represented an unknown tradition among the Utes. I shook my head. When western science can't explain ancient ways, we label it as religious superstition. In fact, we ourselves are proof that primitive people were smart enough to survive. I once attended a lecture where the presenter explained that small, carved fitted wood pieces were an ancient toy. A lowly graduate student suggested they were ingenious traps to catch very small animals but no one listened to him.

After our dinner of trout and ashcakes, Mary sat on a log sharpening a five-inch knife blade, her velvet skirt wrapped around her legs. I grabbed the opportunity to sit next to her, speaking quickly before she could get up and move.

"I see the wisdom in wearing a long, velvet skirt," I began in conciliation. "It's cool during the day and warm at night." The woman didn't respond, continuing to circle the knife against the whetstone. I spoke again, this time directly to the point, sharp like her knife. "You emptied the water from my canteen today. I'd like to know how you did it without me seeing you."

Mary's words dripped with disdain. "I could steal your horse from under you and you wouldn't know until your big butt hit the ground." She flipped the blade to her fingers, steadied her aim, and threw the weapon at a four-inch sapling several feet away. The knife thumped deep into the little trunk and held firm while the tree shuddered at the impact. The woman stood and looked down on me. "You're a bigger target," she finished.

Slowly, with dignity, I stood to face her. Still bristling at her reference to my enlarged posterior, I worked to remain calm. "Why do you want to hurt me?"

"The last time somebody got this close to the temple," she said lightly, as if her story had a funny ending, "our men dragged him to an old log and cut off three of his fingers as a warning. This time, I'll do what the gutless men won't." We locked eyes and she finished her statement in grim anticipation. "If you take the smallest thing from the temple, just one jewel, even a pebble off the floor…" she smiled at the thought, "…I get to kill you. And that will be the end of our trouble." She swung away to retrieve her knife.

My knees wobbled and I sank down on the log. S*he GETS to kill me?* I'd never been hated so thoroughly by a stranger, not even by my husband who became a stranger after I married him. His last words to me were, "You'll never find another man. No one in his right mind would want you." That speech was full of kindness compared to Mary's *"I get to kill you."* Fish and ashcakes burped into my mouth, leaving a taste that reminded me of fear.

Scar and Longnose had left a space by the fire for my bedroll. Four hot rocks and I squeezed together in the wool blanket for the night. By the time they were cold, the first rays of sun had fallen off the tops of the mountains, back-lighting an arrangement of boulders that exactly resembled a castle. A flag was all that was needed to complete the effect. I supposed the Mexican map drew mountains that looked like a sleeping woman and an English castle.

I mounted my horse, still analyzing the trick of shadow and light, when Pox rode to my side holding a lady's sleeping blindfold, shaped like dark glasses with an elastic to keep it around the head. This one had a white ruffle added to the edge.

He raised the silly thing for me to take. "Wear this over your eyes. You can't see the rest of the trail."

"What trail?" I didn't reach for the blindfold. "I've missed seeing even the shadow of a path. If you think I could ever return to this spot---"

His eyes flitted toward the castle and back to me. "It's an interesting formation, isn't it? The mountains themselves give clues to the Temple of Towats. From here, it would be better if you didn't see anything more."

The pretentious blindfold was an affront to my self-respect. "I'll bet Butch Cassidy didn't have to wear that silly thing."

Pox shook his head. "He put a big handkerchief around his eyes and tied it in back."

"I'd prefer one of those."

He let the lady's blindfold hang from his finger by the elastic. "Mary says this is better. You can't see under the fold."

"Why the ruffle?"

"This was the only one she could find." He pushed the blindfold at me. "When you cover your eyes, we can finish the journey." Reluctantly, I slipped the offensive contraption from his hand to my head. Mary was right, the efficient design kept brightness from creeping through or under.

Pox didn't ride off. His horse snorted as Pox said, "It is required that you take a solemn vow not to tell anyone for any reason where the temple of Towats is."

"I'm wearing a blindfold," I reminded him. "I won't know where it is."

"Make the vow." His voice had a sharp edge to it. This was serious stuff to him.

I raised my hand in the Boy Scout oath, two fingers forming a V, the only vow-type sign I knew. "I solemnly promise to never divulge where the temple of Towats is."

"On pain of death," the man added.

"On pain of death," I obediently copied. These people were sincerely serious about protecting this particular treasure.

The horses clopped to their places and we lurched into the familiar rhythm of the last two days. After a while, loss of sight heightened my remaining senses. A slight breeze puffed at my short hair, lifting individual strands from my scalp. I eavesdropped on birds sending messages to each other through the network of trees, the tunes baffling in their variety. The pitch-and-roll sway of Blackfoot lulled my sense of time into oblivion, where minutes and hours blended to a meaningless jumble. I could hear the flat terrain and smell changes in the air. When the horses stopped, there was a pressure of stillness. A living presence approached like a wave, accompanied by the clop of horse hooves.

The deep voice of Pox entered my ears. "Dr. Howard, choose which entrance to the cavern you prefer. The first is an underground tunnel where you crawl on your elbows into a cavern, or we have ropes to lower you into a crevice that leads to the temple from the top."

His voice surrounded me, and I didn't know which way to turn my head to give an answer. I decided there was more dignity in facing ahead than trying to guess where the man stood. "I spent a bad day in a tunnel three days ago," I replied. "I'll take a chance on the ropes."

The man's essence slid away from me, followed by the squeak of leather, the snort of a horse, and the sensation of forward progress.

After an undetermined amount of time, someone took the reins from my hands and Blackfoot began an uphill climb. The horse balked and raised his head to object. I felt his neck stretch forward as the person ahead pulled at him. His hooves added their pattern to the other horses that were…missing. Twenty-four horseshoes should have been ringing against the rocks, but I could only hear four. Blackfoot was the only horse on the trail. The other five must have been left behind.

"Who's leading my horse?" I asked. The only answer was pebbles scraping against dirt. I tried again. "Hey! My horse is the only one climbing. How many people are walking by me?" Blackfoot stumbled, pushing me steeply forward on the saddle. There were sharp intakes of human breath and gentle commands to settle the horse. Judging from the voices, two men escorted the pony at the front and rear. I lifted my legs away from Blackfoot's sides. The left foot hit a solid mass, the right waved through thin air. I was prompted to alter my concerns. "How steep is this mountain?"

The answer came from the horse in another stumble, sending large rocks careening off the ledge. Their slight whistle of descent was like a scream in my over-activated ears. I counted, *one thousand one, one thousand two,* before I heard stones clatter on a shelf and roll to the bottom.

"Stop the horse," I ordered. "I'd rather walk."

"You're safe," an unfamiliar voice said behind me. It was one of the men who hadn't spoken to me, Longnose or Squinteye. Words from the front belonged to Scar. "The worst part is ahead. Hold on to the pommel." I felt the hard angle of a left turn. Blackfoot propelled his body like a swimmer in deep water, a thrust forward, a pause, a drive ahead again. The path had transformed into something so steep I was forced to lean forward against the saddle, clinging to the horn to keep from slipping off the horse's rump. The sides of my little pony wheezed in search of oxygen.

"Crawling through a tunnel is sounding better," I called to the laboring men. "Is it too late to change my mind?"

Nobody laughed.

The end came in a swift clamber to sudden balance. I sat upright, enveloped by the heavy panting of Blackfoot, attended by human gasps and coughs, and the words, "You can take off the blindfold now." I didn't stop to analyze the voice, but ripped the black sleeping mask off my head and raised my face to the cloudless blue sky. We stood on a mountain plateau, shorter than the towering, snow-topped peaks around it. My watch showed the time at 9:03. It had taken less than two hours from the castle monument at camp to this mountain. The two men who had pushed me to the top were Scar and Squinteye, both bending from the waist, breathing hard, hands on knees for support. I slid from the horse. "Thank you," I said. Nothing more was needed. Sometimes, not often, I say the right thing and shut up.

The men nodded in response and removed a duffle bag from the horse, then carried it to the west part of the plateau where they unpacked and set out webbing, cordage, and carabiners for my descent. I'd taken a rock climbing class in college, hated it and quit, but recognized the paraphernalia. Ignoring thoughts of my future use of the ropes,

I walked away from the men toward a scene that stretched into forever, defying all the superlatives I knew: breath-taking, stunning, dazzling, magnificent, awe-inspiring, astoun...I tripped across something hard in the ground. Someone had drilled a core-hole and crammed a railroad spike into it, rusty but still solid, obviously not prehistoric. Maybe an old prospector had found a map, followed the signs, and set the spike to secure a rope for his own try at treasure. Maybe the Indians waited to kill him until he'd finished making the anchor. Maybe his bones were at the bottom of the cliff. Maybe I should have stayed home. I peeked over the edge of the mountain and some new de-scriptors formed: vertical, perpendicular, sheer terror.

"Dr. Howard," Scar stood next to me, interrupting my reverie. He held the webbing and ropes ready. "You need to start. We have to get off the mountain before dark." He wrapped the harness around me like a chastity belt of yel-low webbing. While he tugged on the main cord he asked, "Have you done this before?"

"Yes." It was an honest answer.

He produced a withering gaze through slitted eyes. "This is not the time for the pride you showed with the horse and camping. If you make a mistake this time, you won't just be embarrassed. You'll be dead. Your bones will bleach themselves white at the base of this mountain." My shock must have covered my face because he softened to ex-plain, "We could never find you. This would be your burial place and, believe me, you'd be in lots of company." I stood uncharacteristically speechless and he continued. "If you're not completely sure about this equipment, we need to ei-ther practice or go home."

We practiced. *Lock carabiner to rope. Lean back while men hold rope. Stand up, unscrew carabiner, slip it off webbing, unhook belay rope. Repeat. On…lean…off.* It occurred to me that if they wanted to kill me, all they had to do was push me over the edge. Mary's words leaped into focus, "*…and that would be the end of our trouble.*" But the men were working with me, practicing, giving instructions. It was time to trust them.

"The only place to stand," Scar warned, "will be an old log wedged into a crevice in the cliff face. You need to squeeze inside the crevice before you unclip the carabiner."

"Right. Got it."

"Leave the rappel harness inside the tunnel. Take the thirty-foot belay rope with you. You'll need it to get down into the cavern. Don't use the peg steps."

"Sure. Sure." *I need a thirty-foot rope?*

"When you return, put on the harness and rope. The horse will help us pull you up."

After rehearsals ended, I finally stood backwards on the ledge, my gloved hands divided between the rappel held in my right hand and the belay wrapped around my hip. The Indians held the rope and patiently waited for me to perform the first move.

"Wait," I hedged. "Why am I going into the temple alone?" The question was like the last request from a prisoner already lined against the wall waiting for shots to be fired.

Scar gave a simple, logical answer. "Because you're the one who wants to see it."

Against all survival instinct, I leaned back and took the first step down the sheer cliff face. I slid some rope in my right hand through the rappel device and took two more steps, then five…eight…I looked down to locate the tree trunk and felt my chest contract. It was a hundred foot fall to the slide rock below. The pole I needed was a few feet to my left, fixed into a crack that widened to make an opening in the cliff. Clinging to my ropes, I swung to the trunk and yelled, "Got it!" The old log offered a base of twelve inches to stand on. Only a skinny gymnast with a gold medal for beam could have maneuvered it without ropes.

From the top drifted the words, "Come back at five-thirty."

"What happens," I shouted up, entering the crevice, "if I'm late?" The slit was barely big enough to slip through sideways. I stooped to keep from hitting my head.

Faint words filtered through the fissure. "We have to leave at five-thirty, whether you're here or not."

"Very funny," I shot back.

Safely inside the entrance, I removed the harness and dropped it to the ground. The rappel rope snaked outside and up the cliff of the mountain, a stark reminder of my absolute dependence on the men who waited at the top. I unhooked the belay rope, wrapped it around my hand and elbow, and hung the loops from my shoulder. The flashlight Scar had given me included two beam choices, spot and flood, with a compass embedded in the end of the handle. A small fanny pack held extra batteries plus food and water. Heavy plastic bags with ties were universally used as an outhouse for explorers, to be filled when necessary and carried back to nature for burial. My escorts had supplied everything but what I wanted most: Time. I had eight hours to explore the temple of Towats. I needed eight years.

The crevice opened into a tunnel, man-made judging by pick marks on the walls. At the end of thirty feet, a 90-degree turn kept me parallel to the outside cliff. After twenty feet, another curve faced me toward the interior again. I kept careful track of the twists and turns of the tunnel, counting my steps, estimating the distance. *"The final twenty feet,"* Scar had warned, *"ends suddenly at the top of the cavern. Don't fall in."* I slowed my pace, waving the flashlight beam to reflect against the sides of the tunnel. One more step, then another, and suddenly the light seemed to evaporate. There were no more walls. I lowered the beam to my feet and stood at the precipice of a massive hole.

CHAPTER TWENTY-THREE

I switched to a floodlight. Worn wooden pegs, driven into the sheer sides of the cavern, provided broken or missing steps to the bottom. The hole appeared thirty feet deep with another ten feet over my head. I searched for a place to anchor my rope so I could lower myself down. Back inside the tunnel a railroad spike had been hammered deep into the juncture between the floor and wall, probably the work of the same miner who had set an anchor on the plateau above. I smiled at evidence that the old guy had made it this far, and tied a bowline on his railroad spike, maybe even mumbling the beginning of the magic words, *"This is the rabbit hole…"*

The configuration of rope knots took me back in time to the day in a Girl Guide camp when I refused to make a crown out of pinecones. "I want to learn something real," I had said, stomping away. The old maintenance man found me sulking at a kitchen table and showed me how to make a bowline. "This is the rabbit hole." He grinned as he made a small circle with his rope. "The rabbit comes out of his hole and runs under the log." He threaded one rope end over and under the loop. "Suddenly, he sees a snake. He jumps back over the log, dives into his hole, and disappears." The grizzled old guy smiled at me. "Behold, the bowline." The knot had been useful for twenty years. I never learned how to make a crown from pinecones. The craft teacher wasn't nice to me anymore. You win some, you lose some.

With the flashlight buttoned inside my shirt, the light shone through the fabric like the heart of E.T., who wanted to go home. For me, the alien place waiting for me was better than home. Anticipation made me giddy as the rope slid through the fingers of my leather gloves, the peg stairs visually measuring my descent. When my feet touched bottom, they clattered and slid over hard metal, crunching through something frighteningly familiar. I clung to the rope with one hand and fumbled for the flashlight. It shone on numerous skeletons, still dressed in Spanish armor. These men had fallen or been pushed to their deaths. I froze, waiting for a nightmare, but my mind remained clear of hallucinations. There was nothing here to cause the magnitude of horror that still existed under the Hathenbruck house. Relieved, I let the lifeline flop against the wall and dropped my gloves on the floor, anxious to explore the perimeter of the cavern.

I faced the cliff and moved to my right. Stacks of unstamped gold bullion lined the wall, a repository of unimaginable wealth without an owner, free for the taking, no legal questions involved. I imagined plunking a bar on the assayer's counter. The man would heft it, turn it over, search for marks.

"Where did you get this?" he would say.

"In the Uintas." I wouldn't be able to suppress a grin. *"It's raw gold bullion, no markings, no way to tell how old it is."*

"Were there other gold bars?"

"A few." I am the Queen of Understatement. *"But this was the only one I could..uh…get out."* Get-away-with is more accurate. *"How much will you give me?"*

The man will stare into my eyes, checking for truth, then shake his head as he analyzes the gold content and hands me a six-figure check.

The bubble popped in my face. If Mary planned to pat me down for pebbles, she would certainly notice a gold bar. I dismissed the daydream and swept my floodlight over thousands of bars in various sizes, wondering where the Indians had put my Spanish gold. It should be easy to find, marked with *Ano Dom 1675* and the numeral V, showing that a twenty percent tax had been paid to the Spanish King.

A mummified face startled me. It had a strip of cloth under the chin, tied on top of his head in a knot. My heart dropped a few beats before I analyzed the universal burial practice of jaw wrapping, which prevented the mouth from falling open in a silent scream. His closed eyes were sunk into the eye sockets, the eyeballs liquefied long ago. He slept peacefully, leaning against the rock wall in a sitting position, surrounded by three wives and the bones of his favorite horse. The animal had probably been cut into pieces to get it into the cavern. The abundance of artifacts around the man testified to his wealth and importance. An antique rifle and three pistols showed he had lived in the 1800s. Now he was mummified in the dry temperature of the cave.

I continued my sweep of the walls, counting a dozen Indian chieftains sitting upright, wrapped in blanket shreds and cedar bark. I couldn't take time to study their personal treasures and forced myself past the burials, feeling pity for the families murdered to escort the head of household to his reward. The practice was vile. I would never get accustomed to seeing it.

The floor of the chamber sloped up at the south wall, six openings tunneled in different directions, but I had no trouble deciding which I would follow. One had a carved portal, a large sun symbol on top, with mythical creatures decorating the sides. Some looked similar to the Griffin on a Welsh flag, wings spread, one loop in the tail. I passed through the entrance, sliding downward into a lengthy tunnel, like a skier on a steep mountain. After a few minutes I decided I'd made a mistake, when suddenly my light raised a glint that beckoned from the tunnel's end.

I emerged into an immense chamber. Radiant light bounced from walls and floor covered in gold. The room contained giant pillars, also gold plated, the size of the columns in the Hypostyle Hall of Egypt's Karnak Temple, except these appeared to be set in a circle rather than straight lines. I approached the closest pillar and embraced it with my arms, able to reach only half its circumference. A type of hieroglyphs, more like hieratic script, was etched into the soft yellow metal, wrapping the column like wallpaper. Something about the writing licked at my subconscious. I ran a glow of light up the eighty-foot pillar, catching a flash from the ceiling. My breath stopped at the impossible task of gold-plating the top of a massive cavern. I looked closer at the carvings in the golden pillar and saw what was wrong:

They were too deep. In a burst of perception, I realized the huge column wasn't gold-covered. It was solid gold.

I moved to the wall where my fingers inspected a twisted design. The half-inch deep incisions had not been carved in thin gold plating. A memory of George on the first day we met popped in front of me like a holograph. "*This,*" he had said, spreading his arms to the landscape, "*is the source of the greatest gold deposit in the world.*" I had discounted George as a fuddled fanatic, but now I had to explain my own experience. This chamber was once filled wall to wall with gold, melted over the heat of a newly forming planet. Prehistoric civilizations mined out the room, carving designs in the gold pillars and walls to leave behind a sacred temple.

Placed by the east wall were stone boxes in various sizes. Some were open, filled with colors that sparkled in my light, emeralds, rubies, turquoise, sapphires, and surprisingly, abalone shells. I grinned at the logic of valuing mother-of-pearl in the same category as precious gems and considered putting a shell in my pack as a souvenir. Mary's words flew at my face: "*If you take the smallest thing from the temple, just one jewel, even a pebble off the floor...*" she had smiled at the words, "*...I get to kill you.*" The vision of Mary's knife shivering in a tree unsettled my plan. Considering the risk, I might as well steal some jewels and have something valuable. I gathered a handful of colorful stones, planning to swallow a few, calculating the time needed for them to make their way to the light of day. But Mary would track me into the forest and see the evidence of my theft, watching me sift through...I couldn't finish the thought and returned the jewels to their stone container.

Exquisitely crafted necklaces, rings, gold bracelets, and ear loops spilled from the boxes. Statues of animals stood on the golden floor, resembling dragons, alligators, cats and snakes. Hundreds of masks captured my attention with familiar designs in gold, coral, shell, and jade mosaics, all with large round ear spools attached, typical of the Aztec Empire in Mexico. A tax of ten masks a year was required from the outlying areas, sent to the capitol of Tenochtitlan.

It appeared that the majority of the tribute had ended here, in the American version of Aladdin's Cave. If Cortez saw only a portion of this wealth when he conquered Montezuma, it was no wonder he refused to accept its loss, and no mystery why the Spanish spent three hundred years trying to find it again. But the treasure of Montezuma had been returned to its source in the Uinta Mountains, hidden in the Temple of Towats, guarded by the Ute Indians. I fleetingly considered the idea that the Utes were descendants of the original Aztec group that transferred Montezuma's treasure to the caverns five hundred years ago.

I made my way to the center of the cavern where nine pillars surrounded me, the riches of lost civilizations scattered across the shining yellow floor. My floodlight scanned the area and hit the south wall where it rested dully on a large throne carved of stone, elevated on a platform. The starkness of gray rock against surrounding gold made a conspicuous contrast. At floor level in front was an altar with carved troughs, designed to collect sacrificial blood. I questioned why the gods needed to feed on constant death and examined closer. There was no fresh or dried stain on the rock, indicating sacrifice hadn't been done recently. I turned my attention to other objects.

On the walls at either side of the throne, facing each other, leaned two golden solar disks, about seven feet tall and several inches thick. The disks represented the sun, its rays emanating from the center of a Celtic cross design, ivy vines twined around it. Between the rays, signs and symbols were carved in an obvious writing system, neither hieroglyphic nor cuneiform. Given the Celtic center, maybe the writing was Ogam, which meant that two clues in the temple pointed to prehistoric Wales and Ireland. But diffusion, the theory that ancient world civilizations traveled to America, received no support in the scientific community. The very thought was unprofessional. Celtic creatures and a smattering of Ogam would not be sufficient proof.

I turned my attention back to the massive wheels. It would be impossible to move them into the chamber through the tunnels I had followed. The lower entrance was described by Pox as a belly crawl, so that way couldn't have been used, either. There must have been a third access to bring these massive artifacts into the temple. I let possible theories slide away and continued pawing through the treasures like a child playing with pebbles. My goal was not lost entrances.

At one-thirty I noticed my light was fading, not a problem since extra batteries were in my pack. I still had plenty of time. Scar had instructed me to return by five-thirty, which left three hours to explore with one hour to get back to the real world. Resolving to go as far and fast as possible in my remaining time, I decided to save power and switched from flood to low beam. I cringed at the circle of dark that trespassed into my personal space. A tunnel on the east wall jumped into my vision from the half-lit gloom. I hadn't noticed it earlier because it was excavated from the gold walls of the cavern and blended like camouflage. Without light, it yawned its shadow at me. *"The main room,"* George had said, *"is as big as a three-story house, with nine corridors leading to other rooms."* Nine corridors, nine pillars. I visually lined up the tunnel to the pillar next to me, then walked to a second pillar and studied the wall opposite it. Another opening appeared. Encouraged, I assumed each pillar pointed to an additional room in the Towats Temple complex and entered the cavity.

At the end of the passage was a smaller golden room with one pillar. My beam of lesser light flitted across statues and three-foot high jars full of gems before I saw an Aztec calendar resting against the far wall, the sun god Tonatiuh in the center. Falling from his mouth was a sharp pointed tongue like the tip of a knife, while his hands held the blood-soaked hearts of his victims. The same grotesque calendar was in the museum in Mexico City, but its complicated design was carved in stone, not gold. I returned to the main cavern, determined to see all nine rooms of the temple.

The next corridor led to a 9x12 gilded room with an eight foot ceiling. A long stone table in the center, complete with benches, could seat ten men for…what? Dinner? I glided my hand over the smooth stone and noted that anyone who sat there must have been very tall. I crawled onto the bench, feeling like a child at the grown-up table, my shoulders barely clearing its top. I stood, not believing the table was used for a picnic.

Rows of stone boxes, 3x4x3 feet deep, lined the walls and I peered inside. Round gold plates with holes in the center were slipped over dowels fitted into the bottom of the box. Each box held three dowels of plates in a two-foot stack. Inscribed on the gold plates was a kind of writing in a precision that could only be accomplished with a metal tool. Here was true treasure, the records of a people lost in time.

I transferred two of the heavy round discs to the table. The flashlight's skinny beam created a typical dark circle on the plates. Even though the batteries were nearly spent, I reluctantly switched to the flood lamp for fuller lighting. I kneeled on the cold bench, hunched over the plates, intent on discovering a pattern in the symbols. Circular lines divided the plate into three sections. I turned the disc like an old-fashioned record player to follow the squared letters in their endless positions: an X; an upside-down Y with one arm longer than the other; a repeating Delta symbol in the four cardinal directions. There were no pictographs, no birds or ox heads, only a variety of straight marks representing the probable phonetic sounds of a dead language.

I removed two more discs from a dowel and set them next to their counterparts for comparison. A linguist could decipher this like a mystery code, separating the signs that occurred most often, analyzing frequent groupings. *"If I could smuggle just one plate,"* I thought, *"into the hands of a genius like Champollion, history could be expanded, re-written, the knowledge and skills of past civilizations open to our understand…"* The light dimmed, jerking my attention from the plates to my watch. It was five-fifteen. I had stayed too long at the fair.

Panic provided fuel to fly me out of the room, leaving four gold plates on the stone table. There was no time to change flashlight batteries. Pushing the switch to low, I rushed past the labyrinth of pillars, stumbling over things that didn't glitter back at me. The tunnel I had entered was in the north wall, but the light was too dim to show the flashlight compass. It took an agonizing amount of time to locate the opening and dive onto the sloping incline. There were steep places that required a hands and knees crawl, the flashlight inside my shirt providing a pale glow. When I finally exited, breathing heavily from exertion, I knew the fastest way to my rope was a diagonal run across the room. But I didn't know the size of the expanse. The safer plan was to follow the wall, retracing my steps past the old Indian chiefs.

At the bars of gold bullion the flashlight finally failed. Plunged into darkness, I replaced the now useless piece of technology in my shirt and blindly felt my way along the stacked bars until I heard the rattle of bones under my feet. My hands followed the wall as I kicked aside metal helmets until I found a jutting peg, a clue the rope was near. When I touched its long, rough fibers, I grasped the lifeline in gratitude, bowing my head reverently to thank a god I didn't know and never spoke to. As someone once pointed out, there are no atheists in foxholes…or in this case, mountain bowels.

Stepping lightly against the peg stairs for support, I pulled myself up the rope, wishing I had taken some precious time to find my leather gloves in the dark. A wood step broke under my foot and the rope slid like a cheese grater through my hands, slicing skin from the palms. I cried out in pain, scrambled to find another peg, and worked through the hurt with a mind control mantra I had learned in India. It had rarely succeeded before, but it was all I had and I repeated the hypnotic sound, still climbing the offending rope while resting on unreliable pegs. The trick failed and I moaned my way to the top. I would have to apologize for leaving blood on Scar's rope.

I pulled myself into the black tunnel, crawled along the rope to its bowline knot, and stood upright to prop one shoulder onto the right side of the wall. I left the belay rope on the floor and began my slither home, shoulder against the wall for guidance, hands pressed under my armpits to stop the stinging. I didn't try to recall the number of paces in each turn, but allowed the tunnel to guide me through its endless dark maze until a diffuse light outlined an edge of rock. Stumbling to a slow jog, my shoulder still hitting the wall, I cried out to the waiting men above me, "I'm here! I made it!" Gratitude surfaced again, this time for the horse that would pull me up. I didn't have to use my hands.

During the next few steps, my eyes became accustomed to the filtered light of an ending day. I checked my watch. The dials pointed at six-ten. I hurried toward the exit, yelling gibberish I barely understood, mostly 'no' and "don't leave,' and 'please be there." Crouching through the fissure I reached the slit to the world outside and faced the sure knowledge of what that extra hour in the Temple of Towats had cost.

The harness and rappel rope were gone.

CHAPTER TWENTY-FOUR

There are five stages of grief. The first is denial. I fell to my knees and pawed through the dirt to find the harness, as if it had melted into the hard soil and could be pulled out. My frantic search brought me to the precarious horizontal beam, which I used for support while poking my head from the fissure. I expected to see a dangling rope and harness, hoping it might have slipped from the tunnel passage, unlikely but possible. It hadn't.

"Hey, I'm here!" I yelled up into the empty air, balanced with wounded hands on the tree trunk. "It's a good joke, but it's over." The instruction to be back by five-thirty wasn't a serious threat. Scar wouldn't strand me. I waited. There was no rope, no harness, and no response.

I backed into the fissure to sit against the wall. There was some mistake. This couldn't be happening to me. *"We have to leave at five-thirty,"* Scar had said, *"whether you're here or not."* Denial changed to guilt. The men had waited until their own descent off the mountain became dangerous. My failure to return on time broadened into the malfunction of my entire life. Everything I'd ever done wrong crowded into my conscious mind, compacting me into a ball of remorse. My insufferable behavior, the obnoxious statements I'd made, white lies I'd told to cover blunders, the use of hurtful sarcasm to display my cleverness, all combined to prove I was an ugly frog. No wonder everyone despised me. I wallowed in stage two guilt until shadows from a setting sun entered the crevice and diverted attention from my repellent past to the dismal future.

In the waning light, I removed my small backpack to assess what was left. Two batteries, one stick of jerky, a small bag of dried apples, three protein bars with leftover wrappers, eight mylar packs of water, three empty. In the collection were five plastic toilet bags, two filled. I'd been careful not to defile the Temple of Towats, restricting food and water to avoid using the inconvenient quart bags. But eight hours carries demands, and the needs had to be met. It galled me to know that I'd carried the full bags in my pack all day for later burial, only to find that I'd been the one disposed of.

Sight of the bags transformed guilt to irritation. Surely the Indians knew the size of the caverns. They should have given a grace period, told me to be back at five-thirty, realistically planning to leave at six. What kind of monsters would abandon someone for the sake of a few minutes? The third stage of grief is anger and I flew into fury. "Indian imbeciles," I shouted toward the nearly dark opening. "Callous creeps." Shaking with rage, I grabbed the bags of sewage and tossed them over the cliff. There was barely enough light to see the contents splatter on the rocks below. "That's what I think of you," I shrieked and followed verbal insults with food wrappings and empty water bags. It felt good to litter the Indian reservation. When I returned to the backpack, I found two aspirin wrapped in foil. They had prepared me for a headache. How thoughtful.

The flashlight still hung heavy in my shirt and I removed it to replace batteries. I envisioned leaving the dead batteries on the sacrificial altar of the main temple room. The thought made me smile. I regretted throwing my two plastic waste bags over the cliff. They would have looked great on the lap of a mummified chieftain. I should also have kept the food wrappers to scatter on the gold floor between the pillars, but I could still have a picnic in the library. I laughed out loud at the thought of eating on the great stone table, leaving crumbs and garbage as witness to my sacrilege. The anger phase was powerful. At that moment, I knew I wanted to return to the caverns and find the lost passage out.

The tunnel's twists and turns were familiar and I switched to a low light until the final stretch when the rope tied to a spike stopped me before the drop. I removed my shirt, careful not to pop any buttons, and placed my arms in the upper sleeves, gathering fabric into my palms. For now, the light source was squeezed into the band of my jeans. *"Five days ago,"* I counted the time, *"I destroyed a shirt to save Pope's life. Now I'm shredding one to save my hands."* A crooked grin sawed into the corners of my mouth. *"At this rate I'll run out of long-sleeved shirts before I get home."*

The word "home" brought a vision of my small, three-bedroom stucco dwelling in Scottsdale surrounded by desert landscape. It was the place where sidewalks got so hot in the summer you could smell your sandals burning. Even cockroaches danced across the street. But on Christmas Day people walked to the corner convenience store barefoot. Home was a front room painted red, a bright backdrop for floor to ceiling pictures of world heritage sites. One entire room was set aside as a library. 'Home' did not include the Victorian house in the Uinta mountains.

My feet touched the cavern floor and I put the ruined shirt on. It took awhile to find the leather gloves, kicked aside when I had scrambled up the rope earlier. I put them in my pack and jogged along the now familiar north end of the cavern, passing gold bars and withered Indian chiefs to the carved portal of the Towats Temple. I figured if I kept the beam on low, I could get twelve hours of light to help me find the way out, starting with the nine pillars that pointed to nine caverns. One of them had to be the exit.

The golden room was startling in its beauty, like a tantalizing Circe who mesmerized the men of Ulysses to relax their guard and enjoy the pleasures offered. I shook my head to clear it and strode to the throne, placing my dead flashlight batteries upright in the center of the sacrificial platform. It had to be done, a symbol of my disdain for the ancient gods who demanded innocent blood.

I faced east to follow the route, bypassing the room of records that captivated me beyond the time limit. I explored the fifth cavern and its treasures, yanking myself away to return to the main hall and find the sixth cavern, the seventh, eighth…all large rooms with untold wealth, but no discernable exits. The ninth tunnel in the west wall was my final hope. My watch showed I had already spent three hours in the search for an exit. I stared at the passage, afraid to enter, fearing it, too, would be a dead end.

To my right rested the huge, taller-than-a-man sun disc leaning against the west wall, its twin across the room glinting like an eastern sunrise. I compared the seven-foot-tall golden circle to the little five-foot tunnel that led to the ninth chamber. Earlier that day I'd puzzled over how the huge disc was brought into the temple. It was too big to fit the tunnels leading to the nine caverns. The door had to be…or maybe the sun disc was created in the cavern…but the door might cover its….

Circe had enchanted me into idiocy. Stupid, dim-witted, brainless, obtuse, I had wasted all those hours exploring tunnels that were too small to bring in the huge sun discs. With resolute steps I walked to the edge of the giant gold circle and kneeled to peer into a triangular gap between the disc and the wall. It was large enough to admit me. Two feet of crawling brought me to an opening on my right. I entered, aware of a difference in the air, a feeling of space above my head.

Standing tall, I pointed my flashlight toward the ceiling. There was no gold to reflect back at me. I switched to a floodlight and estimated the height of the tunnel at eight feet, its sides four. An army of ancient men had gouged a tunnel into the rock to bring the treasures of Montezuma into the Temple of Towats. The intensive labor of it left me stunned before I threw my arms up and out, spurting squeals of joy at discovering the exit.

The floodlight allowed me to move rapidly along the straight route, conscious of excavation marks on the floor and walls, alert to any writing that might have been carved.

Suddenly, my light bounced back from a wall of rocks and boulders, a floor to ceiling barrier.

The stage of anger did a lightning return to denial. My hands pressed the walls for hidden openings, repeating the mantra, "*This can't be happening.*" I scoured the blockade with light, hoping to find a space, until the truth could no longer be denied. The exit had been sealed.

Hope raised possibilities. "*Maybe there's a passage behind the other disc.*" I spun to face the interior of the tunnel, stumbling over my feet, crawling back into the golden chamber. With my radar set for the east wall, I barely noticed the dead batteries on the sacrificial altar as I passed. The crevice between the sun disc and wall invited me in to spit me out the other side. I turned to make a slower pass, but the wall was flat. There was no exit. Pulling myself to stand, I leaned my head against the edge of the massive gold circle, thoughts scrambled like eggs with a wire whisk. "*It's a giant disc,*" I thought, "*or is it spelled 'disk' with a 'k'? Disc or Disk?*" The insane self-talk seemed logical at the time. "*I think the British use a 'c' ending. Americans use 'k'. I'll look it up when I get home.*" At the word "home" my situation loomed hopeless and I slid in despair to the gold floor, letting the flashlight roll from my hands.

I entered the bargaining stage of grief, making deals with God and the devil equally, keeping all options open. At some point I noticed that the beam of light traveling across the floor hit my watch. I thought the time would be close to ten p.m. but both dials were on three. Confused, I flicked at the crystal. It couldn't be three in the morning. I counted numbers on my fingers to grasp that I'd been underground for eighteen hours.

There's a report of a French scientist who lived in a cave for two months without a watch, calendar, or the sun. His research showed that in the absence of clocks, psychological time is compressed. When colleagues outside contacted him to say the time was up, he thought he had another month to go. Interesting, but irrelevant. My random thoughts did nothing for a solution.

A quote from the Egyptian Amarna letters came to mind. *"In my brother's country,"* the King of Mittani wrote to Pharoah Ahkenaten, *"gold is as plentiful as dust. May my brother send me much gold in order that my brother may honor me."* Cold from the golden floor filled me to the top of my shoulders. I sat in the middle of more gold than the ancient kings had ever seen and I'd swap it all for a sweater and a warm place to sleep.

My alter ego took over, bless her heart. *"Pull it together, Matt,"* she whispered from somewhere inside. *"Think."* I cast about for something in the cave I could use, anything soft and thick to comfort me. But my surroundings were metals, gems, statues, thrones, and crowns, all hard and dead. The water was gone, which meant I might have three days to survive. The bargaining stage plummeted to defeat. I would die here, my bones added to the mummy collection.

The mummies! Their treasures of animal skins and rotting blankets once came from the living world. I could at least die in comfort. I cranked my stiff body to a standing position and staggered across the great hall to enter the sloping passage leading to the first chamber. It took ten minutes to reach the upper cavern, another ten to find the mummies. Awareness of time became a lifeline to the real world. I remembered the sun and moon, fresh breezes thrusting through tree limbs, animal droppings fertilizing earth. I thought of Zeus, his intelligent brown eyes wide with questions. My life had been plump with pleasure. Gratitude prepared me to accept death.

My flashlight scanned human skin that resembled shrunken apples carved to look like faces. There were animal hides cracked with age and blankets decomposed to near dust. I finally found a relatively recent burial, a chief with three wives and two children, their woven covers still showing muted colors in the Ute design. I removed my backpack to use as a pillow. "Move over," I said to the wives, burrowing between them, their children covering my feet.

A musty smell rose to assault my nose and I pulled my shirt over my face, hoping there weren't any deadly viruses that would kill me like the curse of King Tut. I laughed at the silliness of such a precaution. It didn't matter anymore. I switched off the light and welcomed the blackness, inertia keeping me from moving, my body heat warming the tattered blankets and carcasses of my bedfellows. I shifted to the final stage of grief: acceptance.

Sleep followed. A gentle humming sound, like a tune, drifted over me, a lullaby with words that hovered beyond recognition. My hair ruffled as if a hand swept it off my face. My mother used to do that. She couldn't carry a tune, but she tried anyway and the noise she produced had always soothed me to sleep, like now, a sweet melody that abruptly ended when she kicked my foot.

"Get up," she said.

Surprised at her roughness, I stirred and mumbled, "Mom?"

"Get up!" the harsh voice commanded, her foot punting the seat of my pants.

I rolled to a sitting position, blinded by full light in my face. This was not my Mother. The female voice held venom. "How dare you desecrate the sacred burials."

"Mary?" I pushed to my feet as the two mummies on either side of me flopped into the hollow I had made. "I am *so* glad to see you…" she kept the light solidly in my eyes and I added, "…if I could see you." I tussled with the straps of my pack, flailing my arms in all directions. "Thanks for coming back for me. I don't suppose you brought water."

She reached in her daypack and slapped a mylar bag in my hand, then turned and strode toward the west part of the cavern, the area I hadn't explored. "I voted not to get you out," she said, the words tossed over her shoulder, "but it was easier to bring you out alive than drag you out dead. I didn't want your corpse stinking up the sacred place."

I was too busy tearing the edge of packaged water with my teeth to consider a retort. Almost skipping with joy behind her, I switched on my lamp to follow her retreating figure, nicely rounded in a pair of blue pants, a long sleeved light blue shirt tucked in at the narrow waist. She was a lovely woman, her black hair in a single braid so heavy it barely moved with the rhythm of her gait.

My opinion of her softened. She must have searched a long time for me, considering the size of the Temple of Towats, with caves leading through tunnels moving into caverns. Her gruff exterior hid a softer side. I felt the stirrings of friendship. "How did you find me in this huge place?" I asked.

"All too easy," she answered. "You snore."

CHAPTER TWENTY-FIVE

We angled the cave's expanse, bypassing leather sacks and bags sewn shut with sinew. Gold bars, stacked against the west wall, were marked *Ano Dom 1675 V.* They belonged to me, taken from the cave on my property. I had not forgiven the Indians for their theft, but empathized with their beliefs. Superstition carries surprising power. Towats is like the dragon in *The Hobbit*, gathering and guarding treasure he can't use, rising in fury and vengeance when a single bauble is taken from his cave.

A six-foot high tunnel opening was next to my gold bars. If I had gone left instead of right when I first rappelled into the cavern, I would have seen it. Mary and I entered the opening, the walls close enough to be touched by outstretched arms. The Indians must have transferred my gold by relaying each twenty-pound bar from hand to hand. I felt oddly guilty at the trouble I'd caused them, like feeling pity for a frustrated robber who can't get all your belongings in his bag.

A few minutes of walking brought us to an abrupt dead end. A mass of boulders barred the way.

"Looks like the wrong exit," I said to Mary, my attitude slightly taunting, a touch of glee at her mistake. "The tunnel behind the gold disk in the throne room is obstructed, too."

Mary turned her flashlight in my eyes. "You managed to contaminate everything, didn't you." Even when Mary was wrong, she could defeat me.

"I was looking for a way out," I said in my defense.

She began removing her backpack while spitting the words, "The tunnel you saw was the original entrance, blocked a long time ago."

Mary dropped to her knees to push her pack into a small opening at the bottom of the barricade. She flattened herself to follow the pack, wiggling in a commando crawl until her feet disappeared. It looked like the boulders were eating her as she struggled.

I lowered to my stomach and followed Mary into the breach, trying not to think of what it would feel like if the blocks above my head collapsed. Instead, I mentally counted the squirms of my body. Both Mary and I sounded like a life-support system as we wheezed our way through the hole.

I heard Mary scramble, then the faraway sound of small rocks tumbling against each other. Sudden light surrounded me inside the restrictive channel, not man-made yellow stuff but the warm, white luminosity of genuine sunlight. I pushed my pack through the exit and felt Mary snatch it away. She was already checking for stolen goods.

I slithered from the tomb, the warmth of the sun caressing my arms as I inched on my belly over shale until my passage from the tunnel was complete. At level ground I lifted my head to see the alternate entrance into the temple of Towats. It was invisible behind the barrier of boulders.

Rolling on my back to face the sun, I closed my eyes to protect them from its brilliance. A wisp of satin hit my face. I recognized the feel of the blindfold that Mary had thrown at me. I put it in my hand, still reveling in the glory of fresh air and sunlight. Not even Mary could take that away from me.

When I had strength to sit up, I asked for water while fitting the elastic band of the blindfold around my head. It took massive self-control not to focus on my surroundings, but Mary wouldn't like it if I attempted to identify my position. She put a round canteen of water into my hands and jerked me by my belt to a standing position.

I drank like a pig at the trough, uncouth and noisy, while Mary patted me down. I hadn't been explored like that since the honeymoon with what's-his-name. When she was satisfied, she used my belt to pull me to my horse. Her disappointment at not finding smuggled goods prompted her to speak threatening words. "If you think anything of your life," her voice hissed in my ear, "make this trip your last one."

"You know, Mary," I couldn't resist saying, "maybe I swallowed some of those jewels in the cavern. You might want to follow me during bathroom breaks for the next couple of days, just in case." Her grunt of disgust delighted me into a wide grin. I climbed onto Blackfoot, his muscles twitching, his warm neck pleasant to my hands as I caressed it.

During the next undefined amount of time, the blindfold created darkness out of day. With my horse led by the reins, I held to the pommel with nothing to do but jostle and think. Mary could have planted a small jewel in my pocket to find during her search, giving her an excuse to execute me. But she didn't. Perhaps my cooperation, with arms and legs spread for inspection, diffused her anger. The silly black blindfold with white lace might have added a pathetic, clownish touch to my appearance. Maybe gutting me wasn't worth the effort of having to clean her knife.

Somewhere in the loneliness of the plodding gait of horses, with bird sounds in the air and breezes in my hair, other thoughts appeared. It was possible that Mary started life as a nice little girl, but something went wrong, distorting her into a hateful, vengeful woman. Life is indiscriminately cruel to everybody, either grinding us to tiny particles or firing us into strength.

I heard the squeak of saddles, a rustle and bump of men mounting horses that snorted and stomped the earth. We had reached camp. I touched the elastic around my head. "Can I take this off now?" The sizzle of water on a fire and human feet shuffling through dirt told me the group was breaking camp. No one spoke. I assumed they were angry about the delayed trip home. My broken promise had cost everyone another day.

Air stirred around me when someone passed to the rear of Blackfoot and tied something behind the saddle, probably my bedroll. "Look," I started lamely, "I'm sorry I made everybody wait. Can I take off the blindfold?" There was a tug on the horse when the item was cinched into place and the person moved to my left side. "Go ahead," a quiet male voice advised. I ripped the mask off my eyes in time to see the back of Pox walking toward his horse.

Above him in the morning sun, the illusion of a medieval castle outlined itself in a protuberance of the closest mountain.

Six horses lined up to move west, with me filling my assigned fifth place. The silly sleep mask ended up shoved in a saddlebag while I retrieved jerky and dried apples for breakfast. Someone had already filled my water bottle, in case I survived the Towats Temple. My trusty watch told me it was 10:25, and I enjoyed a renewed fantasy of power over time because I could name it.

While Blackfoot swayed in monotonous rhythm, my mind provided a tune between beats. *"The Old Gray Mare She Ain't What She Used Ta' Be,"* changed to the Latin rhythm of *"La Bamba"* which ended in *"Ninety-Nine Bottles of Beer on the Wall."* That one lasted all the way to lunch, where we took a break and let the animals graze.

In the need to make amends, I tracked down Scar and Longnose. They were sitting on a rise of grass chewing at tough pemmican.

"Thank you, " I began, "for an experience I will never forget."

Longnose answered, his jaw taut in anger. "You'd *better* forget. If you tell anyone what you have seen…" He let the words drop into the dirt.

Scar finished his thought, minus the force. "Do you understand how serious it is if you also break your promise of silence?"

Two promises: one of silence, the other to return on time. "About being late," I said humbly. "I want to apologize for that."

"Why were you late?" Scar's question deserved some worthy reason, which I didn't have.

"There was so much to see," I raised my arms in a gesture of joking, "I forgot to watch the time."

Longnose wasn't amused. "When you return to your world, will you forget to be silent the way you forgot the time?"

They were making too big a deal of my being late. Something else was happening. "I won't disclose the secret. I made an oath to---"

Scar cut me off. "Do you understand our oath?" Emphasis on *our*.

"Uh…not completely." *Actually, not at all.*

"We are the keepers of the yellow metal. We have taken a blood oath to protect it."

"Whose blood?" I tried to speak casually, but the sacrificial altar in the throne room flashed before me.

"Whatever blood it takes," Scar answered, "to keep people away from the temple." His attitude was matter-of-fact. "We prefer scare tactics, like cutting off fingers, but in cases where people have seen the treasure, death is the permanent solution."

A visceral fear stabbed my stomach. "Do you mean me?"

Longnose volunteered his piece. "Mary thought you were dangerous when you moved into the Doctor's house." The tall Indian rose to his feet. "She offered to kill you then, but we voted to wait."

Scar also stood. "Your actions have been good," I detected sympathy in his voice, "but your word is not."

He was right. I had lied the minute they showed up with the horses, telling them I could ride, pretending to know how to camp, staying in the caverns when they had to leave. My eyes had seen Spanish gold bars and the Towats treasure. I knew way too much and they no longer trusted me. "Look, guys," I laughed nervously. "I couldn't describe my own kitchen, much less how to find a cavern in these mountains."

Scar shook his head. "You wouldn't have to give directions." His eyes went dark. "If you tell anyone that you've seen the Towats treasure, the swarming would start again."

"But I promise not---"

Longnose and Scar walked away. I was in deep doom.

The trek continued. I contemplated possible solutions. Apologies had already failed. If I galloped into the mountains, they'd catch me. If I hid, they'd find me. My only hope was to talk to Pox, their apparent leader, and convince him that I could be trusted. The trouble was, I had proven otherwise. Still, Pox was my best bet for survival.

That night at camp we had fish and ashcakes again. They were still feeding me, which I took as a good sign. Surely they wouldn't waste the effort on someone they planned to sacrifice. But the mood was hazardous, like smooth water on the Grand Canyon seconds before you hit a number ten rapid.

After dinner I found Pox sitting on a long log, cleaning his fingernails with a Swiss army knife. I stood before him. He didn't acknowledge my presence so I stayed standing while giving the little speech I'd planned.

"Being an eye-witness to the temple of Towats," I began, "is the greatest honor I've ever had. I hope you know I would never betray your trust."

Pox moved the knife to his little finger and worked on dislodging dirt from the nail. I couldn't afford to leave. My only course was to keep my tongue wagging. "You know, I've never actually met you. After all we've been through together, I should know your name."

That got his attention. He raised his head, eyes unfriendly, to meet my face. "My name is consecrated to be shared with trusted family and friends."

His changed attitude toward me indicated the group had discussed my future and the decision leaned toward bleak. Pox was detaching himself, preparing for what had to be done. Mary was no doubt sharpening her knife.

I hurried into the next phase. "Pope told me the history of his name," I said, hoping that mentioning the young man would soften the mistrust. "I learned how the Indians were used as slaves in the Spanish mines. I'd like your permission to share that story when I get home." *O.K., I've announced that I expect to go home.*

"No," Pox quietly said. He returned to his fingernail duties.

"Fair enough," I fumbled through the words, searching for a point. "I can see that if I mention Spanish mines, it might send people searching for gold." *Two strikes out. Think, Matt.* "I really came over to talk to you about a problem I need help with." *Help me get home again, stop Mary from her blood lust, explain to Scar that I can be trusted.* "I'm in a little trouble," *a lot of trouble, huge.* The next words flowed without thought from an unfamiliar source. "I own a haunted house that won't sell." My eyes rounded in surprise at the direction I was headed. "The IRS wants an inheritance tax too large to pay. I can't develop the gold mine under the house because it belongs to the reservation. I'm wondering if I could ask…if you'd consider…accepting a quit-claim deed to the Hathenbruck Estate?"

There it was. I had called "Uncle" and quit the game before I got killed. Pox paused the survey of his thumb and glanced up at me. "You want to give us the property?"

My smile made a wide cut into my cheeks. "I'm not sure who you mean by 'us.' Does the whole Ute tribe know there's a gold mine under the Hathenbruck house? Do they all know the location of the Towats Temple?"

Pox rested his arms over his knees and spoke to the ground. "Too many of our people no longer believe the traditions of their fathers. The majority can't be trusted as keepers." He flipped the knife blade into its slot and placed it in a pocket. "Traditionally, there were twelve Elders who guarded the temple. There are only five of us now."

I did a head count of five men including Pope. "Where does Mary fit in?"

"Her father was a keeper. She understands how important the treasure is."

"I'd like to know that information myself. It seems to me your people could use the gold now, instead of waiting for the future. Has Towats told anybody his plans?"

Pox straightened his back and considered my question for a few seconds, an eternity in my mind. He scooted over to make room for me in a silent invitation to sit. The gesture was a Hallelujah Chorus to my strung-tight nerves. I felt a faint spark of hope and settled at the edge of the log.

Pox spoke furtively, as if he shared a confidence with me. "Do you know what would happen to my people if they were suddenly made rich by the standards of your civilization?"

My best move was no move. I let him continue. "They would cease to be 'The People.' They have already forgotten much of their heritage. If they had sudden wealth, they would become…" his face turned to mine, and I sensed a slight smile in his dark eyes, "…like your people."

I didn't allow the insult to get below the surface. This was not the time for a debate titled *my civilization is better than yours*. I couldn't afford to win under my current circumstance. I laughed instead. "Well then, what name should we put on the quit-claim papers?"

"I don't want it," Pox quickly said. "None of us do." I watched a calculated evaluation happening behind the man's scarred face. "Pope keeps one foot in our world, the other in yours. Give him the house."

"I'm not sure that's fair," I said. "Isn't that like assigning the hardest job to the person who didn't show up?"

Pox nodded slightly. "He can handle the responsibility."

"Can he pay the $200,000 inheritance tax and property taxes and…" Pox's eyebrows arched as if he questioned my sanity. "Right," I answered. "I suppose Towats will let him take a bag of gold nuggets from under the house when he needs it. There's a supply for several lifetimes."

Pox seemed as relieved at the solution as I was. "Pope's work as a lawyer will make it seem natural for him to own the house and land. No one will question where he gets the money."

"As long as he doesn't get greedy." I shouldn't have released those words into the air. I had to backstroke my way out. "One of *my* people, of course, would steal the gold and run with it. It's a good thing Pope isn't from my civilization." So much for the debate on superior civilizations. One for the red men, zero for the ugly white lady. I stood to leave. Pox also stood.

"My name," he said slowly with dignity, "is Ouray. I am a keeper of the yellow metal."

He had given me his sacred name. There was nothing I could say to such a gift. I bowed my head to acknowledge I understood, and turned to leave as the gentle, kind man sat back on the log.

I didn't notice a pow-wow among the Indians. I didn't even see whispers along a grape-vine, but the doom of judgment lifted. Mary had made herself scarce. Scar and Longnose approached me as I checked my horse. I turned to silently greet them.

"My name," Scar said, "is Nicatat. I am a keeper of the yellow metal."

Longnose stepped forward. "I am Capote. I am also a keeper of the yellow metal."

The statements were too solemn for a smile. I said a humble "Thank you."

I felt the presence of someone behind me and turned as Squinteye announced, "I am Ankotash, a servant of Towats. I keep the yellow metal."

In my mind, I had assigned nick-names to the Indians, but never spoke them aloud. Now, I felt unworthy to use their sacred names. Scar-Nicotat and Longnose-Capote left an opening for me by the fire. I placed four hot rocks in my bedroll and spent a warm night.

CHAPTER TWENTY-SIX

The taste, texture, and aroma of food has its own storage slot in the brain. I can still remember eating a perfect mango in Mexico, taste Massaman Curry in Thailand, and breathe the odor of Durian fruit, like dog breath and vomit, in Cambodia. The impact of food lingers like other memorable events. For me, breakfast of fish and ashcakes that morning at the Indian camp in the Uinta Mountains counts as the best meal of my life. It was also the first meal, considering I was allowed to live beyond yesterday.

Squinteye-Ankotash acted as cook and offered me two ashcakes hot off the edge of the firepit. He knew I'd sneak the second one anyway. As usual, there was an absence of banter, no ribald jokes or verbal plans for the day, but vibrations sent into the space around us reached my soul as a melody of peace.

My clean-up task was to scatter unused firewood back into the forest. I passed Mary washing utensils in a stream. With my arms holding small logs, their dead branches scratching at my chin, I stopped a few feet away from her. Humans have a sixth sense that tells them someone is watching. Mary looked up. Our eyes locked until we both looked away. No one spoke until she finished her work and stood.

"I went to the cave to kill you." She wiped her wet hands on her multi-colored skirt. "Everyone agreed you couldn't be trusted and it had to be done. I was willing." She talked as if I wasn't there, her eyes directed at something across the stream. "It would have been easy. You were already sleeping with the dead. I could have made it permanent."

I absorbed her words and found the courage to ask, "What stopped you?"

She picked up the wash pan full of clean dishes and settled it against her stomach. "They spoke to me."

I did my usual headlong run into a faux pas. "Who could speak," I said, one eyebrow raised quizzically, "in a dead cavern?" Her eyes narrowed and I knew I had stomped on sacred stuff. My next words were formed carefully. "I'd like to know who to thank for saving my life."

It was an adequate recovery and Mary visibly softened. "The spirit of the old ones told me in my heart that Towats had a purpose for you." She shifted the bowl full of dishes to rest against her hip. "The men were surprised when I brought you back alive."

My breathing got shallow at what might have happened. "How can I properly thank Towats and the old ones?"

Mary's reply was as sharp as her knife. "By keeping the promise of silence." She turned her back on me and walked toward camp.

"Mary," I called behind her. "What purpose does Towats have for me?"

She stopped and studied me as if I were an errant child who had missed the point of a lesson. "You will make it possible to keep the treasure safe until the time is right."

"Oh," I said, then covered my stupidity by asking, "How do I know when the time is right?"

"When your civilization dies," she announced with pleasure, "and Towats builds a better one." Mary couldn't have missed the shock on my face and happily shoveled dirt in it. "Your country is sick and decaying from the inside. It doesn't have long to live." I stood rigidly while she launched an addendum. "All civilizations fall. A thousand years ago, ours was not primitive. We had artisans, scientists and architects who built great monuments. We studied the sky to keep time much better than you do. But we caught the same diseases you have: low morals, high greed, pride, and corrupt leaders. Eventually we had wars until we destroyed each other." She offered one of her deadly smiles. "You're next."

I didn't have anything to counter the speech. Mary sauntered back to camp with her clean dishes while I finished spreading firewood through the forest.

Funny thing about journeys, it takes less time to return home…unless you're Odysseus fresh from the Trojan War and need ten years to find Ithaca. Our little group was the rule, not the exception, and our trip was standard. We did a rapid rewind of everything, the circular burial in the sagebrush with the tarnished bell in the center, the forest and waterfalls, the mountain cleavage shaped like a woman's bustline, and the dry, winding riverbed. Before I knew it, we had emerged from the woods to face my meadow and the yellow house half a football field away. The sun was in a three o'clock position, preparing to slide down the sky and disappear behind the cliff. My eyes focused on the dining room window, hoping to see Zeus's large face and paws on the sill. He wasn't there. I wondered how long it would take me to stop looking.

Our horses crushed long grass and tiny wild flowers under their iron shoes until we stopped at the edge of the dead zone. I waited for a ritual, maybe a brotherhood thing where you cut fingers and share blood. But no one moved or spoke ceremonial words. I hefted my numb body from the saddle and clung to the horn until my legs came to life and could hold me upright.

"Thank you." I said the words, knowing how inadequate they were, wishing my language had something more fervent to communicate appreciation. I shrugged off my lack of verbal skills and added, "When Pope is strong enough to sign the papers, I'll pack up and go home." Pox nodded and the group reined their mounts toward the north forest. I watched the six horserumps undulate with each step, their riders swaying on top. After four days of that action, the Shove-it would be a limousine of luxury.

I stared at the front door, loathe to enter and spend another night in the house. The stained glass windows bordering the door represented the colorful jaws of Hades, ushering me to a nightmare. It had been nineteen days since the adventure started in Arizona. My old life there seemed illusory, when the only serious problem was a broken air

conditioner. Taking deep breaths to clear the fear, I un-
locked the front door.

The chaos I'd made in the hall spread itself across the
carpet, the sledgehammer still leaned against the edge of
the wall cavity. Somehow, the disorder of plaster, lathe,
and chalky dust seemed common, even friendly, making
the house mundane in its mess. I grinned wickedly at the
thought that Mary would have to clean it when I left.

Since my pride no longer had anything to prove, I
avoided the hall and passed through the dining room to
the kitchen, hoping something was still edible. The fridge
assaulted me with mold and decay, an open carton of sour
milk seeping its smell into the air. Food had shriveled and
sprouted thin white tendrils, like people whose hair keeps
growing after they die. Or maybe the hair looks long because their heads shrink. Someday I'll look it up. I shut the
fridge door and searched the cupboards for cookies when
I noticed a lumpy burlap bag in the sink. It took a few seconds to recall the contents.

Potatoes. George had given me four potatoes, each con-
taining a gold nugget ready to harvest into, let's see…four
potatoes times maybe a hundred fifty bucks a nugget…a
virtual fortune of six hundred dollars. With plastic gloves
for protection against the quicksilver, I cut into each tuber,
laughing like a child on a treasure hunt when kernels of
yellow metal popped into my palm. Returning the mangled
veggies to their bag, I removed the gloves, washed my hands,
and grabbed clean clothes from the basket by the washer. A
toothbrush and paste completed necessities. I combed my
hair with my fingers and threw some sparse possessions into
the Shove-it for a dash to *Harvey's Hoard* before he closed for

the day. I would trade the nuggets for cash and, if all went well, I could spend the night at Motel Three-and-a-Half and enjoy a long, hot shower.

Thirty minutes later, I re-introduced myself to Harvey, who didn't remember me until I held out two pieces of golden chicken feed and asked for three hundred dollars.

"You know," he said in a deep rumble from his mountain of flesh, "two more pieces lowers the value of the first and I'll get stuck with three worthless novelties."

"No," I reasoned with him. "The buyer will have a unique set, earrings and a pendant. Let's see the first one you bought and we'll check how close the match is."

Harvey's face had the look of a child caught stealing money from his Mommy's purse. "I've sold it," he blurted, "so the idea of a matched set of three won't work. Too bad you only have two. I'll give you two hundred for the set."

"Tell you what," I returned one nugget to my pack and held out the other in my hand. "I'll sell you this single piece for a hundred dollars and go somewhere else to unload the rest."

"The rest?" Harvey's eyes widened. "How many do you have?"

"Four." I let the number settle in his head. "Enough to get me back to Arizona where I belong, if I can find the right buyer." I smiled sweetly at the fat man.

His double chin wiggled when he swallowed. "Where did they come from?" *He must have made a nice profit from the first nugget.*

"Thar's gold in them thar hills," I drawled. "These were in a campfire."

Harvey narrowed his eyes in disbelief. "They were just scattered inside?"

"I had to dig a little." *True. I dug into a bunch of potatoes.*

An ornate grandfather clock ticked loudly, the hands almost pointing to five o'clock. It was time to present the challenge. "Do you want one or not?"

Harvey put his big arm on the glass counter, trying to look relaxed, casual, uncaring. "I see you're in a hurry. I'll take all four off your hands for four hundred dollars."

I took a chance and called his bluff. "Thanks anyway, Harvey, but I think I can find a buyer down the road tomorrow." I put the nugget with the others and slowly zipped the pocket of my bag. I'd have to sleep in the car if Harvey didn't bite the bait.

The man circled his corpulent finger over the glass. "Alright," he finally said, "you win. Five hundred."

I took the cash in small bills, distributing it throughout my pack on the theory that the money would last longer if I had to search for it.

My next stop was the trailer court to find Pox. I walked up and down the dirt roads, passing rectangular metal boxes where families sheltered themselves, and hoped Pox or Mary would see me. An occasional aluminum awning stretched over cracked concrete patios. Strangled flowers struggled to survive in tiny patches of dirt. I paused at a playground where mud-crusted chubby children squealed as they climbed on a rusty jungle gym. Their poverty contrasted sharply with the extreme wealth that lay only a few days away. Two people living in this court knew where the treasure of Towats was hidden, but they would never use it. I stood in the dust to consider the irony of life.

The children pushed at each other in their climb to the slippery slide, toppling on whoever didn't move away fast enough at the bottom. Always there was laughter. Children don't know any better. They haven't yet learned about being poor and being rich.

"What are *you* doing here?" The words dripped hostility.

I spun toward the familiar tone of Mary's hate, trying to salvage balance from my sudden move. "Hello, Mary. I came to give a message to…" *What was his name? Not Pox.* "…Ouray. Tell him I'll be at Motel Six if he needs my signature before tomorrow afternoon." Mary dismissed me with one slow nod and I did a dignified retreat to the trailer at the corner. Once out of sight, I scurried to my car and drove to the motel where I handed over fifteen dollars, recalling the desperation I'd felt digging for small change the last time I'd been there. I considered writing a book titled, *"I've Been Broke and I've Had Money. Believe Me, Money is Better."* It would outsell the pottery textbook.

That night I enjoyed a hot shower, clean sheets, and a television set. I clicked on the one-eyed monster to fill the night with mind-numbing patter, like a mother's lullaby that keeps away ghosts made of vibrations.

CHAPTER TWENTY-SEVEN

A male voice yanked me awake.
"Do you wake up with a stiff neck and dull headache?"

I thrashed my way through tangled sheets to leap up and protect myself.

"Switch from your old, flat pillow to the new Plick pillow, guaranteed to produce---"

The still flickering television showed a pillow floating on sparkles of light. I sank to the edge of the bed, shoulders curled, eyes focused on my toes. When my heart rate returned to normal, I hurled the inferior motel pillow at the TV, suddenly aware of a stiff neck and dull headache.

The clock on the nightstand blinked the time, 10:30 on, off, on, off. If it was still night, I'd had three hours of sleep. A glow escaped the edge of the closed curtains to suggest daylight. I counted from 7:30 last night to 10:30 in the morning and ended up with the number fifteen. I forgot the point of the number and wobbled like a newborn calf to the bathroom.

The tub-shower enclosure was mine until noon so I used it for twenty minutes, relishing in the unending supply of luxurious hot water. At home in Scottsdale, a twenty-minute shower would turn cold. In the Hathenbruck house, a five-minute dribble of lukewarm water represented a celebration. Fifteen bucks of affluence had made me decadent. I planned a huge breakfast followed by ice cream. Then I'd drive to the Hathenbruck house for my typewriter and manuscript, say goodbye to bad vibrations, and return to the motel to work on the textbook until Pox arranged for the quit-claim deed. It was a good plan.

With my backpack flung over one shoulder, I followed the hall to the main desk where I waited patiently to be visible to the middle-aged woman behind the counter. She finally raised her eyes to catch me in full color.

"May I help you?"

I dropped a ten and five under her nose, feeling the power of paper money as opposed to a kid's coin collection. "I stayed in room 202 last night," I said in my best business tone. "I'll stay there again tonight."

The woman checked her register. "That will be fine, Dr. Howard." *Life is good,* I thought. *I'm titled and momentarily rich.*

I moved toward the exit and caught a peripheral vision of something large headed for me. I turned to face Pox-Ouray.

"We can go now," he said, his head bent slightly toward me. "Our Agent will meet us in Pope's hospital room when I call him."

"How long have you been waiting for me?" These guys were famous for hanging around.

Pox exhibited the smallest wrinkle at the corners of his mouth. "Mary told me you were here. You slept a long time. I guess we tired you out on the journey."

"Actually," I countered, "your threat of violent murder was an emotional drain. I needed time to replenish my life force."

His mouth moved from a slight smile to neutral. "It would not have been violent murder," he said. "Your death would have been swift and painless."

I soared to sarcasm. "How thoughtful of you."

Pox lowered his head and shook it, probably to get me out of it, then strode to the desk where he used their phone. I regretted the breakfast I was going to miss and grabbed several candy bars from a vending machine. We rode in his car, which was slightly uglier than mine.

Lack of conversation pickled me in acid discomfort. My culture doesn't do well with silence. Two people together, not talking, is a signal that something is wrong. There's a breach in the relationship, a crack in camaraderie. Attempts to repair the problem are required, including meaningless prattle or loud music.

Desperate for words to fill the air, I rummaged through my memory for a topic and settled on meaningless prattle. "So...uh...Ouray," I couldn't call him Pox out loud. It was my mental nickname for him based on his facial blemishes. "What's your opinion of the 1970s protest at Wounded Knee?"

He didn't answer immediately. "Dr. Howard," he finally said, "in the Indian world, if there's nothing to say it's okay not to speak."

We drove the curving canyon road to the valley below in one uninterrupted hour.

━━◁┼▷━━

The hospital was a no-nonsense gray building with six floors. Pox knew his way to the elevator and pushed the button for the trauma ward, fifth floor. The doors opened on a small visitors' area with couches and tables, a public place for families to collect and cry over a loved one. Every person who got off the elevator witnessed the mourning process. Maybe the designers planned it as an object lesson to discourage accidents.

I followed Pox around the corner to a reception counter. One of the nurses looked up as we passed, then went back to her work. It was clear Pox had been there before. The hall dead-ended into a forced choice, right or left, like Robert Frost's poem *The Road Not Taken*. At the end of the left fork, a man with a gun sat in a chair outside a closed door. I stopped and stared. "*...long I stood... and looked down one as far as I could.*" Pox noticed my interest. "The end room is for felons from the prison. They're as brutal with each other as they are with society. Sometimes they fight with forks, or gouge out eyes with spoons."

I considered the kind of choices that would land a person in a lock-down trauma ward. "*...and that has made all the difference.*"

Pox took the opposite hall and kept talking. "The human species is the worst kind of animal. Personally, I'd rather be attacked by a bear."

We entered a room that held one sleeping occupant trussed up like a turkey for Thanksgiving. Traction cables held up a leg. One arm carried a white cast, the other was connected to an assortment of gadgets, including an IV bag hanging from a shepherd's crook. A head bandage wound its way asymmetrically to hide one eye. An oxygen tube snaked from a nostril. The rest of Pope's face was still bruised after a week, colored russet, coffee, and chocolate.

Pope opened his uncovered eye and silently acknowledged Pox, then turned his attention to me. "Hello, Dr. Howard. I understand you're here to make my life harder than it already is."

I ignored his futile attempt at humor, resisting the urge to remind him I was about to make him the richest man in the world, even though he couldn't spend it. Instead I said, "Hello Pope. What have they done to you? You looked better after the bout with the bear."

"I let them pin some bones and sew my skin together," he replied, "but I refused plastic surgery on my face. The scars will give me a professional edge."

"Good financial move," I agreed. "Disfigurement will make you recognizable. People will hire a lawyer who survived a fight with a bear. After a few years, the story will evolve and it'll be the bear that ended up in the hospital."

We grinned at each other before Pope got sober. "I'm sorry about Zeus. He was more than an ordinary dog."

"I wish I'd understood that. I didn't know much about dogs when I got him." A respectful silence ensued between us before I picked up the pace. "I saw the treasure of Towats. It was beyond amazing. The most valuable items were written records that could keep archaeologists in Nirvana for a hundred years." A palpable pall filled the room and I scurried to cover the gaffe. "Naturally, I won't tell anyone, and that will make *my* life harder than it already is." I smiled hopefully. "Will there ever be a time I can tell about the adventure?"

Pope stared at me long enough to make me squirm. "In twenty years," he began, "I think the time will be close. When you see the signs of..."

A tall, thin man breezed into the room, interrupting our private conversation. He had a nose like a parrot's beak and skin the color of his leather briefcase. He placed three pieces of paper on the meal tray and wheeled it across the bed for all to see.

QUIT-CLAIM DEED

Dr. Matt Howard, GRANTOR, of Maricopa County, State of Arizona hereby quit-claims to...

Pope's legal name turned out to be Richard Tabby. I thought of the portrait of his great-grandfather, Tabby-To-Kwanah, hanging in the landing by the second bedroom of my house. Zeus and I had hidden in that room during the oily darkness haunting. Why would a baby crib with a lop-sided angel painted over it provide safe refuge?

"Dr. Howard?" Pox-Ouray brought me back from the reverie and nodded at the paper. "You need to sign the document."

WITNESS, the hand of said grantor this twenty-second day of July, 1992.

With a few cursive lines of a black pen I gave away Hathenbruck's living gold, condemning myself to teach about dead things for the rest of my life. The parrot man stamped his official authorization in the bottom right-hand corner. We repeated the motions, distributed copies, and tiptoed from the room as Pope dozed into a stupor.

The drive up the canyon was done in silence. I leaned my head against the vibrating car window, my teeth knocking together as I mentally rehearsed why I had nothing but my original poverty at the end of a journey full of guaranteed wealth. Money is power, freedom, a cushion, the root of all evil, the sum of most blessings. Money talks. Why does mine say goodbye?

When Pox-Ouray dropped me off at the motel I had convinced myself that I was the victim of an illegal scam and all the people in town were laughing at me. "Life isn't fair," I said bitterly to myself. "Get over it," myself answered, and we enjoyed our last night at Motel Three and a Half. Next morning I climbed into the Shove-it and drove for the last time to the Hathenbruck Estate.

The car chugged up the path to the meadow and I parked it on the south side of the house, planning an entrance through the kitchen door. A pounding in the direction of Zeus' grave kept me walking the length of the porch to find the sound. I stood frozen at the sight. Four Indian men and a red-haired hippie were placing a heavy wood tombstone at the head of my dog's final resting place. George saw me first.

"The game is up," he announced to the other men, who stopped shoveling dirt around the edges.

I took a few steps forward. "What are you doing?"

"Come," George invited me, "and see the tribute."

I walked around the six-day old gravesite until I could see a full view of the monument, it's face carved in letters scorched with a wood burning tool, adding deep dimension to the words.

Here lies Zeus, an important dog.
Saigneleceur fondeur.

I recognized the foreign words engraved on the brass bell at the center of the burial in the mountains. *"My father,"* Scar had said, *"thought the words on the bell were a mix of Latin and French. The bell says, 'It grieves me to the very heart.' My father said an important man lies here."*

The sight of these dirt-encrusted men paying homage to Zeus made a beautiful scene. Drops of salty tears slid off my nose. I wiped them away with my hand and smiled stupidly at everyone. I knew my dog's tombstone actually said, "Here lies Zeus, an important dog manufactured by the foundry in Saigneleceur, Switzerland." It didn't matter. I cried anyway.

The group returned to finish the grave while I packed my things from the house into the car. Without Zeus and his foam bed, the Shove-it seemed empty. Pox-Ouray transferred Pope's dried-blood quilt from the back of the car to the kitchen floor. "Is there anything you'd like to take with you?"

My response was quick. "I'd love to have Hathenbruck's gold watch fob," I said, "but it belongs in a museum." I realized I couldn't take it. It was valuable, but only if it was melted down. I couldn't do it. "Would you give it to Old Ben for his museum collection in town?"

I remembered another interesting piece of equipment. "There's a Cornish Miner's lunchbox hanging inside the hall closet. Could I have it?" Pox carried the worthless antique to the back of the car and shut the trunk. Outside, the sun hit the half circle of dead zone, evidence of buried brass cannons. I watched the light move across the meadow, where Spanish arrastras were hidden under tiny wildflowers. Pox waited patiently during my last long look at the house. I silently scanned the faces of the Indians I had grown to admire and respect. Then I made the inevitable move to give him the door keys.

George stood on the cake-icing porch where his yellow scarf had once convinced me he was a serial killer. It had been a long time ago, at least two weeks.

"George," I called to him, "your empty potatoes are in my sink. I can't thank you enough." I crouched my way into the car, then struggled out again to stand upright for my final parting quote. "Where your treasure is, there will your heart be also."

George wrinkled his eyebrows in concentration. "Is that Shakespeare?"

I shook my head. "The Bible."

The Shove-it and I disappeared over the edge of the meadow and drove into the sunset.

Thus ended twenty days to treasure.

I slid, exhausted, into the driveway of my little Scottsdale house. It was good to see the desert landscape still sprawled in my front yard, it's fake river lined in round boulders, the mesquite trees alive in faded green. It took very little time to carry my belongings into the house, but when I tried to lift the Cornish lunch box, it barely budged. The thing was way heavier than it had a right to be for a seven inch tall, nine inch wide tin bucket. That hundred- year-old miner's lunch must have turned to stone.

I scooted the box to the edge of the tailgate and opened the cover. The top section held about twenty gold nuggets, all somewhat bigger than a quarter, but mangled into various shapes. I hefted one and guessed an ounce, three-hundred-thirty-three dollars worth. A muted cry of joy moved from gut to throat to air and I quickly removed the tray to reveal the middle division, filled with raw gold pieces. When my shaking hands lifted the center section, I got the sight I expected: gold in a variety of sizes, three inches deep in the tin lunch box where hot tea had once settled.

I sold a few pieces of the gold in the top section to buy a genuine air conditioner, not a swamp cooler. The remainder of the gold stayed in the Cornish lunch pail, like a safe deposit box, to be used for special occasions. It was a good decision. Last year, gold rose to $1,531 an ounce. But I don't really need the money. I do pretty well for myself. The pottery textbook is required reading, sending me enough royalties to eat out at a medium quality restaurant once a week.

My hierarchy of ownership rules were fatally skewed. Instead of starting with a fish, a bird, a cat, a dog, and a husband in that order, I messed it up going backwards. The husband left, the dog died, and there didn't seem much point to the cat, canary, and fish. I did, however, decide to use some gold to go to China and adopt a little girl. It seems to have been successful. She's still breathing. So am I.

I wonder if Candy ever went to the Junior Prom, and hope Ezra is still conducting sunrises. I worry that George might slip into a cold stream and drown while pulling his gold-encrusted sheepskin to shore. I find myself thinking about the Towats treasure and the Ute god's plans for its future. According to Mary, it has something to do with starting a new civilization.

By now, Mary has probably choked on her own acid bile and is buried under the rusted swings in her trailer court. Pox-Ouray was an old man twenty-three years ago and has no doubt gone to his happy hunting ground. I think he deserves better, but then, I'm not a hunter.

The other keepers of the yellow metal were fine young men, but not given to much outside reading and probably won't see this account. Pope, on the other hand, will. I hope I haven't misinterpreted his unfinished sentence in the hospital. *"In twenty years,"* he said, *"I think the time will be close. When you see the signs of…"* and we were interrupted. If I am murdered next to my computer, which I finally had to buy, Pope did it.

I think about the Spanish gold mines that dot the Uinta mountains, and the granddaddy of them all, the lost Rhoades and Hathenbruck mine cleverly hidden under a haunted house. I remember the fabulous treasures in the Towats caverns, and wonder when the Indian god will bring forth the mysteries and records of those ancient people.

I repeat to myself the treasure hunter's motto, "Today is the Day," and consider going back to see what's left, what's changed. But today is not the day. Neither was yesterday. Tomorrow isn't looking good either.

But I still think about it.

BIBLIOGRAPHY

Boren, Kerry Ross and Lisa Lee. *The Gold of Carre-Shinob.* Springville, Utah: Bonneville Books, 1998

Boren, Kerry Ross and Lisa Lee. *The Utah Gold Rush.* Springville, Utah: Council Press, 2002

Hooper, Vicki Huntington. *Quest Beyond Our Reach.* Copyright 2012.

Peale, Norman Vincent. *The Power of Positive Thinking.* New York: Prentice-Hall, Inc., 1952

Rhoades, Gale R and Boren, Kerry Ross. *Footprints in the Wilderness, A History of the Lost Rhoades Mine.* Salt Lake City, Utah: Dream Garden Press, 1971

Skarin, Annalee. *Ye Are Gods.* New York: The Philosophical Library, Inc, 1952

Thompson, George A. *Lost Treasures on the Old Spanish Trail.* Salt Lake City, Utah: Western Epics, 1986

Thompson, George A. *Faded Footprints.* Salt Lake City, Utah: Dream Gardens Press, 1991

Zukav, Gary. *The Dancing Wu Li Masters.* New York: HarperCollins, 1979

AUTHOR'S NOTES

SEPARATING FACT FROM FICTION

CHAPTER ONE: (1) Quotes from Ahiqar and the Egyptian father to his son are authentic. (2) The Hathenbruck name, introduced in this chapter, is real, but Hilda Hathenbruck is a fictional character created to provide Matt with a house in the isolated Uinta Mountains. (3) The town of Kamas is a lovely little town in the Uintas full of gold lore and legend. Many of its tales are written in *Footprints in the Wilderness*. (4) The Uinta Mountains could also be spelled Uintah. I chose the shorter version.

CHAPTER TWO: The Kanab Chamber of Commerce recommended the book *Quest Beyond Our Reach* by Vicki Huntington Hooper, which supplied the story of Freddy Crystal and the town's hunt for Montezuma's treasure.

CHAPTER THREE: (1) Dialogue in this chapter gives valid history of Cortez and Montezuma. (2) The carved steps of Johnson Canyon are real. (3) Antique bells from the horses of Spanish explorers are scattered along the Old Spanish Trail. (4) Artifacts in the novel's fictional cave were described from discoveries in a variety of locations in the Kanab area.

CHAPTER FOUR: (1) Ezra Snow is a fictional character who tells factual stories. (2) The 1842 journal of Margaret Ann Adair is the source for the story of pioneer settlers wintering in hand-dug caves until Spring, when snakes dropped from the ceilings and walls. (3) *The Gold of Carre-Shinob* contains the Indian legend of mazes under Manti hill leading to treasure. (4) The Hathenbruck mansion is fiction, designed to allow the novel's plot to spread from a central location. (5) The dead half-circle of ground in front of the house introduces a true puzzle found throughout the Uinta Mountains. (6) I added the trunk in the house to hold contents that are key to the actual life of FWC Hathenbruck.

CHAPTER FIVE: (1) George Murdock, the Shakespeare quoting prospector, presents factual backgrounds on theories about Aztec origins, the Uinta Mountain gold mines, sheepskin mining methods, and Greek explorations. (2) Mel Fisher was a treasure hunter who traced Aztec gold to the Uinta Mountains, but died before he could finish his work. (3) Isotopes within rocks of different ages show that Earth's gold is not native. A recent theory is that a firestorm of gold-laden meteors bombarded the planet 3.9 billion years ago. (4) I used the character of George to introduce Towats, the Indian god, and the temple caverns where ancient treasures are hidden. The cavern's Indian name is Carre-Shinob. (5) Fourteen men are said to have seen the

Towats temple, but my sources only named eight: Thomas Rhoades, Caleb Rhoades, Isaac Morley, Aaron Daniels, Pete Miller, Butch Cassidy, FWC Hathenbruck, and Kerry Ross Boren.

CHAPTER SIX: (1) A story in *Faded Footprints* concerned Jed Hickman, who saw the barrel of a cannon protruding from the ground. (2) *Faded Footprints,* page 136, also presents the idea that a buried brass cannon poisons vegetation. (3) The Coronado account is historical. (4) Jack the Real Estate Agent gives additional facts about Hathenbruck. The house, as explained above, is a fabrication.

CHAPTER SEVEN: (1) Prospector journals identify Kamas as the closest town to several rich Spanish gold mines and caches. The Towats Temple itself is about a three-day journey farther east into the mountains. (2) The museum is real, the characters are fiction, the stories are fact.

CHAPTER EIGHT: (1) House hauntings begin with the sound of the chandelier crashing to the table. This experience happened to a family in southern Utah that moved into a haunted house. They couldn't buy another place and ended up living with the ghost. They should write a book. (2) Landmark cairns for sighting cave entrances are common in the Uintas. (3) Harvesting gold nuggets from baked potatoes was an intriguing side comment from *Faded Footprints*. Hathenbruck used the method with a mercury amalgam. The technique is also described in *The Gold Panner's Manual* by Garnet Basque, written in 1974. (4) IRS tax rules on raw gold was found in *Faded Footprints*.

CHAPTER NINE: (1) *Faded Footprints* describes a cave hidden behind a large boulder. (2) Pope is a fictional character who tells the true history of Indian slavery. An Indian warrior named Pope organized a widespread rebellion against the Spanish in 1680. The story is also detailed in *Lost Treasures on the Old Spanish Trail.* A second uprising of Indian slaves happened in 1844.

CHAPTER TEN: (1) Spanish cannons are reported to be in the Uinta Mountains, indicating that the Spanish traveled farther north than scholars believe. (2) The large portrait of Hathenbruck and the photograph of Chief Tabby were printed in *The Utah Gold Rush.* Also included were photographs that describe Hathenbruck's life, his family, the Robber's Roost gang, and his Indian friends.

CHAPTER ELEVEN: (1) Spanish gold is again mentioned as originating in the Uinta Mountains. (2) Bears in the Uintas are a problem. Warning pamphlets are given to campers.

CHAPTER TWELVE: (1) The cruelty suffered by the Indians is unimaginable. Various methods of torture by the Spanish and later Mexicans are documented in *Lost Treasures on the Old Spanish Trail* and *Faded Footprints.* I tried not to use too many examples. (2) The Spanish warning on the cliff face was found during a library search and written on scratch paper, but I didn't note the source. I decided to use it anyway. The verb should be "hablan," but "habla" was written on the cliff.

CHAPTER THIRTEEN: (1) Spanish and Mexican arrastras are spread throughout the Uinta Mountains. (2) *Footprints in the Wilderness* claims the Lost Rhoades Mine was close to a meadow, with the Towats temple about sixty miles to the east.

CHAPTER FOURTEEN: The idea of the sliding trunk was taken from a story I heard as a child. It has frightened me ever since and I enjoyed repeating it here.

CHAPTER FIFTEEN: FWC Hathenbruck was a major player in the goldmines of the Uinta Mountains. The biography reported is true. Condensed quotes scattered throughout the chapter are from diaries, letters, and newspaper reports found in *The Utah Gold Rush, Footprints in the Wilderness, The Gold of Carre-Shinob,* and *Faded Footprints.* I organized them chronologically to tell the story. Hathenbruck was a good man, the illegitimate son of the Crown Prince of Germany, known as "Frank" to his friends.

CHAPTER SIXTEEN: (1) The trunk is fiction, but the contents contain historical facts about Hathenbruck. (2) "De Re Metallica" by Agricola is a classic book on prospecting, and includes dowsing and pendulums. (3) The gold nugget watch fob is part of the Hathenbruck legend. I put it in the trunk with his books. (4) The idea that powerful vibrations of the past can influence a person's mind was suggested by three books: *The Dancing Wu Li Masters*; *Ye Are Gods*; and *The Power of Positive Thinking.*

CHAPTER SEVENTEEN. The mine entrance through the closet was assembled from several sources: (1) Carved steps leading down to a tunnel is from *Lost Treasures on the Old Spanish Trail.* (2) A sixty-foot tunnel, opening to an underground chamber is from *Faded Footprints.* (3) The gruesome mine entrance guarded by a skeleton chained to the wall is from *Lost Treasures on the Old Spanish Trail.*

CHAPTER EIGHTEEN: Matt's experience in the mine under her house was compiled from various stories in the bibliography.

CHAPTER NINETEEN: (1) Hathenbruck didn't build a brick house over his gold mine, but according to *The Gold of Carre-Shinob,* he and Rhoades really did build the back wall of their cabin against a ledge. I allowed my imagination to run with that detail and used it in the novel. (2) It was Benjamin Franklin who said only two things are certain: death and taxes. Both are motivational.

CHAPTER TWENTY: (1) Landmarks described during the journey to the treasure cave are from journals and letters of gold hunters. (2) The double circle of rocks with a brass bell in the center is reported in *Footprints in the Wilderness.* The bell was inscribed with *saignelegier chiantel fondeur,* but the meaning is debatable. I eliminated *chiantel* in the novel.

CHAPTER TWENTY-ONE: (1) *Faded Footprints* provided the story of the prospector who died from mercury poisoning when he camped near a stream contaminated by Hathenbruck's amalgam techniques. The longevity of mercury and its deadly effects are well known. (2) History of the Rhoades-Hathenbruck Mine is accurate. It was on the Ute Reservation. (3) *The Utah Gold Rush* explains the difference between Carre-Shinob and the Sacred Mines: Carre-Shinob, called the Towats Temple in this novel, is a series of nine huge caverns where the treasures of the Aztecs are stored, along with ancient artifacts of a prehistoric civilization. It also contains mummies of leaders of the Uto-Aztecan nation. The Sacred Mines, including the Lost Rhoades Mine, comprise seven rich deposits of gold.

CHAPTER TWENTY-TWO: The anecdote of the man who had three fingers chopped off as a warning came from *Faded Footprints*. (2) The blindfolded trip to the top of a steep mountain was the experience of Aaron Daniels, in *Footprints in the Wilderness*. He dictated the story to his daughter in 1895. (3) Pete Miller was an old prospector who found the upper entrance to the Towats temple, hammered a spike in the ground, and rappelled down a cliff to the crevice entrance and tunnel. His story is in *The Gold of Carre-Shinob,* which also includes the account of a runaway squaw who said the great cavern was situated in a large crack and the Indians had to lower themselves with ropes in order to get to the gold. *Faded Footprints* describes the top entrance as facing East, where the early rising sun sends light into the entrance tunnel.

CHAPTER TWENTY-THREE: The contents of the Towats temple is described in *The Gold of Carre-Shinob*. Author Kerry Boren reveals his personal experience inside the great caverns.

CHAPTER TWENTY-FOUR: Stages of grief have been determined by numerous psychological studies.

CHAPTER TWENTY-FIVE: *The Utah Gold Rush* states there are typically two entrances into old gold mines, a tunnel below and a vertical shaft above.

CHAPTER TWENTY-SIX: Money is power, freedom, a cushion, the root of all evil, the sum of most blessings. Too true.

CHAPTER TWENTY-SEVEN: The adventure ends.

Clues to the location of the Lost Rhoades mine are listed in *Footprints in the Wilderness*. It is near a road, close to several natural caves. The gold vein runs through a meadow with the mine itself at the base of a cliff. The mine is on the Ute Indian Reservation as it stood before 1905. Indians are reported as saying, "Stupid white man look high up. Mine low down." Caleb Rhoades stated publicly that the mine was in such an unlikely place, he didn't worry about anyone finding it, not even geologists. Given these clues, I put the Lost Rhoades Mine under the mythical Hathenbruck house.

To those who don't believe in lost gold mines and caverns full of ancient treasure, consider yourselves fortunate. Believers waste their lives in the search. And even if they find treasure in the Uinta Mountains, they can't keep it. Towats has other plans.